MW01120821

The Ice Widow

A Story of Love and Redemption

Anne M. Smith-Nochasak

ANNE M. SMITH-NOCHASAK

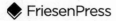 FriesenPress

One Printers Way
Altona, MB R0G 0B0
Canada

www.friesenpress.com

Copyright © 2022 by Anne M. Smith-Nochasak
First Edition — 2022

All rights reserved.

Spelling and usage of Inuktitut expressions are taken from:

Labradorimi Ulinnaisigutet: An Inuktitut-English Dictionary of Northern Labrador Dialect. August Andersen, William Kalleo, Beatrice Watts, eds. Nain, NL: Torngasok Cultural Centre, 2007. It is noted that there are many variations according to region and age group, and these do not always reflect current usage.

Biblical references follow:

The Jerusalem Bible (Reader's Edition). New York: Doubleday & Company, 1968. This version is chosen for its fluid style and its popularity during the time of the character Terrence's studies.

No part of this publication may be reproduced in any form, or by any means, electronic or mechanical, including photocopying, recording, or any information browsing, storage, or retrieval system, without permission in writing from FriesenPress.

ISBN
978-1-03-916038-5 (Hardcover)
978-1-03-916037-8 (Paperback)
978-1-03-916039-2 (eBook)

1. FICTION, ROMANCE, CONTEMPORARY

Distributed to the trade by The Ingram Book Company

Dedicated to the People of Home

And, always,

To my son, Noah

TABLE OF CONTENTS

Notes on the Text   **vii**

Chapter 1: A Snow House Filled with Light   **1**
From Anna   1
Ice Woman Today   4

Chapter 2: Woman Baptized into Endor   **15**
Eyes North   15
Face to Face   19
Tonya's Dream   28

Chapter 3: Woman of Earth Awakening   **31**
Terrence's Hope   31
Quickening   34
Winter into Spring   42

Chapter 4: Woman of Steady Flame   **47**
From Anna   47
Lessons in Stories   48
Leah: Low Fire Burning Long   51
Joshua Hebronimiut   59

Chapter 5: Woman in Waiting   **62**
Mattie's Dream   62
Terrence As Hosea   64
Catherine: Mother and Grandmother   67
Photo Moments   70

Chapter 6: Horizons without Mountains   **75**
Joshua's Lament   75
Anna in Galilee   78
Mountain Sketches   82

Chapter 7: Independent Woman Seeking Home   87
  From Anna   87
  The Passing of Catherine   91
  Mattie's New Dream   96

Chapter 8: Independent Woman as Pilgrim   98
  Aaron's Hidden Years   98
  Anna's Wandering Years   101
  Mattie's Promise   104

Chapter 9: Woman on the Edge of Life   107
  Moments and Memories   107
  Marta's Nativity Play for the Streets   110
  The Persistence of Mountains   114

Chapter 10: Time and Water Flowing   116
  Roads to the Sky   116
  Leah: Low Fire Burning Bright   120

Chapter 11: Women Overlooking Waterfall   123
  Mattie's Return   123
  Journey in the Present   128

Chapter 12: Working the Rapids   139
  From Anna   139
  Gateway Emerging   142
  Facing South   147

Chapter 13: Seeking Calm Waters   153
  Homecoming of Sorts   153
  Change of Direction   157

Chapter 14: The Failings of Nostalgia   162
  Rabbits and Coyotes   162
  Cougars and Axes   165
  Great Christmases   170
  Winter in a New World   173

Chapter 15: Travellers Facing North   **176**

The Narrow Portal   176

Time for Terrence   182

Sarah, Wife and Guardian   187

Two Leahs, One Rachel   190

Chapter 16: Within the Gates   **193**

Elusive Landmarks   193

Joshua's Way   198

Chapter 17: Stories of the Last Days   **201**

Introduction by Mattie   201

According to Terrence   203

According to Miriam   209

According to Aaron   213

According to Sarah   214

According to Anna (Northern Magnificat)   216

According to Joshua   218

According to Mattie   219

Appendix: Joshua's Family Tree   **221**

Acknowledgements   **222**

About the author   **223**

NOTES ON THE TEXT

The capital K in Nunatsiavut has a guttural pronunciation. It resembles a /h/ sound pronounced deep in the throat, with only a hint of /k/. Arctic char, for example, is *iKaluk*, not *ikaluk*. When you see the capital K, this is not a typo. In Nunavut, this sound is represented by a capital Q.

This raises the question: Is Joshua Kalluk in the novel *Kalluk* (eyebrow) or *kalluk* (thunder)? I assure you, he is *kalluk*, but because it is a proper noun, it is written *Kalluk*.

I have not used typical Nunatsiavut surnames; some are drawn from names heard during my time in Nunavut, and some, like *Ullâk*, I have constructed. I did this to allow more latitude in character development.

Endor is a fictional place, which allows me some freedom in building the setting. Hebron and Okak are actual place names, though, recalling locations of profound history.

Within the Labrador dialect, there are variations in spelling and pronunciation within regions and age groups. Language is dynamic and in a constant state of change. I have, therefore, used the resource *Labradorimi Ulinnaisigutet: An Inuktitut-English Dictionary of Northern Labrador Dialect* (August Andersen, William Kalleo, Beatrice Watts, eds. Nain, NL: Torngasok Cultural Centre, 2007). I have used it as a standard and acknowledge that many will have different spellings and expressions.

~~~Anne M.

FROM ANNA

"I will put an ice wi'dow in my snow house wall," my friend says. "Then I will have light in my snow house all day."

I shiver in my parka, there in his northern spring with snow piled around me—no daffodils here. His words draw images; his voice carries mystery. His ice widow could be many things.

"I see her pale," I declare. "Eyes cast down, trembling, as he wedges her between the blocks; he is snickering as he packs the snow about her body.

"But then I see her brittle and bitter, scowling hard, and he heaps the snow around her face, patting it over the piercing eyes.

"Maybe she is, instead, an ice queen, a demon lady, a dark spirit turning to ice. His fingers burn as they touch her frozen skin.

"Or she could be like the grass widow we have in the South: maybe her husband is always off on the Land—ice fishing or hunting or being—and she is left behind."

My friend's eyes are troubled, and he points to the wall of the snow house he is building. "I will put the ice there, for that block. I will chip it all around, and I will seal it with snow, and I will have light in my snow house all day. A ween-dow. You need to read less and spend more time on the Land. Maybe go fishing, in the spring, and camp."

He pauses, tilts back his head, and laughs into the sky. "Then you won't be an ice widow."

M

Ah, my friend, I have become an ice widow anyway.

I am an ice woman, who has carried love all her life like a dead coal, never allowing its light or its heat. I have lived, my friend; yes, I have lived. I have climbed mountains, dear one, but not your mountains. For in your mountains, beings far older than those of the Bible stalk the bleak rockscapes; they scratch at your tent door in the shadow world before daybreak, to breathe dreams of madness into your defenceless brain. You have faced the dark ones; you have received their horrors and spat them back.

I have climbed lesser mountains.

Yet I have lived rich and full, I tell you, without love, without communion, a strong and solitary woman. I stand on my own little mountain, back straight and shoulders squared.

I knew passion, in that perfect, dazzling spring with you. I can smile now, precious one, and shake my head at our young-ness. You were shining eyes over me as the Land quickened with spring, and I was free.

My engagement was far from me, my joy all around me, that special, special spring. I laughed, and I was so free. You were engaged, but that did not matter to me. I was engaged, but that had been a different world, before our world. We belonged to each other, allies in a world that would stifle us. We were free, there in the spring sun where all dreams were possible.

Do you ever recall our first passion there in the brilliance of an early northern spring, our innocence, our perfect intimacy? Oh, the promises and the dreams we made, far from the walls and locks on our lives. We could run away, I said, live as wanderers on the Barrens, the sky our only roof and the voices of order not even a whisper on the wind. I laughed when you shot a glance toward the town and said that the mosquitoes would be thick in August. The wind will hold them off, I said. You chuckled, and then you laughed full into the open sky.

I said I would swear loyalty to you and cast off my old loyalties. I had chosen you as you had chosen me, there in the shadow of your mountains. What did I think I would do in winter when the slop pail froze in the porch, and you were hunting for days on end? What about your grandmother and the parka she was even then embroidering for sweet, sad Leah? What would I say to them? Oh, I was young.

"You are in love with life," you said, "not with me. You love the feeling of love."

"Then I will go home and marry my fiancé," I snapped, "since you only want an affair and care nothing for the things that matter."

I wanted to shock you. You were supposed to sweep me into your arms, proclaiming undying love. I waited, but perhaps you did not understand. Finally, I decided to tell you, without pretense, that I loved you and wanted to live with you forever.

Thus, I came to your grandmother's house in the village that day. I ran up the steps and pushed open the door. I stepped around the buckets and firewood and swept aside the curtain to your room. Our room. Her head was on our pillow, turned to one side as the tears trickled from her closed eyes. You murmured in her ear as you stroked her cheek.

It seemed this day that you were embracing the stifling.

"I love you," you murmured. "It will be all right."

You were not murmuring to me. I stepped back from the curtain. I tiptoed past the wood box and the water buckets. I closed the door and sauntered up the road, hands in my jacket pockets, eyes on the harbour. It was a good day for a stroll. I smiled and said that to everyone I met.

I finished packing my trunk, and then I was gone.

I offered you every dream I had, but I did not ask what your dreams were. And I walked away, never having asked. There is freedom in not asking.

I moved on; I lived. Do you hear me? I lived my life on my terms, and I stayed free. I had a career many, many times. I worked, I paused, and I listened, but I did not hear your laughter, and so I moved on and worked, paused, and listened again.

Now we are old—can you believe it? Your wife lies in the churchyard, my discarded fiancé is probably still teaching, I am retired and have a little garden finally, and you, my friend, my stranger-friend, my occasional-message-or-text-friend, you are dying.

Now we are young again, and it is time to walk with you.

I am an ice woman, my friend, so please do not drop me or press me or I will burst into shards, and the wind will scatter my fragments over the sea ice. Hold my hand gently, for when your grey face is near mine, wisps of long hair straying in the wind (for you never cut it again, when it grew back), and when you close your eyes against the gathering night, you are young and beautiful and laughing full into the open sky as you build a snow house and fill it with light.

You called for me, and for some reason, here I am. We have stayed in touch, as long-ago friends do, as sharers of parenthood will, but suddenly we are young, and here we are, starting our life together at last.

If I am supposed to be the one supporting you, then why am I the one asking to be held?

Ice women should be made of stronger stuff.

ICE WOMAN TODAY

Anna Caine rises to the musical refrain of her alarm, to the golden dog pressing an eager face to hers, feathered tail whipping the side of the bed. *It is time; it is time! The breakfast song is playing. Oh, do get up and see the beautiful morning.*

Anna always does, even now in this first September of her retirement.

She is a retired teacher and a senior citizen. She knows her own mind, and she follows her heart. She has created a corner of Paradise, right here in the woods, and this will be her home forever. She is not packing, drifting, and searching; Anna Caine has arrived. She is satisfied.

She is strong now, confident and vigorous. Perhaps she should be pudgy curves and dimpled knees, plump cheeks puffing out as she rolls another piecrust. Maybe she should don flowered gloves and straw hat and waddle into her flower garden after a breakfast of muesli, yogurt, fruit slices, and herbal tea. That, however, is not the way of Anna Caine.

Anna swings tanned, muscled legs over the side of the bed, groping for denim shorts. She peels away her sleeping shirt, squirming into sports bra and baggy sweatshirt. The well is low, so tomorrow will be shower day. Today is splash and sponge day, but there will be water for coffee. There will be bacon crisping, eggs sizzling, cheese melted over the works, and two cups of coffee. She will take a three-mile walk and then march into the garden in her faded, paint-spattered cap and rubber-palmed construction gloves. She is retired, she is a senior, but by God, she is Anna Caine, so maybe she will kayak across the lake after her walk with the dogs.

The garden will wilt by then, and it will be too hot to water it. So, she will water it, walk three miles, and then kayak across the lake. She will read important works after a light lunch, then weed and mow in the late afternoon. Yes, she will be busy.

She wonders what her son, Aaron, is doing today, and if he dreams of visiting her. She wonders if he and his father, Joshua, are having breakfast together, planning a hunting day.

No, Joshua is working on the new elders' centre; Aaron will be in the office already.

You are supposed to slow down and die if you stop teaching. She is ready to risk it. For the past nine years, she has done short contracts, supply teaching locally in between. She passed a few of those nine years scrubbing hands and even locked down as the pandemic rose and fell and rose again. She spent the last winter waking in the night to a raw throat and pounding headache, sure signs of the new virus that was pushing into their lives. She gargled and swallowed acetaminophen and learned the power of her imagination. She has loved teaching, and she has loved being online and in the classroom in her teaching life, but finally, she has had her fill. Now, she is going to live in her house and harvest her squash. Maybe she will paint all the walls when winter sets in.

She might put in a few days' work, in fact. But she will not develop dimples in her cheeks or on her knees, and she will buy pies if company ever comes.

She will read in the afternoons but will tell people she is looking into quilting. She will leave partially knitted dishcloths out, to be snatched up should anyone come to the door.

She will have a historical text handy, to replace the mystery novel.

She will post photos of jars of jam on social media. She will hint that she is gathering ingredients for her grandmother's Christmas pudding.

She does not have to invent excuses for avoiding church suppers anymore. They have all been canceled again since the beginning of this phase of the virus.

She does miss those church supper potato salads. Could she make one, maybe? And then watch the many ingredients gather dust and mould until her next craving?

She will get one at the deli.

She will fill up her days with all the hiking and reading and exploring she has meant to do for years.

When Aaron was with her, she did all those things, and camping too. Kids need to do things. Other mothers, though, still made jam and always had the ingredients for anything you could possibly want to cook. They had cheese graters and colanders and spice racks too.

But she can still make excellent *panitsiak*, thanks to her time in Joshua's community.

She made *panitsiak* once for Terrence, her long-ago sweet and scholarly fiancé. *"Why are you frying tea biscuits in lard?"* he asked. *"Perhaps if you cut in just a little shortening, added a little sugar, and baked them, they would be lighter. You should not smother them with butter and jam like that. That, my dear, is a heart attack in the making."*

Terrence would not be dragging a *Kamutik* up a waterfall, so perhaps the *panitsiak* would settle in his arteries.

Such are the hurts that Anna Caine has brought to Terrence's heart: *panitsiak* steeped in cholesterol, and the news that his fiancée had played the harlot under every bush and rock pile.

That had been a time to remember.

She will never regret her time with Joshua, there in his Labrador. Nothing was ever more right.

She should have made her claim right then and there. She should have been an honest woman, grabbed Joshua by the hand, picked up the phone, and said, *"Terrence, I owe you many things, but I am now a fallen woman, and I am leaving you. I am going to marry a carpenter, just like the mother of Jesus."*

By then, the carpenter was marrying his sweetheart, as planned; after all, Anna had said she would leave in the spring to marry *her* fiancé. And had she really wanted to live in Joshua's room in his grandmother's little house, which was scrunched between the shore and the slop bank? With Joshua's girlfriend weeping in the doorway, clutching his daughter in her arms? Be honest. How long would Anna have stayed? Especially knowing as she does now how territorial some men can be, even when far away.

Joshua was married by the time Anna, back in Halifax, realized that she was carrying Joshua's child. Anna notified him in a brief letter, claiming she had no wish to maintain contact.

In sentimental moments, she still pictures Joshua appearing at her door, ringless, to bring her home. Then she thinks about something else.

She will never regret that time, but didn't her life turn out for the best, after all?

She can, at last, shrug off the past. She has made mistakes and is probably better off without Joshua in her life. She has said that for years, but this time, she means it. She has decided. Again.

She closes her eyes against the glare of the spring sun on the Labrador ice, turns her cheek from the lips that nuzzle along her jawline. *Oh, Joshua.*

She pours water into the French press and starts the bacon. She does her first physio set for her knee—left knee and right arm up, then change. Hold the rhythm. People will see her as they drive past the patio door, but she will not close the curtains; after the intense heat of summer and the darkness of blanketed windows, she craves light. All curtains must be opened to greet the sunrise, with the coffee brewing and the bacon crisping. This is retirement, safe and uncluttered. This time, it is real.

Golden Joy inhales her kibble as the dish reaches the floor; Petra, the husky, minces to the deck and awaits her portion. Hers must have a light drizzle of bacon grease. Petra is not spoiled, but she has a discerning palate.

Now Anna starts the gentle bends. She does not extend her knees past her arches. She straightens her back and sinks to a squat. She rises on her toes to a full extension, then eases her heels down and starts again.

She pours the first cup. She swings arms and right leg forward, now wide to the side, now back. Oh, this feels good on the hip, the knee, and the chest. After ten vigorous sets, she switches to the left. Petra stands nearby with eyes half-closed. Is she counting? Pitying? Amused? Joy, an affectionate dog of collie and retriever origins, hovers near the bacon. A trace of drool drops to the floor. Her eyes focus on the pan.

The phone on the table pings. Then a staccato burst, seven pings in all. People cannot write a full message. Oh no! The message must be broken into little phrases to ensure the listener will respond, if only to shut them up. She has turned off notifications for several people for that very reason. *Ping!* "*I need to get away.*" *Ping! Ping!* "*I am coming for a visit.*" "*I can't take it here.*" *Ping! Ping! Ping!* "*I only need three days.*" "*We have a lot to talk about.*" "*I am so depressed.*" *Ping! Ping! Ping! Ping!* "*I am not going to stop!*" "*I am not going to stop!*" "*I am not going to stop!*" "*I am not going to stop!*"

Didn't she block the one who used to do that?

She finishes the set, turns the eggs, and takes a sip. She picks up the phone.

The messages are from Joshua. They do communicate sometimes. After all, they are the parents of Aaron, and although Aaron is grown now, they should maintain contact. Joshua had sent her a message before going north with Aaron in April, and again when they had returned.

Joshua goes north each spring to the ancestral lands, into the dark spirit mountains and into the storms and nightmares scraping at the tent door, for eight years ago, Joshua defeated the great tumour behind his eyes, and his pilgrimage each year celebrates this truth.

M

In that long-ago desperate winter, Joshua lay limp in a hospital bed, his body poisoned and collapsing. The tumour was killing him, the chemo was killing him, and life itself was rejecting him. The dark ones came for him. They dragged him into a shadowed and solitary world, where his body tossed in an unseen current, buffeting against jagged rocks. At the turning of the tide, at the very moment of his death, he had burst to the surface, eyes wide, fists raised high. He had thrust out the scarred, gaunt limb that was his arm, eager for the needle, and he gritted his teeth and smiled. "Their power is gone," he had whispered, and his laughter had been a rasp because the feeding tube had scarred his throat. They would not give him the needle, knowing it would kill him, but his grandfather had been a 1918 Okak survivor. He had been a strong man, and he had taught his grandson well. Joshua rose, and he ate, and this time, there was no nausea. Then he slept, and soon they dared to start anew.

Eight weeks later, Joshua went home. His hair grew back, into long grey wisps, and he never cut it again.

Anna wonders if Joshua ever knew that she dropped to her knees on an old logging road and screamed to God for his life. She wonders if he knew that she imagined herself with him, holding his hand, and his eyes opening, his bewilderment turning to joy as he beheld her. Leah was gone; Anna could move in and keep house with him. Aaron might return to university as his father grew well again. Joshua's eldest daughter had her own household—she was a principal-in-training and did not approve of the Anna Caine teachers—and the youngest son was in college in St. John's. Joshua's middle daughter and her children did live with him; Anna would be helpmeet to Joshua and mentor to this daughter, while her little ones tumbled around their feet. Family would wander in and out. The kettle would always be steaming, and a pot of stew would be simmering on the stove. Laundry and floors would be unending, and the babies would wail in the night.

If they could just sit side by side, holding hands and smiling into each other's eyes, that part would be nice. But Anna Caine was not good at being matriarch of a family home; it would be like working a church supper that never ended.

Therefore, she had just screamed for his life and left him to it.

Aaron had probably been relieved. His mother had not been part of his life with his father, and it would be hard for him.

∧

Joshua is fluent in Inuktitut, but sometimes he struggles with the nuances of English, especially in written form. When writing, he applies question marks and commas to reflect inquiring tone and pauses, and reading his texts is like hearing him speak, with the hesitation of one whose natural language is the musical flow of Inuktitut. She likes this practice, although she rolls her eyes and says it is annoying.

> *Going Saint John's soon.*
> *Wondering, how r u?*
> *I need escort, but hard to find?*
> *Scan not good, this time,*
> *Looks like Chemo again, ugly chemo,*
> *Miriam, she can send the times, going for 2 weeks,*
> *Let me know? Pls? and tks*

Anna sits on the kitchen chair, staring past her deck, studying her yard and her dogs capering in the garden. This is not the first time that Joshua has pulled a stunt to get her to St. John's. Last time it was a PET scan, and yes, he needed companionship, but saying his cancer had come back and spread, and this was the end, had been manipulative. She had taken the first week off her new contract in Ontario citing family emergency, and the day she arrived, Joshua wanted to tour all the hardware stores in search of the perfect framing hammer. He was possibly in better shape than she was. Still, he was sweetly grateful to her for sitting in the waiting room, masked and distanced, while he sat alone in a little room with tubes pumping chemicals through his body. And they looked like a real couple, taking meals in the hotel restaurant while the staff smiled over them. *"He was so lonely until you got here,"* they said.

She had just made it back to Nova Scotia before they closed off the historic Atlantic Bubble, or she would have been self-isolating for two weeks in Nova Scotia or Ontario, and possibly both. That happened four years ago, just as the second wave of the pandemic was finding its stride.

Anna was at that Ontario contract during the third wave. Everyone out there felt the strain that time. They thought it could not get worse. They thought it could not get worse, but in those days, they always had enough to eat, and they should have known better.

The pandemic-weary world stumbled forward to a rough fall followed by a winter of anger and despair, and then sank down into the grind for a long, dragging year. Last autumn brought a lull, but this spring had been the worst of all. In this newest wave, she had gone back to scrubbing every surface with bleach until her fingertips puckered and withered. Sometimes, she had wanted to scoop all the masks into one heap and burn them in the yard outside her little trailer at her contract location. She had eaten porridge and made soups. She had watered the soups and stuffed the emptiness that remained with plain bannock. She had not been sure if this was a new pandemic or a new phase of the old one.

What a way to spend my senior years. That is a selfish thought, she knows, for she has been safe and comfortable every step of the way. She has been masked and vaccinated and never crowded into a multigenerational household. She has had ready access to clean water. She has not lain helpless in an intensive care unit while her son struggled for breath in another room in that same unit. She has not, with her last conscious breath, begged for prayers for her dying son. Her system has not been weakened by intergenerational ravages to body, mind, and spirit. Her immune system is not compromised by chemotherapy. She can have another booster, if they start that again, but this latest variant seems to outpace the research. There is no working vaccine. Will a cart roll by, gathering the dead? Should she buy a pellet gun, to finish off the rats at the garbage box, before they bring down the plague?

Perhaps she should, instead, water the garden.

Anna does not want to step out into the world, although at this moment, things are quiet. She likes being home, going out once a week, disinfecting the masks once a week. She can have good meals each day. She washes, masks, and steps away—and wonders if she needs to. Everyone looks so healthy. *Stay away; stay away. They will breathe death into your lungs.*

There are carriers, dark figures skulking in the shadows. She must not trust them; they look healthy, but they will infect her with one breath, one touch. They are ubiquitous. She stays away from everybody, just to be sure.

Anna does not want to go to St. John's and develop mask rash and puckered fingertips. She does not want to leave her dogs with the neighbours, let her garden go to seed, and dig deep into her savings. She dreads checking flight alerts and exposure sites. She will probably sit beside a carrier on the plane and fan a new and devastating wave through the city of St. John's. *The seatmate of Anna Caine on Monday's flight to St. John's had the virus, and she will now be responsible for unspeakable waste and suffering. Everyone else should be fine.*

Anna does not want to go to St. John's and share a hotel room with Joshua, the dazzling young lover who became the rigid critic of her childrearing skills. She does not want to hear what a gentle and beautiful person he is, when she has been angry with him most of her adult life. She has been cast as a wanderer because of him. She has lost joy in parenthood because of him. She has not been able to form an attachment because of him. She has been an introspective and bitter woman because she has let herself be one. Like the prophet Jeremiah, she has let herself be seduced. She has manipulated the seduction, if she admits the truth.

She wants to see Joshua with the jet-black hair spilling over his forehead and his brown eyes glowing, Joshua with the shoulder muscles smooth and rolling, the abdomen flat and tight. She does not want to see him with stringy grey locks and tattered goatee, eyes dull and squinting, body sagging just a little, for then she too will be old, and they will have missed their life, and it will be too late to reclaim the missing years.

They have lived those years, for better or for worse, and they cannot start a future now, when they are suddenly and inexplicably old. If they never see one another, she can roll through retirement in her new life, and she and Joshua will be fresh and young forever on the Labrador shore. Nevertheless, she taps out a message. Anna chooses her words; Joshua has a functional understanding of

English, but misunderstanding is a constant possibility. She still uses one finger, poking at the screen and correcting:

> *Hi. That is too bad. When are you going? Is this eight-day chemo again?*
> *-what bad? Me? Cancer? No, 2 bottle chemo 1 hour, then, steroid pill 3*
> *days, then, 3 days, and then, half hour chemo, 1 bottle*
> *-see you then, and tks*
> *I do not know if I can come. When is this? And sorry you have*
> *chemo again.*
> *-Idk? Talk to Miriam, tell her, you be escort? She tell u everything*

Oh, please do not make her send a message to Miriam, the child of Joshua and Leah. Leah might have wept in the background but was probably so smug presenting Joshua with that howling little bundle thirty-eight years ago. Miriam Kalluk went straight through teacher education and became an elementary teacher sixteen years ago. She has dedicated her skills to her home community and made a difference. She is balanced and compassionate with her students, but she has no patience with Anna. No, she has a low opinion of opportunistic adventure seekers whipping in and out of Endor, breaking hearts and confusing children. Miriam is grateful that teachers are more carefully screened in these times.

A muffled *bong* announces an email. Lovely. It is Miriam. She probably has a letterhead and a signature listing her credentials in colour. Anna opens it anyway.

> *Good morning, Anna Caine.*
>
> *My father informs me that he is asking you to be his medical escort, and the family thanks you for accepting. It is difficult to find an escort, as there are active cases of the virus on the island, and most of us do not have the time to get away for two weeks, due to family and work commitments. As you know, I am beginning my first year as principal at our school, and with my Beth now in Grade 7, I am kept busy. I am so pleased that you are retired from teaching now and able to help too.*
>
> *You will be flying Monday evening; they will be sending your electronic ticket. You will get a meal allowance, and as per policy, share the room. That is because you are there as a support—physical and emotional*

support. So, the escort should not go off visiting and shopping. You will be flying back Friday of the following week, so it is a twelve-day trip for you. Please let me know the outcomes of my father's appointments.

With thanks,

Miriam Kalluk-Peterson

That does sound like Miriam: *So pleased that you are retired from teaching now and able to help too.* She *would* be pleased, no doubt. And she would see it as an opportunity for her family to use too, no doubt. But Anna is still going to fall into line, no doubt at all.

Anna misses Joshua. That is natural, she reasons, for they are the parents of Aaron. And thus, she taps out her reply, deleting and correcting as the morning warms.

Hello, Miriam.

Thank you for your letter. Congratulations on your new position. I know you will do well.

I look forward to Monday. Could you please include your father's flight agenda and appointment times? If there are any allergies or special circumstances that I should be aware of, please include those. I will, of course, send you a summary each day, and I assure you that his care will be my priority.

Sincerely,
Anna

She nearly chokes on the opening, but it is the truth. Miriam is a homegrown teacher with vision and commitment. She is open and supportive with the staff but has no time for day trippers. Miriam and Anna have never bonded.

Visiting and shopping indeed. Anna has poured her savings into house renovations and car payments. She is not a handyman. She cannot tinker under the hood. She spends on causes. She leaves things behind and then replaces them. Her personal retirement funds plummeted in the first wave of the pandemic. She is damned well not going shopping.

Another subdued *bong* summons her attention.

Anna:

All that information will be in your package, which you will have by Friday. Dad needs compassion and support. This is very hard for him. I must go. I do look forward to receiving your updates.

With thanks,
Miriam Kalluk-Peterson

Anna will receive the information by Friday, which is tomorrow. And Monday, she will arrive in St. John's.

September means messy weather on the North Labrador coast, so she hopes Joshua will be able to fly to Goose Bay on the smaller hospital plane to get his flight to St. John's.

The eggs are cold and rubbery; the coffee is tepid. The lake is so far away, and the dogs now lie by the door, watching. Miriam and Joshua have screwed up Anna's perfect retirement day.

Dad needs compassion and support. This is very hard for him. Anna's heart constricts. What if Miriam is losing her father? What if Joshua is facing his death? What about her own son, Aaron, who is so close to his father? Anna picks up her fork and knife and pokes at her cold breakfast. She pictures a world with no Joshua, and it is a little lonely, a little grey. She sees Joshua with the jet-black hair spilling over his forehead and the brown eyes glowing, the shoulder muscles smooth and rolling, the abdomen flat and tight. He is building a snow house and filling it with light. His laughter echoes over the harbour, and it is dazzling spring. They are young, and the future is vibrant with promise.

Her eyes burn, and the dogs hover at her side as the sobs rip from deep within her body.

EYES NORTH

"You are going to the end of the line!" Terrence exclaimed, brandishing the map of coastal Labrador. "*End*or. End of world," he chuckled.

Anna gritted her teeth. Terrence loved his little word plays. Almost as much as his precious biblical jokes. She sensed one of these coming.

"So, will there be a witch, I wonder? . . . And you can go and see her in disguise, and she will recognize you, and say, 'You are Anna Caine! And your fiancé wants you back. Right now.'" Terrence snickered in breathless little gulps, arms reaching to draw her close.

Anna sidestepped, pretending not to see.

"And I would be in disguise, why?" she asked.

"Well, Saul had outlawed witches, and yet it was Saul who visited the witch of Endor, you see. Only he wanted to raise the ghost of Samuel. . . ." Terrence was frowning, trying to follow the hopeless scriptural tangle that he had created.

Anna relented, and planted a firm kiss on his right cheek. "Never mind. The sentiment was sweet." She did not add, *"And I promise not to raise any spirits from the dead"* because that would undermine what was, undoubtedly, a chivalrous declaration of love. Terrence was a sweet boy, trapped in the mind of a stilted scholar.

She loved the sweet boy, although at times the scholar could be tiring.

M

During her junior year at Dalhousie University, Anna Caine had become a disciplined English major with a preference for twentieth-century poetry. She had not been a disciplined student in her first two years; in those times, she had frequented Celtic pubs downtown, occasionally mellowing in candlelit coffee houses. Her love of the ballad form in its raucous political moments had found an outlet in the pubs, and her affinity with its haunting love sentiments had drawn her to the coffeehouses. In her third year, it had been time to put away the things of the child, boost that average, and get some decent references. It had been time for a disciplined student phase, and she had found it satisfying.

Since she had been pursuing a minor in mathematics, an elective in logic had seemed fitting. As a fourth-year theology major with a minor in psychology, Terrence Sutherland of the University of King's College had decided that a course in logic at Dal sounded practical. After all, arguing was a logical exercise, and he would undoubtedly be doing plenty of it in his future career. The minister was always hunted at social events; arguing him down represented the triumph of the secular mind. And thus, Anna Caine and Terrence Sutherland had met.

Their relationship had begun as mutual awareness, but logic class was not the most romantic setting, even for students sitting beside each other. Venn diagrams, subsets, and intersections did not kindle feelings of warmth. Neither was the type who could sit over coffee, chortling as they created a valid syllogism that came to an unsound and absurd conclusion. *No news is good news. Impending world annihilation is no news. Therefore, impending world annihilation is good news.* Instead, Anna had been absorbed in the mathematical forms, while Terrence had found unlikely syllogisms a little sad.

Then one day, Terrence's elbow had bumped her binder, and it had tumbled to the floor with a resounding whump. The rings popped, and papers scattered on the damp, slush-patched floor. It was a very full binder.

Their eyes met. Her lips parted. "You damned clumsy moron," Anna Caine began.

Then he was on his knees in the slush and water, head bowed as he plucked the sheets of paper one by one, shaking them and draping them on the arm of his chair, muttering comforts and apologies. "Well, the ink didn't run." "We'll have it straightened out in no time." "Yes, I am. Oh yes, I am." It was this last remark that thawed her heart and the next thing she knew, she was muttering back, "No, you're not. No, no, you're not. Oh, no. It was me. Really. Let's go for coffee?"

Groveling and apologizing show true love. Anna and Terrence are groveling and apologizing. Therefore, Anna and Terrence are showing true love. Perhaps they should have questioned the soundness of the first premise. Anyone in Endor could have told them that groveling and apologizing do not show true love; true love is the ability to accept and stand by the brokenness in the other, even if you must go away.

M

So, here were Anna Caine and Terrence Sutherland, three years later, preparing for Anna's northern adventure. They were in love but not lovers. They were intimate minds and hearts but not bodies. They had been classmates and friends. He had gone on to study for the ordained ministry on the Northwest Arm; she had finished her degree and transitioned to the education department at Dal. Now she was qualified to teach English and math, she had not been pubbing in three years, and she hoped that Terrence never figured out all of her past. She was a good person and a moral person, but she had also danced right through closing time, even occasionally as a disciplined third year student. Not long before she met Terrence, she had invited a classmate in for coffee, and he had misunderstood the reference. Thus, Anna had lost her virginity on her kitchen floor, with the toast crumbs pressing into her back. That had been her first and only sexual encounter. She had tugged her clothes back on and said she did not want to have sex anymore. The classmate had been angry when she had refused to continue, for he had found her reluctance exhilarating. She had invited him to do it, he had explained, and she owed him the rest. In the end, Anna had let him finish, although she did not agree. She had lain on the floor, the grit digging into her skin, and watched the ceiling until he finished rocking over her. She had been waiting for her period the day Terrence had sent her binder tumbling. Terrence had knelt before her, red-faced and babbling as he offered her the remains of the binder, raising it up on his hands. While she and Terrence had been having coffee that day, she had felt the welcome flex and the dampness and known she was safe. Safe from the past, safe for the future. Terrence would be her safe place.

She enjoyed a little wine now, at functions. She volunteered evenings at Terrence's street outreach. She played basketball and tutored in math. She was safe, safe with Terrence. He would be ordained soon and would age soon—a little balding and naïve but always sweet. He would be an assistant in a church and would probably pursue graduate work and teach, too. She would go on this one-year replacement contract to Endor, and when she came back, there would be teaching for her, studies and ministry for him, a little apartment at first, and sex that was gentle and uplifting and sweet. This would be on her terms, and hopefully, not too often.

But first, Anna was going to Endor, as far north as the planes flew on the Labrador coast. Terrence would be the beacon to guide her home.

FACE TO FACE

Anna stumbled from the bobbing float plane and struggled for balance on the wobbling dock below the wharf in Endor. Rounded hills and mountains enclosed the harbour, locking her in place; glitter of blue and splashes of white foam on the water dazzled her eyes. She turned shoreward, and gazed up, up into the eyes of all the people of the town staring down.

The faces were fixed and silent that day, for how many bewildered countenances had gazed up at them over the years? Could they discern that she had a hangover? Did they know that she used to be a youth volunteer with an enthusiastic track record but had still managed to drink her way into the book of records with near strangers the night before? Her companions last night had assured her that people drank a lot in the North, and had pressed drinks into her hand as testimony to that truth.

The faces above her today had seen these things and knew these things and so they were silent. A cigarette shifted to the right hand; the left hand steadied the ladder.

Up the hill, on a ladder resting against the church roof, a carpenter paused, slid his hammer into his belt, and raised a hand in greeting. By the nearby fish plant, a ragged woman, stooped with age, face creased, and eyes squinting, took measured puffs from a cigarette stub, leaned back against the wall, and chuckled to herself. Anna kept her eyes on the carpenter. If she looked at the woman, she decided, that would encourage her. The woman would walk up to Anna and embrace her while haranguing her with stories and requests for drink money. Anna knew; she had been warned.

An Elder detached herself from the crowd, tugged the knot in her headscarf straight, and smoothed the skirt that almost covered heavy trousers and skimmed loose rubber boots. She smiled, extending one twisted hand. Anna clambered up the ladder to the wharf, hearing the thump of luggage hitting the floating dock.

"They will bring it," the Elder said, "and you and I will see the town. Welcome to Endor, Miss Caine."

The Elder laughed as she slid her arm through Anna's and drew her near. "Welcome. Welcome, welcome, Miss Caine. I like your boots! Be careful though; those good hiking boots will slip on our rocks! And that anorak—very stylish, very nice, but it will not protect your kidneys. No. That is a nice backpack. Lots of things you have, good things. But the main things, those are in the heart."

The Elder paused, squinting up at Anna. She nodded. "Maybe you got a hangover, I think."

Anna pulled away, just a little. Along the periphery of her vision, bundles and duffle bags were rising to the wharf. The crowd turned toward Anna and the Elder, who now stood on the rough planks where the wharf met the road. "I need to take my things to my apartment," Anna said.

The Elder's grin exposed stubs of yellowed teeth. She leaned closer, hissing in Anna's ear: "We have seen, Anna Caine, and we have watched and endured. We know the stories, old and new. We do not judge Tamar; we do not celebrate Rahab. We walk with the Magdalene.

"We are here. We do not know how, sometimes, but we are here. See those houses, the little ones like boxes on the hill? Do you know, Anna Caine, that those little houses, which your people call charming, are cold? Did you know that we are careful, washing the floors in January, because they freeze along the edges? Did you know that sometimes, when people are homesick for their Land, they make homebrew?"

The fingers gripped hard, through the anorak sleeve, as the Elder breathed into Anna's ear. "Or perhaps they were children in Okak, when the Spanish flu sucked the life from their parents and the dogs were hungry in the streets, and they do not know how they survived but here they are. And they are lonely, Anna Caine, and homesick for a childhood that was over too soon. And there are horrors in their days and in their nights, images and sounds burned into their eyes and their ears. Do you know the sound that a starving dog makes as it claws under your door, and you are five, and your family is dead around you? No? That woman, the one over there leaning against the shed? The one you will not see? She knows. So do not judge her, Anna Caine, and we will walk with you then.

"Do you see that man, so lean and straight? The one on the ladder there, who looks over to the wharf and waves? Yes? That is Joshua Kalluk. That word, *kalluk*, that means thunder. His family came from the north communities; they were strong on the Land, but the mission closed, and the government told them to come here. Joshua's father was very homesick here. Joshua Kalluk was raised by his grandfather and grandmother then. His grandfather was a young man in Okak, in the days of the Spanish flu. And he taught Joshua well. Joshua is a good man, strong on the Land, and he can read any blueprint there is. Oh, the eyes of the young women are on him. Watch yourself, Anna Caine; it will not do for them to see you looking at him like that."

The Elder gave Anna's arm a little shake, stepped back, and grinned anew. "Beatrice is coming now. She's going to show you the way. I will see you, sometimes." The old woman shuffled off, wrapping her thick cardigan close in the breeze freshening over the harbour. Her laughter was a cackle. "Try not to stare so hard, eh?" she called over her shoulder as she scuffed along the gravel in her rubber boots.

"Ms. Caine. Welcome. We got busy getting your luggage sorted." A middle-aged woman with smooth features framed by a colourful headscarf came striding up. "The truck is here now, and they'll load it up and drop it off. And I was seeing my son; he just came in today too. Well. I see you've met our Deborah. She's very friendly. She likes to talk; I hope you don't mind. She doesn't have much English, though. But she's nice. She wanted to welcome you and make sure you felt at home. We'll walk up to your apartment now."

And with that, Anna Caine was hurrying up the road, trying to match the eager pace set by her guide. Anna looked everywhere, but Deborah had vanished into the crowd or among the houses. For someone who didn't have much English, Deborah had been remarkably eloquent. Anna was not quite sure what had happened, but perhaps Deborah had secrets unknown to this Beatrice, her fast-walking new guide.

She did not see Deborah after that, and did not think to ask.

Thus, Anna Caine arrived in Endor. With poetic speeches from mysterious Elders. With faces pressed together, looking down from the wharf, and mountains all around. She felt crushed; she couldn't breathe. And yet there had been a hand steadying the ladder above her, and a twisted and arthritic hand pulling her close. There had been another hand waving from that ladder by the church.

21

Anna Caine was welcome—her wrong boots, hangover, and anxieties embraced and allowed. She must remember not to stare so hard.

M

There were real mosquitoes in the North in August. Anna prayed for wind as she shuffled along the dusty road, nodding to passersby who gave brief smiles and continued passing. She waved to children in windows; they clutched the sills and studied her movements. They did not wave. Not yet.

The mountains and hills surrounded her. She looked from horizon to horizon and suddenly understood that this was the size of her world for the next four months. She had toured her apartment, which she would share with two other teachers. As returning teachers, they would not be here until the weekend. Her guide had seen that Anna had food, directed her to the store for produce and meats, and hurried off to family time with her son. The apartment had been heavy with silence, and so Anna had gone out to walk on the road.

Her head throbbed as she walked. She had enjoyed draft beer in her pub days, slugging it down as the music pulsed around her, when she had still been innocent and reckless. She had mellowed in later times to a glass or three of dry wine at evening engagements with Terrence. Last night, though, she had gulped her way through rum like a despairing and faithless soul with a plane going down and no parachute.

Her drinking partners from last night, it seemed, had crash-landed in helicopters in the Mealy Mountains several times. They had been stormbound on the south coast for weeks on end and survived on one bottle of rye and two cans of beans and an unending poker game. At other times, they had frozen their fingers while working on transformers and been unaware of arterial cuts until they had noticed the blood jetting from the wound. Most of all, her new acquaintances had been authorities on the Indigenous populations of the entire territory. The lads had ordered another round—was that the third? No, it was . . . oh, my, the fifth—and they had explained that "Those People" drank hard when they drank. *"Oh, yes, they get out of hand, pretty fast. Yep. They drink hard. Say anything, get crying even. No control. Nope, no. Bad stuff. Drink up now, girl. Don't wimp out on us."*

And so, Anna had drunk up.

Today, her stomach was still churning. Oh, God, she was going to puke, right here in the main street of Endor, between the school and the church. Six. Six rum and colas, and then she had gone weaving off to the washroom, where there had been vomit on the floor in front of her, and a concerned someone asking if she needed anything. Perhaps it had been the soft drink that had upset her stomach, but after retching into the toilet bowl for several minutes and washing her face several times, Anna had coordinated her way back to the table. One drinking colleague had departed, having started a fight with an innocent at the bar, one had been a homesick shambles droning out poignant love songs, and the third had been ready to deliver a fresh lecture on the Dark Side of the North. Anna had said that she was expecting a phone call and set a course for her room.

Thankfully, she did not puke today on the roads of Endor. It was a passing twinge. She turned, however, to face the harbour. The breeze was rising, fanning her face, slicking back the moisture, brushing the mosquitoes away. It was sweet to stand on the side of the road and feel the breeze sweep back the mosquitoes. It was a benediction on her. She closed her eyes.

"Grandmother says you want pick red berries?"

Anna opened her eyes and looked down at the child, who was arrayed in a frayed T-shirt bagging over cotton jeans. An oversized ball cap wobbled about the ears. Scuffed sneakers, no socks. Anna shivered.

"Aren't you cold?"

The child shrugged, snuffling back a bubble of mucus bulging from one nostril. A thin hand rubbed across the nose. "It is summer."

Beside the child stood a bent figure, blue skirt hanging over brown slacks, a grey cardigan, a headscarf of bright flowers. "New teacher." Anna was not sure whether this was a question or a declaration. "Berries. Endor Hill. Lots for you. Bugs!" The woman grimaced.

"Grandmother says, come pick berries with us. Gonna find lots up there. But maybe too much bugs for you up there. Not like town," the child explained.

Anna tightened her jacket hood around her face. "More than here?"

The grandmother spilled out a speech in rapid Inuktitut.

"Good you pick berries, good Inuk ways. She says you homesick, makes you get that bad headache, red eyes," the child translated.

The grandmother nodded, a little smile playing around her mouth. "You come. You see."

And so, Anna Caine, who was welcome to Endor, hangover and empty heart included, walked beside the bent grandmother and the skinny child. It was good to be here and to ascend with these people, here in the presence of mountains.

M

Red berries were not sweet and succulent, but they were strong and cleansing. They added texture to a muffin and made fine jams and preserves. They were partridge berries, but here they were called red berries. You gathered them for the winter ahead.

The mosquitoes were dense on the hill side, and the child flapped the battered cap at them. The grandmother squinted her eyes a little but had either learned to ignore them or was impervious to their presence. "Ah, Mattie," she chuckled.

"Is your name Matthew then?" said Anna Caine, scraping a pulsing layer of mosquitoes from her sleeve.

The child's face crumpled. "I am *Mathilda*," she wailed. "Matthew! Eeeee. That is *boy's* name." Tears were close at hand.

Anna was glad that she was teaching high school. Her body tensed when she was confronted with tears. She did not know yet that tears were part of all life, from birth until the final breath. She sighed.

"Aw, I'm sorry, Mathilda." She groped for a way out of this. The situation called for Terrence. Terrence would know what to say. Terrence would have noticed the femaleness of the child; he would not have blundered into this situation. Stilted scholar he might be, but he had the heart of a child and a heart for children. Children adored Terrence. He was a charming curiosity, and a little like a hopeful puppy. "So, your grandmother lives with you?" she offered.

The little girl, Mathilda, known as Mattie, lowered her gaze. "My mommy is dead now," she said. "And my daddy went away. I look after my *anânatsiak* now."

"Ah. You have one, then?" Perhaps it was a family pet.

"*There.*" Mattie pointed to the grandmother. "I look after *her*, 'cause she's old. She needs me. And I look after myself."

Here was Anna Caine, breathing mosquitoes on Endor Hill, picking tart but healthy berries, hurting the feelings of little girls who were dressed for berry picking. Now Terrence's solution rose in her mind. "I used to have a basketball group for young people where I come from. You think you and your friends would like one here?" Anna smiled and felt her parched lips cracking.

Mattie pursed her lips, considering. "Mr. King got one already. Since last year."

Of course, of course. All the fun things were all set up. Anna was not needed.

Mattie drew in a long breath. "What we need most of all," she declared, "is a Christmas play. Not shepherds and stuff. Not that one. A real one. About us. With lots of kids in it. And grandmothers too. And we could all be in it, with lights and songs and lots and lots of beautiful stuff. The story of Christmas, but our story, you know?"

"Songs," Grandmother added. "Story songs. And church songs. But drums too, like time way back. And time coming. *Hebronimiut. Uvani.* Here. Always gonna be. You know?"

Anna did not know, but it sounded like a wonderful plan. So here was Anna Caine, scrubbing away mosquitoes on Endor Hill, tasting tart but healthy berries, sharing a dramatic vision with a little girl in an oversized ball cap and an elderly woman in a flowered headscarf. She had arrived, and now she had two friends.

ᒥ

"You do a Pagan thing like that, and you will be in so much shit," Clarence the social studies teacher said, and squeezed his eyes shut and belched. He was young to have such puffy features and a receding hairline.

Several teachers had gathered in his apartment the first Friday night of the school year to sip liquor and listen to music. Anna had been included because she was new and had no group. Perhaps she would find a place with this group. Anna was not too sure as she numbed her mind with rum and missed Halifax.

"You see." Clarence pursed his lips as he studied the bottle and picked at the label. "You have your church types and your not-church types, and your people relocated during resettlement, and your settlers from way back, and everyone gets along, but you can't put them all in one story on the same stage; that's some weird fantasy old Ida Amarok's got going, and she's warping that kid she's raising. Mattie. You know about her? Skinny little kid? Weird baseball cap? Lives with Grandma—Mother found frozen, hit her head on the ice or something, and the father's been in St. John's since she was a baby. Not sure about him. Anyway." He paused and tipped back his beer. Anna wanted beer right now, but rum had been more portable to stuff in her backpack. "You'll alienate everybody in this little town, and that is not smart because you are going to need friends. You could help after school with sports and games. Everyone loves sports. Great leveler." He nodded.

"I was thinking the Grade 11s could maybe set up some scenes—"

"Aww. Geez. No." Clarence flapped one hand. "No, you are not going to turn this into a project for Grade 11 English. No. They do research papers; they don't turn their research into plays. My God, have a drink and listen. Mary! Talk some sense into this woman. We've got another one saving the goddamn town."

Mary, a slim woman perhaps thirty years old, with thick blonde hair pulled back from her face in a loose ponytail, widened her eyes and lit a cigarette. "Clarence, despite his great lack of tact, is probably right. Maybe do it after school, tone it down a little, make it a nice little history with hymns on one side and throat singing in counterpoint—"

"Mary, you are not helping. You are not helping at all." Clarence hefted the now empty bottle and drifted off to the kitchen.

Anna sipped her rum and wondered what Terrence would say. Undoubtedly, he would counter with a nice quotation from T.S. Eliot's *Journey of the Magi:* *"This birth was hard and bitter agony for us, like death, our death."* Terrence was a remarkably well-read man as well as a humble man of profound faith; he loved Christmas, as a child did, but also saw in the Incarnation the transformation of humanity, the birth of something new and powerful in the cosmic order. Yes, Terrence would have no trouble with a historical play that connected the Christian experience with a radical change in Inuit ways.

With hymns and throat singing?

Mary took a long swallow from her rye and water. Her words were neatly spaced when she spoke again, each pronounced with care. "Clarence is part of a dying breed. Drinking like that went out of style here a few years back. *You* want to slow down, maybe, cut back on the rum a little. Like, Ralph was saying, he said, you know, you got really wasted in Goose Bay."

"Ralph?" Was Ralph one of her new friends from that night? Was he the crooner? Possibly. No, he was the fighter. She distinctly remembered they said Ralph. Oh. Wait. It was the lecturer.

"Yeah. He said they told you a few stories, shocked you a little, woke you up, and you got hammered and puked on the club washroom floor. Like, either you don't know how to drink, or you've got a serious problem."

Anna placed her glass on the table. "I have to go phone my fiancé," she said. "There is something I want to ask him about Eliot."

"That your cat?"

"The poet."

Mary shrugged, draining her glass. "I never cared much for that English lit. Make sure you focus on the outport themes. That part is real. But I'll help you with the music for your play. We want to make it real. Hard part will be getting the kids to do it right. They don't take direction that well."

"It will have to be their voice."

Mary sighed, opening her cigarette pack. "My God. Clarence was right. Another one. *Listen to the people*," she announced in a sing-song voice. "*Let me teach you how to teach.* You damned well make me sick."

Oh, dear. Where was this coming from? More important, where was it going? Mary was no longer mellow; perhaps that last swallow had put her over the edge?

"And stay the hell away from my guy, OK? No more cozy little binges. Damned tease."

Please, dear God, let her guy not be....

"My Ralph told me all about you. In Goose. When we were *together*. You know?"

Perfect. Anna was going to spend ten months in isolation with mood-racing Mary, who was thankfully not her roommate, who was besotted with Ralph, who hopefully would spend the winter stormbound on the south coast with his meagre portion of rye and beans and an endless poker game.

This was a very small group. Anna's goal for Saturday would be to find a very different group, but right now, she needed to be with Terrence.

TONYA'S DREAM

That evening had ended, Anna heard later, with Mary weeping in the hall closet, and Clarence cooking a massive midnight breakfast, which only he had consumed. Clarence had been outraged when his colleagues snubbed his hospitality like that. Others had cleared the mess, got Mary home, and assured Clarence that he was the best host ever. Anna soon learned that Mary's Ralph was always out to charm someone, and that Mary had been in love with him since she met him just after her arrival two years before. Mary lived in hope. Ralph was friendly but always moving on. However, a nurse had now captured his heart, although time would tell about the rest of him. Ralph was a free spirit.

Best of all, Anna learned that these parties, though legendary, were atypical and rare. Music, camping, and community involvement were more the norm.

Mary had either forgotten or withdrawn her musical commitment to the play, and Anna did nothing to reopen that conversation. One of her Grade 11s emerged as the visionary who would bring Mattie's play to life. She was Tonya, a remarkable and vigorous young woman, shimmering with promise. Tonya, just turned nineteen, had come back to school to finish her education. With a talent for volleyball and a smoker's cough, with a mixed reputation and a passion for history, Tonya could balance toddler on hip and textbooks under arm. Tonya, rising from the ashes, committed herself to the project.

It was Tonya who suggested that the class, instead of completing independent community research papers, divide up the eras and create a comprehensive history. So, instead of three papers on the history of the church in Endor, four on the development of the fishing industry, and so on, there would be a series. One paper would focus on pre-contact life, technology, and culture; another would deal with early interactions with fishing and whaling cultures; one study would describe the establishment of the mission in the district, another would focus on the residential school models for the Coastal Peoples, and yet another would trace the community shifts during resettlement. Finally, one would examine the direction the community was taking today. Partners would share the research and collaborate on the writing. Ms. Caine's task was to keep them motivated and approve the final edits.

Ms. Caine was glad to oblige. The others respected Tonya. She had gone down hard, but she had pulled herself up by her own hand. Tonya was the future her fellow students aspired to. She loved all Inuk ways, and she spoke the language. She had also decided to get the best education there was. She had gotten a restraining order on an abusive partner, had lived down the gossip about her past, and was planning to study law. The others knew Tonya was the one who would make it.

It was Tonya who arranged the play in seven scenes, one for each of the first five research papers and two for the sixth—to mourn the losses and to celebrate the accomplishments and the aspirations of their people.

"Do it with narrators, with the main points, not the whole paper, with a diorama thing and maybe just a little moving around, you know? Don't go giving everyone lines in case they don't come or get stage panics or something. That way," she concluded, "we can work on the costumes. And find the music."

M

Anna stood in the wings the night of the performance and watched the dream unfold. On one level, she was grateful to Tonya, for the play was exactly as it should have been. On the other, she resented Tonya, because it was Anna's dream first, and Anna secretly did want to be the one to save the town, even as the teachers Clarence and Mary had seen.

Still, as her fiancé Terrence said, it was a birth. Not, as it was for the Magi, a realization that the old ways could no longer satisfy, but a realization that the old ways would come again, in a new and profound way, to astonish the world. There had been birth and death, and then birth again.

When little Mattie and her friends shuffled onto the stage, a little shy in their snowy *silapâks* and ceremonial *kamiks,* while her grandmother chanted a story song of joy and finding the way home, Anna's throat closed with emotion.

As the ceremonial hood of doctor of laws was draped over the child's shoulders, the tears spilled from Anna's eyes. Thank you, Tonya, for you bring the past into the future with beauty and hope. *And a little child shall lead them.*

ᴧ

One January morning, the body of Tonya Ullâk was found along the trail between the old quarter and the new school. She had sustained a cranial fracture, the wound at the base of her skull raw and angry, and she had been dumped there beside the path.

Restraining orders are legally binding, but they cannot call the dead back to life.

Anna cried for a long time then, for the hopes and the dreams crumpled on the side of a deserted trail. She cried for the long emptiness that lay ahead for them all.

ᴧ

Thus, Anna Caine arrived in Endor. She had broken through the crust and found the raw wounds torn deep into the earth. What she would do about it would take many stories, seen by many eyes, told in many ways . . . until Anna was ready to live the last story.

TERRENCE'S HOPE

Terrence stood in the lounge at the Halifax airport that January morning, hands deep in his overcoat pockets, as he watched the plane roll down the runway, carrying his beloved Anna back to Labrador. Six months. Six long months lay ahead, and then they would be together forever.

He sighed, turning toward the exit. Six months and this adventure would be over.

Not a moment too soon.

Anna had seemed different when she came home at Christmas. Her eyes had looked past him, seeking. It was as if she had grown up, put aside the things of the child, and grown quiet inside.

She had been listening.

An elderly woman in the village had taught Anna beading, and she had presented Terrence with duffle slippers encrusted in flowers. *"I will keep them safe always,"* he had assured Anna, *"but they are too fine to wear. Gifts of the heart should not be worn out."*

In truth, he simply could not put the glittering things on his feet.

Anna had talked much of a little girl called Mattie and her English student Tonya Ullâk. *Ullâk* meant "morning," and indeed, Tonya had seemed a dazzling morning of light, come to shine over her people.

She had enough devils in her past, in Terrence's humble opinion, to shock even his Lord and Saviour. Jesus would have had to grit his teeth to seize the courage to cast those out. Tonya drank. Hard. She walked the roads. She dared the night things. She had put herself under the protection of a man who shared her with his companions. She did not seem a nice girl, but Anna had told him that Tonya had been a pretty and happy child, clever in school and much loved. This had not shielded her from the darkness of the world, and she had been deep in anger since that darkness had ruptured her at the age of fourteen.

Terrence shuddered. She had been *fourteen*.

Tonya had a baby when she was eighteen—by whom, no one truly knew. Apparently, this child had been her epiphany, her chance at redemption; Terrence saw that birth as the hand of his Saviour casting out Tonya's darkness and pouring in soothing light.

Tonya had been a visionary, and she and Anna had brought to life the encounters that had changed the world of Tonya's people. Their play had been dazzling—with ancient songs, hymns of Europe, and anthems of the universe. And that had made sense to Terrence, for wasn't God, after all, Lord of All Creation? The true work of the Cross was to transform, and therefore, Terrence believed that it was his Lord who was leading this People forward, not with sandals and incense and a camel or two but with the Creative Power of the Universe.

For such was the work of the Kingdom of Heaven.

And then, as Anna had been preparing to return to Endor, the news had come: This Tonya had been crucified, not with nails and wood but with a tire iron, after all the wretched crucifixions of her lost years, and the light was gone until the end of time from the glorious promised morning, and Terrence suddenly knew his Saviour lay crucified beside Tonya, curled in the snow in her blood, weeping for the loss of the beauty she had brought to creation.

A passage from Jeremiah rose in his heart—verses about weeping as the children of Israel passed into captivity:

> *A voice is heard in Ramah, lamenting and weeping bitterly; it is Rachel weeping for her children, refusing to be comforted for her children, because they are no more. (Jeremiah 31:15)*

To Terrence, Jeremiah's words expressed the despair that Anna felt, the despair of the whole community of Endor, as Tonya faded from their midst.

Terrence found the rest of that passage disturbing, not comforting, for Jeremiah had gone on to tell his people to turn from their despair, to take comfort in the promised and distant future—*Generations from now, it will all be fine; don't cry.* What comfort could this possibly bring to the family of the Ullâk girl, dead in the snow? *At least she has a little boy; find comfort in that and dry your eyes.* No! Lament! Weep until your heart runs dry.

How could the death of Tonya ever inspire anyone to hope? It was a brutal loss that should and would be mourned until its time was fulfilled, and words of hope were perhaps not the best words at this time.

May your memories comfort you. Why did people say that?

The passage from Jeremiah moved him especially to think of Rachel the woman, not the symbol, who yearned for children and despaired as her body and her arms remained empty. On her knees on the jagged rocks, her arms stretched for heaven, there was no comfort that could lift her pain, until its time was fulfilled.

Thus it was with Anna, he knew. She had wept down into a deep hole of sharp edges and total darkness. She could not be comforted, for Tonya was no more.

Terrence loved her even more for the greatness of her heart.

He wished she were not going back, but she would not be Anna if she did not return to Endor after this.

Then he pulled his collar tight to his throat and strode through the exit to retrieve his car and return to his own world. The world with Anna in his future.

Even though she looked past him these days.

QUICKENING

When the school opened after the funeral, Anna was unable to comfort her students. There was no kind and uplifting word for this time, and so they stared at the walls and the floor, each in a separate cell of despair.

Thus, the first class passed in silence and in darkness. Anna had been told that she must reach out to her students and support them, but her own heart was empty. The minutes dragged by; the hour was nearly gone when Carla, a pale, thin-faced girl with long, straight hair, cleared her throat and said: "I weep for you, my sister, for you are a bright and shining star, soaring straight to heaven."

"You write that?" Martin, her classmate, cleared his throat as his voice broke. "She was. She is."

Carla held up a plain folder. "She was my cousin. We were *best* cousins, cousins close like sisters. I been writing ever since. Like I can't stop. I talk to her that way, and then I don't have to go to her and hurt my family so bad."

"We have to be strong, Miss." The girl beside Carla slid an arm around Carla's shoulders, but she was addressing Anna.

Anna touched the box on her desk, where all the drafts and pictures lay tucked away, awaiting the promise of fulfilment in the new year.

"We could finish this," she whispered. "We need to edit and revise, polish every page. Get all the references in form. Work in the pictures. Make it strong."

"The last chapter was hers," said Martin.

"Carla's poems," another student offered. "And our stories, maybe our poems and thoughts, some artwork too. You know? Picture and thousand words?"

"A tribute," another said. "Our history. Our story. For her."

"Where is Bobby?" Anna's voice was still hoarse.

"*Anânatsiasuak* Ida's got him," Carla explained. "Tonya's mom and little Mattie's mom were sisters. Mattie's mom wasn't drinking, you know, the time she fell; they said that, but it wasn't true. And Tonya's mom and dad were good people. Not their fault, what happened when Tonya was a kid. They took it hard, what happened to her. Sick guys, doing sick things. But she was strong, she rose above, and she—oh, she was beautiful."

Carla was gulping in deep breaths, the girl beside her rocking her. "He had the cancer, her dad," that girl continued, "two years ago. Gone now, and her mom isn't well. So, her mom's mother, that's Tonya's grandmom, is raising Tonya's little Bobby. That's Mattie's grandmom too; she's already raising little Mattie. Hard for that woman, one daughter in hospital long, other one fell like that. But a new little brother for Mattie—cousin, brother too."

"He should visit here, sometimes, like he used to," suggested Martin.

"This is going to be beautiful," murmured Anna. Her eyes throbbed, the last tears long wrung out of them but aching to create and shed more. There were not enough tears in the universe for this grief.

And yet, these young people who had grown up with Tonya, who knew all her story and all her dreams, had a much deeper grief, and they were walking into her future for her. Thus, her classmates chose to honour their bright and shining fallen star.

M

January slipped away to February, to exams and projects, conferencing and editing and marking. Anna walked on the road and ventured on the snowmobile trails out in the hills. The cold enveloped her, probing her down-filled parka and snow pants for weakness. She shuffled on the trail, her breathing shallow, for the throat and lungs ached with the sharp air.

She was walking one Saturday out to the lake chain that meandered between the hills, leading to the country where the community went to cut their firewood. That was a long way, but she would walk to the first lake. She would climb the hillside and walk along the rounded granite top, see for miles, and pronounce the name of Tonya Ullâk. She liked saying that name, hearing it on the morning air and imagining that, somewhere, Tonya herself stirred and heard.

Tonya would smile, knowing that she was remembered and loved.

Anna was ashamed then, for surely little Bobby would call forever for the faceless being in his memory, the being who was Mother.

A snow machine droned in the distance as she started up the hillside, wishing there was a trail for this part. Her legs sank deep into the drifts, so she spread out on her hands and knees and crawled. At the top, the snow would be blown clear, exposing the rocks.

Anna was halfway up, and the machine would be passing now. She knew she should turn and give a pleasant teacher smile and wave to show friendship and goodwill, but she hated the machine sound this morning. This was a morning for her to name Tonya, the daughter of the morning—her joy.

A loud monosyllabic roar sounded below. A shrill, piping voice rose behind it: "Oh, Miss Caine, Miss Caine, come down! Joshua says come down."

She turned. This Joshua had most certainly not said to come down, although his elemental growl suggested urgency. He was standing with one knee on the seat and gripping the handlebars with huge sealskin mitts. His hood was thrust back, but his expression was still hidden by wolf fur trim and full goggles. Behind the very basic snowmobile was a long wooden sled, a *Kamutik*, coil of rope neatly strapped down in front of chainsaw and gas can. Beside it, little Mattie Amarok, the girl of the berry hill and the play, the girl who was cousin to the late Tonya Ullâk, was managing to dance up and down, arms thrashing against the stiff parka sleeves, legs straining against snow pants and puffy boots. The eyes shone from the tiny gap between scarf and hood.

Joshua pushed the goggles back on his forehead, and his eyebrows lowered. "Lots of crevasse there, deep, down till spring."

"We never go that way," Mattie added. "It is very, very dangerous. You must listen to Joshua. My cousin knows. He is my grandmother's favourite nephew. My grandmother and his grandmother are sisters. And we are getting wood. We look after our grandmothers." She straightened her shoulders within the mass of fabric.

"You should go back," Joshua stated. "Stay on the trail, going." He indicated the way back to Endor with one mittened hand.

"Come wooding with us!" Mattie exclaimed. "Hey? Joshua?"

"Too cold." The voice was flat. The mittened hand pawed down the goggles and tugged the hood forward. "Get on the *Kamutik* now. Hold tight." This last was addressed to Mattie, who drooped her way down onto the sled, gripping the crossbars hard.

The engine buzzed, and they were gone. Little puffs of snow stirred on the trail and enveloped their passing.

Anna was left to call out the name of their cousin to the wind and ice, but not from the hilltop that was forbidden to her.

She yearned to sink down into the crevasse; her gnawed bones would emerge in the spring. There was a peace in that thought that she could never share with Terrence.

Terrence could never push back goggles and squint into the returning sun. Terrence was not of Endor.

Joshua was. Oh, Joshua was, and Anna sensed that he knew the seduction of the crevasse, but he would never submit.

M

February was long and silent, with days of clear skies and wind stirring the snow on the harbour ice. On other days, great flakes heaped and piled until Anna wanted to scream for them to stop, and still they piled, grim, smug in their power. Planes were rare. People waited for their letters, their parcels, and their medicines. They waited to go to hospital for treatment, for surgery. The People had always waited. Anna paced and hated the wind and the snow, and the ex-boyfriend who had taken out his rage on Tonya. She walked near the town, when she walked at all, but wherever she walked, someone was sure to drive by and point out the dangers that she was missing. Oh, she wanted to appreciate their concern and coaching, but she clenched her teeth behind her teacher smile and wished that they would drive by or away or somewhere else.

The new term began, with new units and fresh starts, but Anna lacked ideas. She felt like parsing sentences for parts of speech for the entire period or developing author biographies in literature. Something dull. Something harmless. Something safe.

Adolescents and young adults do not enjoy dull and harmless things. They like to live and learn in three dimensions. They did the dull tasks Anna assigned, and appreciated the predictability, but her classroom became deadening. Her students began to sleep in because who wanted to rise at dawn and charge off to school to underline verbs?

Teachers also do not enjoy dull and harmless things. They dare not sleep in, but in isolation, they can become sensitive. A small thing can become a great thing: Clarence, the social studies teacher of the long-ago first party, left a package of ground beef thawing in the fridge. His roommate Larry left a dish of butter on the shelf below. This Larry found his butter with spatters of blood coagulating on and around it. Larry went raging off to tell Mary, who was upset because "her" Ralph was now engaged, and she sneered at Larry's outrage. Their raised voices and creative expletives awakened one of Mary's roommates, who somehow connected this episode to Mary's demands for her share of the phone bill. Therefore, this roommate now refused to contribute to the phone bill. Anna steamed long and repetitively to Terrence when her neighbours accepted her dinner invitation one Saturday, and then they suggested a different menu and time. The light remained shadowed, the food all needed ketchup, and the endearing habits of one's roommates were now hateful.

The television service was intermittent at best, but the Saturday night hockey always came through. Anna stared, even though she did not know what a blue line was. She stared, because the world was ending, and this was all that remained: a dot flickering on a thirteen-inch screen and insects on skates scrambling after it.

M

One Saturday afternoon in late February, Anna met Ida Amarok, the grandmother of the berry hill and the play, in the store. Ida was a little more wrinkled, a little more stooped, since the morning they found her granddaughter Tonya. From deep within her parka and wrappings, Ida scrutinized Anna.

"Got partridge," Ida announced. "Lots of partridge. Joshua bring them. You come, my house." A smile flickered in her eyes, then faded.

Anna considered. Was she coming to Ida's house to eat partridges? To get partridges? To meet Joshua there and receive partridges? Now? Some time?

"Sure." Anna nodded. "*Nakummek.* Umm, *mânna?*"

Ida grinned. "You come. Mattie and Baby watch cooking. Lots of partridge. As many ever as you want to eat."

This was infinitely preferable to watching shadows gather in a tense apartment while waiting for "The Game." Anna was eager to get there, for Ida's house would be light and calm. An eight-year-old and a toddler were watching the cooking? They should get there fast. Or was the bringer of partridges watching them all? Anna wanted to get there right now.

M

Joshua was playing checkers with Mattie while her little cousin Bobby studied the board with the absorption of a master chess player. A young woman, her parka open in the heat, sat near the stove, where rich aromas steamed from a pot. Her oval face was framed by long, lank hair parted in the centre, and she hunched over a sealskin project that she was working. Her lips parted to reveal even, white teeth.

"Ms. Caine." She bobbed her head. "I am Leah. You like to sew?"

Anna wetted her lips and shrugged. "I'm not very good at it." She inclined her head toward the project, which was a *kamik*. "Are those for the craft store? They're beautiful."

Leah offered a shy smile. "I don't know. Not good enough, maybe. Maybe good enough for his big feet." She tipped her head toward Joshua. "This is Joshua. He is a carpenter."

"She knows," Mattie sang out, her eyes never leaving the board. "We saw her on the ponds, when we were wooding."

Leah frowned. "You must never go off alone. Sometimes, there are wolves, in the day, too." She brightened. "You should come with *us* sometime."

Us. What sort of Us were she and Joshua? Family us? Friends us? Forever us? Leah had a dull face, Anna decided, flat and conventional. Anna's lips pressed in a tight smile. "I wouldn't want to be a bother," she murmured.

"Too cold for her," Joshua observed, deftly clicking his king over his cousin's remaining pieces and sweeping them from the board. "Maybe in the spring."

Leah laughed. "We will dress you warm. You should come," she urged.

Joshua was laying the board for the next game, while Mattie and her grandmother set the table with bowls and spoons, a dish of butter, and a platter of *panitsiak*. He frowned, suddenly. "You should help her," he snapped at Leah, indicating the table. "Make tea."

Leah tucked her sewing into her satchel and shuffled to retrieve the kettle. She should not encourage Joshua to treat her like a doormat, Anna decided. Perhaps she was a woman of weak character, no spirit, no match for a man like Joshua.

"Good strong tea, for my Joshua. You must be a tired man. Always like that when you get tired," Leah sang, dropping tea bags into the pot.

Joshua stared for a moment, and then his face relaxed in a smile. "You would know," he murmured.

He pushed the thick hair back from his forehead. His frame was straight and wiry; his eyes glowed with warmth as he studied Leah making the strong tea. His smile broadened.

The muscles beneath that sweater would be smooth and rolling, taut with energy. Anna could slide a hand up the back of that sweater, tug the shirt free, slide, and caress. Terrence had fleshy skin; it would be a little like caressing a flabby rabbit. Joshua, now, he was a wolf, lean and tough. A hunter.

Anna felt Leah's eyes on her, and she did not have to face her to know that those eyes were troubled. Anna's cheeks were warming; they must be red.

"Take off your jacket if you are so warm," Leah purred, clunking cups down beside the bowls. "Some people are not strong enough for the heat," she added with an apologetic smile. "It is not their fault they are like that."

∧∧

The light grew back over the Land, some days delicate and shimmering with a promise of spring, others thick and oppressive and smothered in ragged snow-flakes or wisps of blowing snow. On the delicate and shimmering days, Anna walked the shoreline with her students, studying models for descriptive writing. Little writing was done, but the mood was bright as the students shouted their oral descriptions over one another.

Their powers of observation amazed Anna. "Look," one of the Grade 9s called out. "That's Joshua Kalluk, heading up Endor Bay!" All Anna could see was a speck on the far side of the bay, winding around the ice slabs. It was easy to tell, the class explained. *"Hear that engine? Got the gas set high for more power. See the way he kneels, the way his shoulders are set over the steering? Only Joshua Kalluk drives like that, always ready, in case maybe bad ice opens up. And his hood is rounded, not pointed, and pushed back a little."*

"The girlfriends can tell it is Joshua in the dark, with their eyes closed," someone twittered.

"I don't see Leah," another added. "Must be still mad. She needs to have a baby for him, then he will love her forever." Nervous laughter rose, as they eyed the teacher.

Anna was supposed to stop them, but she had drifted across the ice to mount the snow machine behind Joshua, sliding close while his body pressed back against hers, knowing his presence with her eyes closed. . ..

Her eyes snapped open.

"That remark is inappropriate," she declared, scowling in the required reproof.

Her student smirked. She had seen Anna's face in the moment before the reprimand.

Anna did not feel sorry in the least for dull-faced Leah. There was no fire in her, nothing there for a man like Joshua. Who would want to husband a bland little seamstress like Leah?

Terrence would.

She thought of Terrence and felt herself sinking into the crevasse, the snow packing her nose and mouth. She thought of suffocating, without a sound.

WINTER INTO SPRING

March quickened into April, and the days softened. Yes, the winds could still blow rough and bitter, but the days of light grew and thrived. Hunters and families ascended to the Barrens to intercept the caribou, and faces tanned in the glare from the snow.

And thus, one Saturday afternoon in late April, when Anna was sharing tea with Ida and Mattie, Leah shuffled in, beaming, a bundle wrapped in plastic shopping bags under her arm.

"*TuttuvimiKuak* for Auntie," she declared. "Good frozen caribou meat to make little Bobby strong! Soon, he will hunt for you. My Joshua will teach him."

Ida pursed her lips and patted her hands together. "Good, good. Put down now. Heavy."

Leah shrugged. "I am Inuk. I am not afraid to work, not even now."

She gazed around the room and her eyes settled on Anna. "Ah. Miss Caine, our teacher. Joshua and I are going fishing up the Bay tomorrow. You come too. You can't go back to your big city without seeing a little of our ways. You can ride on the *Kamutik* with Mattie. Joshua will put the big box on, so you won't fall off. Don't worry. We will go very slow!" She laughed, beaming harder than should be possible.

Ida chuckled. "Yes, go slow now. But you go *Kamutik*; teacher go Joshua."

Leah's eyes narrowed. "I ride with him. So, he will go slow. For the teacher," she added, a scowl starting around her eyes.

Anna listened to the conversation, and although it was in English, she knew she was missing the main points.

Perhaps it was a dialect issue.

M

It was good to relax in the spring landscape, to feel the power latent in the sun's rays, to cast off parka and hat and feel the air soft on her scalp. She was safe now, and the Land could not harm her.

"Hey! Keep your parka on!" snapped Joshua. "You can die like that."

"It feels nice, but it's not safe," Leah elaborated. "The chill creeps up on you, and soon you are shaking. Pull off a mitt, sometimes, but don't strip like that."

Joshua's eyes widened, and suddenly, he tossed back his head and laughed. "Strip!" he exclaimed. "You think the teacher strip?"

His laughter rose, reaching over the ice, soaring into the sky. Leah pushed her shoulder into his side, grinning. "You make my words bad."

They tumbled together, swaying, his arms encircling her. Light laughter and approving nods rose from the people scattered along the shore. Ah! To be in the spring sun, to know most storms had passed, and to see young love, hopeful love, the future coming into being. Ah, life was good today.

Anna squirmed into her parka and tugged her hat around her ears. She sprawled on her side as some others were doing, leaning on an elbow as she gazed down into the swirls and bubbles in the ice hole. Joshua had tunneled with a hand-operated auger through nearly three feet of ice to make these holes. She let the line sink down into the darkness, swung up the hand that held the stick, and flicked it to yield a gentle tug, then paused, lowered her hand, paused once more, and swung it up again.

Now Joshua was stretched beside her, staring down into the hole. "Good," he said. "You learn fast. Just down a little more."

Anna unwound more line from the stick. Joshua nodded. "You like our ways. And you're a good teacher. The people liked your play."

Anna turned her face toward the low mountains across the bay, blinking. "It was Tonya's." She sighed.

Joshua nodded. "My cousin," he said. "Our family misses her. But she was happy, you teaching her. She said she could grow, learning with you."

Anna's vision blurred. "I miss her too. And I wish we had never done the play, if it made her ex-boyfriend so angry."

Joshua shrugged. "He was angry anyway. A long time. Angry man, angry boy. Problems in the home." He rolled to his feet with a sigh. "So many angry people. They need to be out here; people get strong out here, but lots get stuck in town

43

and no way to get out here. Maybe the school could help. More time on the Land, time with Elders, build things, with their hands."

Anna was leaving in less than three months. Did Joshua expect her to organize funding and spearhead a program now?

"I'll be gone end of June," Anna said.

Joshua grinned. "You could stay. Teach again. Learn. You could live with us."

"I'm getting married this summer. He's a minister in Halifax. I don't think he would be good at hunting or fishing."

"So, you could both live with us, till you get your own place. He might be a *hunting* minister." Joshua's laughter rang out across the bay again, and Leah saw him standing over Anna Caine. The smile that had begun on her lips stopped there, for she saw in Anna the free spirit that Joshua yearned to be. He wanted a secure home, and a comfortable home, but sometimes, she knew, he gazed out over the mountains and in those moments, he dared the old spirits, drawing in their nightmares and laughing them down.

Leah knew that she belonged to Joshua. He loved her now and would love her even more later when she was sure of her news. At the same time, she knew that, although he might scowl at Anna Caine, still the woman drew him. Leah would just have to be stronger than Anna, inside, in her heart.

ᴧ

The following weekend, Anna came upon Joshua as she walked around the town. He was on the slope behind the house where his great aunt lived with little Mattie, unloading heavy blocks of snow from the *Kamutik*.

"Not deep snow in town," he explained. "You need strong snow, many blocks."

He gestured to the two layers he had completed, indicating a gap. "I put the ice wi'dow there," he said, "so my snow house will have light."

Anna burst into laughter. "An ice widow? My God, won't she freeze, packed in the wall like that? What sort of person is that? And," she added, "what sort of person would put her there?"

Joshua did not joke well in English. His face fell. "I am saying 'ween'dow,'" he muttered. "You should not make fun when I say it the best I can."

Anna lowered her eyes. "I am sorry," she offered. "We joke about words in English, but it isn't fair when you are learning."

Joshua glanced out across the harbour, then turned to Anna and smiled. "Come with me to get more blocks. Ride with me and learn on the Land," he urged. Again, his voice lifted in that ringing laugh. "So you won't be the ice widow."

M

Now is the beautiful springtime, and there is no storm today, but Anna bundles down in her parka and leans close to Joshua as he drives. She is supposed to hold the strap on the seat between them, but she decides she is afraid and hugs her body to his. This is a moment beyond Terrence, beyond Leah, the moment of Anna and Joshua awakening, and the dark moment in Halifax when she was scrambling from the floor and brushing the crumbs from her shoulders is forgotten, and when the blocks are cut and stacked, and she lies back in her parka on the loose snow, there is a scent of spruce, and the light glinting on the ice, and the rhythm of their bodies in the rhythm of spring. This is right; this is what is meant to be. Anna Caine exults in the power of her young body. Joshua rises above her, and yes, the muscles are smooth and taut. She loves this moment, this man, and this is the entire world, now and forever.

Then they drive back to town and speak only of the snow house while they work. She returns to the teacherage, and he goes home to his grandmother's house. Leah will be cooking. Terrence will be waiting for a call.

The world shrinks back to a tumbled moment in the loose snow, and these realities are just noise in the background.

M

May pulsed with soft warmth. The People journeyed often up the bay, and camps sprawled in the light of the spring night. Children scurried from tent to tent, and then out to the holes to fish in careful imitation of their elders, until restless, they scampered among the campsites again. Visits were made, and many cups of tea consumed in the shadows of late evening.

The stars were white gleams in a pale sky, and Anna slept soundly on a bed of fir boughs in *Anânatsiak* Ida's tent. Ida wove together the fir tips in a perfect mat on the snow, sharp bits carefully tucked under each frond, row upon patient row. No dampness or chill permeated. Anna rolled into her sleeping bag while Mattie and her little cousin-brother Bobby tucked into a bag nearby, and Ida curled near the door beside her sister Lisetta, their voices soft, the Language rising like music in the night. Across the fire pit, Joshua and Leah shared a tent with some cousins, and Anna pictured a tent for just her and Joshua, far from the main camp, where their voices could rise in the night to the rhythm of their lovemaking.

Joshua spoke to her, he fished with her, and he told her ways of the Land, but he did not touch her again. He did not cast meaningful glances her way. Anna reminded herself that they were both engaged, and that this behaviour was totally appropriate. Perhaps he thought that they had made a little mistake and would be wise to put it behind them and get on with their lives. Perhaps he did not imagine her naked on the boughs, and their bodies pulsing together as the Northern Lights rippled over the sky above them.

Did he know that she was taut and trembling, living for his touch, and that she did not think of Terrence or care?

Chapter 4: Woman of Steady Flame

FROM ANNA

The Bible is rich in stories of women who did questionable things but took a stance for the winning side. There is Rahab, who made her scripture debut as the harlot who hid the spies sent to scout out Jericho. There is the widow Judith, who apparently flirted with the enemy Holofernes, got him drunk, and cut off his head. Yet, pregnant widow Tamar was denounced for harlotry, and dismissed to be burned—until she proved that she had disguised herself as a prostitute and her father-in-law Judah was the father. Suddenly, burning was off the table. It seems if you are a harlot, you are allowed to act like one. If you are merely acting like a harlot, you are not. It all depends on the point of view.

I did not set out to save a kingdom or a heritage. I was not a harlot or playing the part of one. I loved. I did selfish things, but everything I did, I did for love. I loved, and I have spent a lifetime trying to move past that love, yet seeking the strength to claim that love. I have known many teachers, heard many voices. I have been many stories. Yes, I made mistakes. But please, do not judge me.

I have spent a lifetime judging me. Is that not enough?

LESSONS IN STORIES

"**I** am not kidding," Lisa, Anna's neighbour and colleague, said. "It seriously happened just that way."

"Mary does not manage rejection well," Lisa's boyfriend Tom expanded, breaking off a chunk of *panitsiak* and slathering butter across it. "My God, this is good. Leah taught you this?"

He paused, and he and Lisa exchanged a look. "We were talking about Mary attending Ralph's engagement party," Lisa said.

"His stag," Tom corrected. "She crashed his stag. Do not dignify it with the title of engagement party."

"She got past the security guys, who were probably plastered anyway, and made a rather embarrassing scene—"

"Professing undying love, and enumerating the sins of the nurse-fiancée—"

"And said things we won't repeat here."

"But would love to. It was a night to remember."

"And I still want to know how you got invited."

Tom's eyes widened. "I just did a lot of winking and nudging and made appealing references to the good old days."

"You mean the one time you flew into Endor together, on the mail plane, on a calm and sunny morning."

"It was a little windy, a little dangerous."

"So, is Mary OK?" Anna interrupted.

Tom pursed his lips and lifted one shoulder. "She is a little older, a little wiser. But perhaps only a little. It could be awkward, but it might pass."

"My God!" Lisa exploded. "Don't you have any empathy, Tom? She is hurting."

Tom gave his head a quick shake and reached for his tea mug. "She made her bed—well, not really, which is perhaps the problem, since she clearly wanted to. . .." He approximated a leer.

Anna reached for the jam. She had never grown close to the teacher Mary; that first party and Mary's accusations about the beloved Ralph remained awkward between them. Yet she felt for Mary as a woman, in the grip of unreturned love and unable to work past it, while people smirked in the background. Was this how people would talk about her and Joshua? Would colleagues shrug and snicker and never ponder the depths of their love?

"So," Lisa remarked, tracing one finger over the pattern on her mug, "you do a lot of camping with the happy couple. She gets jealous, you know."

"Of everyone. Leah has a suspicious mind," Tom elaborated. "She and Joshua are the 'matched from infancy' types, and in her opinion, the whole world is after her man."

"Watch yourself," Lisa recommended. "Don't give her any reason to think you *are* after her man, because she has enough gossipy aunties and cousins to wreck your chances of working here ever again."

"Were they the family that scratched up the visiting consultant's face that time?" Tom queried.

"That never happened. That's just gossip." Lisa shook her head, pushing back her bangs.

"Ah. You hide your eyes like that when you are lying, you know," Tom observed, nibbling around the edges of the slab of *panitsiak*. "Well," he sighed. "Just don't give them any reason to start talking. Or scratching."

"By going camping with the whole family?" Anna's eyes widened in what she hoped was an expression of innocence.

"Or travelling off alone. On the ice. Hanging on for dear life. Stick with that story anyway," Tom suggested, placing the bun on his napkin and pushing back from the table.

Lisa gathered up a few crumbs and rubbed her palms together over her plate. "This was great. We need to get together like this more often. This type of thing would be good for Mary. Fortunately for her, Loose Lips here was the only staff member to witness her total humiliation. What happens at the stag is supposed to stay at the stag."

"And I trust my favourite girls to carry my burden," Tom concluded with a gallant bow. "Lisa, get the recipe from her, will you? Ida's bannock is just so good."

Then why did they say Leah? Why did they even come here? To warn, to shame, to gloat?

This is what happens when there is so much ice and so few trees.

This is what happens when you learn your moral compass only works when you do not test it.

LEAH: LOW FIRE
BURNING LONG

In mid-May, the water pooled on the ice at high tide and froze to shell ice. Sometimes this ice shattered, and then you panicked until you hit the solid ice underneath. Other times, the rising tide soaked the snow, and the ice was heavy with slush. This mid-May morning, Anna decided to walk along the shore. Now perhaps she had seen Joshua working over his snow machine from her bedroom window, but perhaps the encounter was by accident.

It was early morning, but most people had left for the *iKaluk* fishing camps while the tide was still low. Joshua was adjusting the tension on the drive belt, for it was worn and stretched.

Anna took a stance in front of the snowmobile. "Do you like me?" she demanded.

Joshua looked up, his eyes going wide. "What kind of question is that?" he said.

Anna pushed her hood back and straightened her toque. "I mean . . . you just walked away after we—were together out there, and—like it didn't happen, or you got what you wanted and that was that—or like maybe—I was nothing to you? You know?"

Joshua bent over his tool kit, seeking a five-eighths wrench. "I walked away," he murmured. "I thought we drove, eh?"

"No, you know what I mean. You were like, you didn't care." Anna was now scuffing at the crusted snow like a child being scolded.

Joshua bent over the engine again. "And you sat way at the back, not like before. Hanging on before, but then, no."

"We need to talk about it," Anna said.

Joshua eased the wrench in a cautious quarter turn. He pressed one hand to the belt, nodded, and then straightened, tossing the wrench back in the kit.

"You talk about making love? Like the movies? When they tell how good it was, yes or no?"

"No, I talk about love, and feeling love, and wanting to hold someone I love."

"You love the feeling of love. You want it, on the ice, all exciting, and you don't care. Not really." Joshua strapped the tool kit tightly in place and worked the choke. "Lots of people want adventures with us, and we are left with the sad feelings when they finish." He pulled the cord in a strong sweep. The engine sputtered and caught, idling.

"It's like a movie for you, and then you go home. You get us to care, and it is all good for you, and then you go." He lowered his goggles and gripped the throttle.

Anna lunged forward and squeezed the brake with both hands. "I am not like them," she snapped.

"Hey, that's bad for the engine, what you do!" Joshua yelled.

"I care," Anna hissed. "I do not go away. But maybe I should. I should just go home, and marry him anyway, because *you* do not care—"

"You care, eh?" Joshua shook his head. "You care for nothing. Try to break things, get your way? Maybe I feel too? But I know your ways."

With that, he drove off, leaving Anna standing in the exhaust trail.

ᐱ

That evening, as the light was fading, he was at her door, holding out a plastic grocery sack with three *iKaluk*, the bodies split and cleaned, the pink flesh gleaming. "I like to be friends," he said. "I don't like people using people, hurting people. Hurting us, hurting other people."

She knew he meant Leah and Terrence. "I understand," she said, reaching for him anyway, and they were silent and thorough in her small room, and he left her in the pale light of early dawn.

ᐱ

Leah did not go wooding these days with Joshua, but they decided that the teacher should accompany him to learn their ways before she went back to her city. Leah muttered that she did not feel like riding on the snowmobile, but surely the teacher would enjoy the fresh air and take pictures out there. She bent over the duffle slipper that she was embroidering with beaded flowers, her lips pressed tight together.

"Leah is kind," Joshua's grandmother Lisetta stated in their language one day over tea in their kitchen. She was a spare, bent woman, with deep creases in her weathered face. "Never hurt her. Always remember that she holds your heart. No other one can do that. Never look for another."

"Leah is the one, always," Joshua affirmed. "All my heart belongs to her."

Anânatsiak Lisetta frowned, lowering the heavy mug and staring out the window. "Be careful, Joshua. There are no second wives in this time, and the teacher is not like a wife at all anyway. She likes sleeping with an Inuk man; she likes adventures. She is hungry, deep inside. She will never be satisfied."

Joshua nodded. "I will take the teacher wooding," he said, "but I will be true to Leah."

Being true to Leah, though, was becoming more a matter of touching a hand to Leah's face, after laughing with Anna Caine on the spruce boughs on May afternoons. Yes, Anna was hungry, deep inside, but there was the innocence of a prayer on her face as she took him in her arms.

М

Anânatsiak Lisetta did not like it when she rose one morning to a scuffling by the wood box, and there was Anna Caine, tugging on her boots. That was the week when Leah was in Goose Bay for her training with the clinic.

"Ahh," the Elder spat. "You think you do all good. Joshua-Leah do fine, now you come. Not good."

Anna stood her ground. "She left him."

"Ahh, you! You go sometime, you come home, he have babies with you friend. You like?"

As Anna walked up the road that day, she knew that every man, woman, and child in the village was watching; that hunched figure dragging on a cigarette, with squinted eyes scrutinizing the harbour, was in fact studying her.

And what had she done to Joshua? Did they hate him now? Would a gang of relatives swoop down with sticks and fingernails?

What did it mean when each person she met smiled and said, *SilakKijuk?* Were they cursing her, belittling her?

Anna did not know that the People did not judge as she did. She was judging herself, while claiming the eyes of judgment were theirs. They smiled and commented on the beauty of the morning, for they had been here always, and had seen all things, and they knew that this, too, would find a way to peace.

ᴍ

The June sun was strong in the late afternoon; the earth was drying, and smells of tar and green things rose in the town of Endor. The heat was intense yet caressing, the lightness of a lover's hand on the face of Leah, who stood on the front step of the apartment of Anna Caine. Leah tugged her oversized sweatshirt down, smoothing it over her abdomen. She was not angles and curves and flat planes like the teacher, but her body was strong, rounded by hard work, not lithe from trotting around the hills like the teacher. It was a mother's body and would enwrap children in its cushioned folds and then release them to be. She would be stooped when her years came to her, and she would wear her hair long, caught back in a clasp, with streaks of grey for a husband's fingers to trace while they sat together, remembering.

Why did the husbands run to the angles and curves and flat planes, the belted jackets and hiking shoes, the bobbed hair, and the fitted jeans? Leah scrutinized her well-worn sneakers, neat and faded grey, no logos; she brushed at her jeans, thin at the knee and sagging a little. They were clean, but they were not the clothes of Anna Caine.

Would Joshua ever share the sunsets with Leah Piguk? Would Leah and Joshua laugh together as they selected treasures to pack into Advent stockings, anticipating their grandchildren's delight?

Leah pushed her shoulders back a little, ran her hand over the dark hair that framed her face this day, took a deep breath, and knocked.

One of Anna's roommates opened the door. Leah almost smiled to see the woman flinch, clutch the frame, and drop her jaw. "Oh," the roommate said, her voice flat, casual. "Hi."

"Hello," Leah began, giving a formal nod. "I am here to see Ms. Caine. I have something for her."

She held up a small bundle, and the roommate drew back a little, eyes fixed on the plain plastic wrapping.

"It is slippers," said Leah.

"Oh." The roommate's face brightened. "Oh! You are selling slippers? I love crafts. Let me see." She extended a hand.

Leah pulled back a little. "It is a gift," she explained, "because she will be leaving us soon. And so, she will always remember."

"Ye-es," the roommate said. "I'm sure she will." She startled and turned. "Anna. It's—you know—Leah Piguk. She wants to see you. With slippers," she hissed.

"Will you excuse us?" Anna said in an even tone, stepping past her onto the step.

Leah pulled herself straight. Anna cast a critical eye over her; she took in the limp hair, the shapeless sweatshirt, and the bagging jeans. Scrubbing floors, picking berries all day, and carrying wood and water made the body very strong, but Anna saw flab and sloppiness. Anna sighed. "OK. You want to talk here or inside?"

Leah's eyes widened. "I do not come to talk. I come to say goodbye. I have loved you, and been your friend, and Joshua has been good to you. He was your friend too. Now, it is hurting all of us. You do not do this to your friends. You hold their hearts; you do not break them. You go love *your* man, now. When you wear these slippers, you remember Leah, who loved you and was your friend.

"Because she does not think she can be your friend today."

The slippers spilled from the package, and oh! Anna's beadwork was an infant's clumsy scrawl, for Leah's beads danced across the fabric, weaving hints of love and sunshine into the intricate stems, the delicate petals.

"This comes from a life," Leah said. "Not from an hour, not from a day."

Anna lowered her head, scuffing at the peeling paint on the step. "I love him, Leah. I love him with all my heart."

"You love the feeling of love," Leah whispered. "You like that feeling, all that, like it is everything. But love also means you will smile for him when everything you know is ending, and you will know his heart, his thoughts, as you, Ms. Caine, want to know his body."

"I love his spirit," Anna insisted.

"You love your big adventure. Go home, and love your husband." Leah turned, and said over her shoulder, "You break all our hearts, Ms. Caine."

There were tears in her eyes as she hurried down the road, leaving Anna in the doorway, clutching the beaded slippers in her hands.

∧

Anna Caine and Joshua Kalluk never walked the road, touching hands together, swapping little smiles and intimate looks while the community beamed approval for the joy of young love, good love, love grown in hope. Anna and Joshua spoke when they met, for the teacher was friends with Joshua and his family, and if Anna dropped by to see *Anânatsiak* Ida and Mattie, and Joshua was there, she did not ignore him, yet she did not collapse into his arms. They whispered, sometimes, in her room, their bodies close after loving, of all the possibilities. At least, Anna did. They would have a small cabin, way up the river. She would write children's books, and publish them, and he would create beautiful furniture that would be sold everywhere. "We would have to build a factory out there?" Joshua chuckled. "With a road, and lathes, and power tools?" Anna delivered a soft punch to his bicep. "An' work crew, an' shifts, an' a whole little city?" he continued.

Anna sighed. Joshua would not enter the spirit of the thing. And although he cared for her, she felt his distance; he was baffled by her, sometimes. As he listened, his eyes would cloud, and she wondered if sometimes he still saw Leah.

And he always left, although she wanted him to stay.

Little Mattie did not chatter, these days, and when Anna dropped by, Mattie's grandmother was often going to the store, or the clinic, or had been summoned by her sister. Mattie asked if they were going to do another play, maybe one for summer, a happy play to make people smile. Anna asked if her *anânatsiak* was well. "I look after her," Mattie told her. "And I look after our little Bobby, too. Me and Joshua, we look after our grandmothers and everyone in our houses."

Was that defiance in Mattie's eye? Or was it reproach?

Anna tried to recall the face of Tonya, dead these six months, but her features were fading. When she did picture Tonya, her eyes were looking away.

Was that defiance in Tonya's eye? Or was it reproach?

Anna realized it was pity for Anna Caine, who should be alive and didn't seem to know how.

ᗰ

The school year ended with graduations and celebrations as the community gathered in the gym to celebrate the young. All the love in the community was poured into these precious days. The teachers were a good group, they decided, who cared for the young. The teachers believed in the young, and that was good.

Oh, there had been a few rough spots, the community admitted, but what was life without a few rough spots? In not so long-ago days, people had held snow in their mouths until it was water, then spilled it out onto the *Kamutik* runner, and buffed it with a scrap of skin until it was polished and smooth. Smooth took patience, and yes, those teachers Mary Sanderson and Anna Caine would take patience and a lot of polishing, but Mary Sanderson was settling down since Ralph was getting married, and now she hardly drank at all. She seemed peaceful, most days, only a little sad. And Anna Caine—Ah! She was confused, these days, and she should not sneak around with Joshua Kalluk like that. Maybe, though, when she saw her own man again, she would settle down too.

And Joshua—well, the eyes of all the young women were on him, and sometimes he did get on the wrong road. But he was learning. Leah was looking thicker in the waist, they agreed. Joshua would see soon. He would see Leah, and he would see that he should not go looking any more. *Taima,* Joshua! He would see Leah, in the end. He would know.

ᗰ

The Elder Deborah chose each step with care as she eased her way down from her daughter's porch. She did not come out often, these days, as arthritis ate away the cartilage in her knees. She paused, and tipped back her face to the warmth of the morning. Ah! *SilakKijuk!*

She smiled to see Anna Caine walking in the sunshine, eager and excited. "Watch yourself, Anna Caine," she muttered to herself, "for Joshua is true, and he will not trade off his lifetime with Leah for the season he shared with you. He has been troubled, Anna Caine, and although he has love for you, he is ashamed as a man. He and Leah have always loved, and as her belly fills, he will soon know. Ah, Anna Caine. This is how heartbreak feels. You are young. The world will not end for this."

Deborah waited. This should not take long. Sure enough, Anna Caine was soon coming out of Lisetta's house, where Joshua had grown up and still lived, and soon his new wife would join them. Ah! Anna's mouth was smiling, but her eyes were not seeing the harbour even though she was looking hard. Anna Caine walked right past Deborah, her first greeter in Endor, and she did not recognize her. Anna did not remember, and she had never come looking for Deborah, or asked for her. Deborah shrugged. Youth forgot age, then youth became age and wondered how it happened.

"Ah!" Deborah murmured. "I am sorry you are sad, Ms. Caine, but you will be all right one day. Our People have lost too, and we know that in time you *will* be all right. We still feel the fear that was in us back in 1918, and the despair when no one came for us. We were abandoned, Anna Caine, and we still feel every bit of it, but we can smile in the morning, and you can too. Not today, but sometime.

"You will always remember, but you will not die from this."

She pulled herself back up the steps, clutching the worn railing. It was easier, saying this in her language. She had had to work hard, that first time at the wharf, to say everything that Anna had needed to know. But it had not made much difference anyway, Deborah decided.

JOSHUA *HEBRONIMIUT*

Joshua paced the hills overlooking Endor. He had been raised there, but his roots ran deep in the lands North. His father had been a man of Hebron, *Hebronimiut*, brought down to Endor during resettlement. His mother's father had come down from Okak, one of a handful of survivors of the flu of 1918. Joshua Kalluk was a strong man, strong in the ways of his ancestors, strong in his work as a carpenter. The very word *kalluk* meant *thunder*. Yet today he was troubled.

"As for me and my house," he murmured to the sky, "we will be true to our ways."

He nodded. Those words were strong, the words of the minister, but made over for his world.

Yes, he would walk in the ways of his forefathers, in the land that was shown to them from the beginning. He would walk unafraid among the mountains, for living and dying, he belonged to them. He would dwell among them always.

Now he smiled. When he had a son, he vowed, he would teach the boy all the ways his grandfather had taught him; here in the presence of mountains, his son would learn wisdom. He would read the ice as his book and know each shade and texture and its message. The ripples in the snow would set his direction when the stars were hidden. He would know that when the white bear ran from him, he must look over his shoulder then. For that was where the bear would be.

Oh, yes. The Land was alive, and every moment of every season was dangerous, even as it was good.

His son would know these things.

And his son would go far in the new school too. He would be skilled in all the new ways, the southern ways, and he would have friends in many worlds, friends for each world that an Inuk boy must know if he was to survive at all.

But his son must start here, in Joshua's Labrador. Then he would walk strong in all the worlds, here and there.

Joshua paused on the rough path along the hilltop and seated himself on the sun-warmed gravel. He sighed then, tracing his finger through the pebbles, flicking them away into the caribou moss. The teacher Anna Caine had left. He had thought that they had more time because she had planned to stay for a week when school ended, and there was much he had wanted to tell her. But the people on the road said that she had left on the plane that morning. "She was right there," they said, "and suddenly she was on the plane. Why weren't you there to say goodbye?"

That had been a surprise, and it had hurt him, because he and Anna had been friends. Joshua had enjoyed teaching her about the Land. He had liked to see her face light up, and her laughter in the spring sun had brought the Land to life.

He had liked her. A lot.

There had been love there too.

That had been hard on Leah. Leah and Joshua had gone to school together. They had gone to church, played, and fished together. They had grown up together. Yes, he had always liked Leah very much.

And then, he had grown to love her.

He and Leah had always planned to get married later and have their own little house. For now, Joshua was still living in his grandmother's house, where he had grown up with her and his grandfather. It was a good house, and perhaps he and Leah would live there at first, and she could help his grandmother. Old people like his grandmother, Joshua knew, should not be alone. Leah was quiet and gentle; his grandmother was fond of her.

Grandmother had not been happy when Anna Caine had stayed at night. It had only happened a few times, and Joshua had not been comfortable because Anna's head on Leah's pillow had seemed wrong. He had loved his friendship with Anna Caine, and then he had loved her in a special way, but not a husband way. She was like the mountains, drawing him.

He had not known what to do about Leah. He had not wanted to hurt Leah, and he had not wanted to give up Leah.

But he had wanted Anna Caine, and she had wanted him.

Joshua had decided to go to the teacherage, and explain to Anna that he and Leah had loved each other all their lives. Also, he had just learned that he was about to be a father. What he and Anna shared had been special, but now he was going to look after Leah and their child. He had loved being with Anna Caine, when winter had passed and the sun was blinding against the snow, when glad songs were sung in the *iKaluk* camps up the Bay, in the season of good things. She had awakened a need in him, to know her and walk awhile in her land. That had been one season, though, and he must not trade a lifetime for one season. He was going to marry Leah, but he would be Anna's friend. Always.

Perhaps Anna's man, Joshua would say, could come here, and they would all grow old together and smile to remember this special spring, the one that was named for all of them, now and forever.

He would have liked growing old with Anna Caine, just the two of them, their children growing up around them, but that was a dream for another lifetime. In this one, Anna and Joshua would be friends forever, and Leah and Joshua would be wed.

He scooped up dust with his palms and let it trickle away into the breeze as he stared at the mountains that ringed his home. That would have been a good speech. In his mind, it rang with all the dignity and grace such a moment deserved.

Yet Anna Caine had left that day. Just when the People were starting to know them, the new ones always left. They never seemed to say goodbye.

He missed Anna. The world had been more alive when they had walked through it together. Would she tell her Terrence about her time with Joshua? Would she think of Joshua, now and then?

Yes. He missed Anna. He wanted to marry Leah, but sometimes he imagined Anna Caine as the one under the veil.

He and Leah had a baby coming. Joshua had a feeling that he was going to have a son. He would like to name him Aaron, for his grandfather, who had been a young man in Okak that dark November of 1918. Aaron *Songujuk*, a man strong in mind and body. A strong name, a strong man.

MATTIE'S DREAM

Little Mattie Amarok huddled among the willows along the shore, long after Ms. Caine's plane had disappeared between the mountains. She had helped Ms. Caine, her first day in Endor, the day Mattie had been taking her grandmother berry picking. She had helped her make a wonderful Christmas play, given her partridges, taken her fishing, and made her part of her family. Yet, Ms. Caine had climbed on the plane without even looking back.

There by the shores of Endor Harbour, little Mattie rocked and wept as she remembered her beautiful Ms. Caine. The willows swayed and mourned over her, and Mattie knew she could never be happy again. Her Ms. Caine world was gone, forever.

The funeral of Mattie's mother had been hard, and the whispers had pounded on Mattie's ears, for her mother had fallen on the ice that time and she had died there on the road. The teachers had looked upon Mattie with pity, and they had said her mother was a drunk. She was a drunk and neglected her daughter, her teachers had insisted, but the People knew that ice was slippery even when you were steady on your feet, and rocks still broke bones when you were sober. You spun in a moment, and then you were gone.

Mattie's father had been in St. John's since before her memories began.

That was why Mattie looked after her grandmother. And now she also looked after her cousin Tonya's child, because Tonya had had a really mean boyfriend, and now Tonya was dead.

Mattie also helped her cousin Joshua, and his girlfriend Leah was always kind. Leah acted like a sister to Mattie, and Mattie was going to be her flower girl. Ms. Caine had been her cousin Joshua's girlfriend for a while, and that had been hard because Leah cried lots when Ms. Caine went off with Joshua, and Ms. Caine seemed to forget Mattie; she looked right through her and didn't talk about plays and berry picking and the good things they shared. Mattie had planned to get Ms. Caine to leave Joshua alone, so she would be friends with Mattie again. Mattie had felt uncomfortable while everyone was looking everywhere but not at each other, and no one was talking to her.

She rubbed her eyes with her fists and sniffed the mucus back into her nostrils. *If I fell on the ice and hit my head, would you cry for me, Ms. Caine? Would you remember me forever and write plays about me?*

Mattie had been at the plane, and Ms. Caine had not seen her or said goodbye. Mattie had run in the shadow of the plane all along the shore and seen the plane lift and sway and vanish beyond the cliffs.

Mattie was eight years old. She didn't have a mother to hold her, and her father was far away and never ever called. Her grandmother was all bent over with sadness, and Mattie did her best for her and for Tonya's little Bobby. She would help Leah with her baby and help Joshua wooding.

She would have helped Ms. Caine and been her friend forever.

Mattie stood and drew a long, shaky breath. When she was fifteen, she would go to St. John's and never think of sad, sad Endor again. She would live in the city and have high school adventures and then become an explorer and discover new worlds.

She would be kind to all the people in those worlds, she vowed, and when she had to leave them, she would hug them and tell them she loved them.

Then they would smile, and their hearts would always be warm.

"You never looked back, Ms. Caine," Mattie whispered. "You made my grandmother sad. But I can look after myself; yeah, don't you ever worry. I always have.

"And I will make a great story about you one day, Ms. Caine. I will take all the stories I can find, and put them in a book. With all sorts of beautiful stuff. And all sorts of sad stuff too, all about us and Ms. Caine."

Mattie pushed through the bushes and back to the dusty road. Ms. Caine had left her. That was a little sad, but she needed to check on her grandmother now.

TERRENCE AS HOSEA

Terrence slumped in the middle of the sofa in his little living room, staring at the door that Anna had just closed. The apartment was drab now, a minister's sparse furnishings, books and papers scattered on the surfaces, no plants or splashes of colour.

He had been so happy when his beloved Anna had returned, his gentle prophetess back from the wilderness. She had journeyed into Endor, inspired by God, he knew, but perhaps inspired a little by God's humble servant Terrence. It had pleased Terrence to think of himself as the catalyst of faith for Anna Caine.

Oh, what a catalyst he had turned out to be.

He had pictured Anna reaching out a cool hand, drawing the struggling, seething mass of northern humanity up into the Light.

It had not occurred to him that she would pull them down into her own hidden darkness, not uplifting but reveling in impurity, and now she had told him it was not new to her. But this time, it was sacred.

Had he become Hosea, most inept husband in the whole Bible?

Had he become like God to a wayward people? *I will not love her children, since they are the children of whoring,* Hosea declared on behalf of God. *Yes, their mother has played the whore, she who conceived them has disgraced herself.* (Hosea 2: 4-5)

Hosea lived his life as a model of God's relationship to his covenant people. Or so, Terrence considered, Hosea would have us believe. God *told* Hosea to marry a whore—this was a deliberate, calculated act. He also told him to take her back. That was supposed to represent God's willingness to take his wayward people back. Hosea was not a fool. It was not bad judgment or naiveté that made him such a luckless husband. It was God's will!

Terrence wondered whether Hosea was simply a man obsessed and desperate to justify his obsession.

Perhaps Gomer was in truth a meek and chaste wife, and her lust and deceit were idle speculation on Hosea's part. Or repressed hope. Terrence wondered what Gomer thought; she had finally gotten away from Hosea, and then, while she was waiting in the marketplace, he appeared, jingling coins. Perhaps she thought, *Oh, no, not you again.* Perhaps she hoped for another buyer that day. Perhaps she was a desperate woman, doing desperate things.

Terrence decided that he must not dabble further into the Book of Hosea; he was not supposed to pity Gomer.

He disciplined his mind to consider the Book of Hosea as a theological statement, not Hosea's personal memoir. The Book of Hosea was not a treatise on marriage. Faith in scripture did not compel Terrence to choose a whore. Or her offspring. Or to explain the complex psychology of an angry prophet.

Terrence rested his elbows on his knees and buried his face in his hands. Had Anna been so broken by the brutal death of her student, so lonesome out there in her wilderness? Had that Joshua preyed on that loneliness—beguiling her with mystery, with signs and wonders? For Anna had been so sweet, so happy, laughing when she and Terrence had walked arm in arm through Point Pleasant Park in the morning sun. Anna had seen the love her unworthy Terrence held for her, and she had honoured it. She had loved him—her fumbling, unworldly, unwise Terrence. *Her* Terrence.

He must not think of that. Or the child that was coming.

Anna had cast aside his love one day, and embraced the love of another. Not a slightly pudgy, prematurely balding scholar, but a wild and piratical man of the North.

He had a sudden urge to run into the street after Anna, grovel at her feet, and beg her to return. That would make him a fool like Hosea, and at least Hosea had salvation history as his excuse. Hosea's remarriage was supposed to be a paradigm for God's forgiveness of His covenant people, but no one past, present, or to come, would believe that Terrence was marrying Anna and claiming her child · to demonstrate that God loves and forgives everyone, whores and all.

Anna had not liked his idea that the child could be sent to Endor to be raised among his own people. She had started for the door when Terrence then suggested they tell people that they had adopted this northern child.

He twisted his hands in his thinning hair and groaned. What had he been thinking? What insensitive fool told a mother to forsake her motherhood and embrace an archaic convention?

Terrence had believed he embraced the universe. Now he knew he was locked into a little church box, after all.

"But I can't, Lord God of Hosts," he moaned into his hands. "I cannot accept the child. I cannot accept Anna. I cannot take my faithless covenant people back. I am just a humble minister and part-time lecturer; I am not the prophet of the Most High. I cannot love or lie with her."

He began to sob. "Besides, Lord, she says she does not want me. My Anna has turned from me. I loved her, God, and she has turned her back on me."

Anna had walked out that door, right over there. They had been going to live here, in this little apartment. In the corner of the kitchen, the light streamed across the table for two. That was going to be their table, where she would smile and pass him his tea. Every day was supposed to start like that, but instead there was just a lonely fool, staring at the empty chairs through his tears. Just him, and his own personal wilderness.

"She doesn't want me, God," he sighed, "and now I am all alone.

"Is this how you feel, every time?"

CATHERINE: MOTHER AND GRANDMOTHER

Anna's mother, Catherine, had always loved the way her name was spelled with a C and not a K, with an I, and not a Y. It was a comfortable name, a safe name. It was a humble name, without pretense.

Catherine had served her community, her church, and her family. She had never been overweight or underweight, and she had provided her household with plain, nourishing meals. Her cakes were firm with a thin scraping of frosting; her bread was light with a crisp crust.

After she had completed high school, Catherine had studied bookkeeping. To this day, she kept the books for a few small businesses. Her columns were always neat and clean, up-to-date, and balanced. Her ledgers always matched the spreadsheets she included in these times.

She had married her high school beau, and they had set up house in a semi-rural area just outside Bridgewater. Evenings had been idyllic times, as their daughter Anna played in safety under the neighbourhood's watchful eye.

There had been a restlessness in Catherine's daughter, a need to fit in while breaking away. Anna had never been overtly rebellious, but she had skipped faster than her peers in the playground, and she had hitched at her swing to make it soar above the others. She had run hard in high school track and field; her hems had always been within the rules but only just.

In her last year of high school, Anna could hardly wait for university. Catherine suspected that was because Anna had wanted the freedom of the city, although she had claimed the academic possibilities thrilled her. Catherine had not thought her daughter would stay buried in the library for long.

Yet Anna had stayed home for two years after high school. Catherine was still ashamed that she had wished her only child would leave home. That was because Catherine's husband had been diagnosed that first year, and had been often in the hospital, and frankly, Catherine had wanted the time with him to herself. At the same time, she had not wanted to be alone.

The second year, no matter how many people were in the house, no matter how many things were packed away and photo albums alternately thumbed through and thrown across the room, no matter how many events Catherine had attended or stories she and Anna had told, Catherine did not notice anything but the hollow ring of her life partner's absence, and it had been nice to have someone there in the nights.

Anna had worked those two years as a waitress in Bridgewater. Some nights, she had worked late, and Catherine suspected that Anna made a few stops on the way home. Perfume and breath mints could only cover so much.

Anna had been a good girl, and a moral girl, so Catherine had not worried much about her.

Anna had also been a driven girl and a very intense girl, and so Catherine had worried a little.

Anna had finally left for Halifax and university, and at first, she had come home weekends.

Then she had just come home for holidays.

Anna had claimed her studies kept her busy, and Catherine suspected that became true in the third year, when Anna had met Terrence. That was the man Catherine had prayed for—stable, kind, humorous, and a student minister as an added bonus. Terrence had been a little hard to take, at first, for he made clever jokes, and Catherine was lost in them. When he saw how lost she was, Terrence switched to plain English. His smile simply glowed, and Catherine had been delighted when they slipped into engagement after a few years.

Terrence, Catherine felt, was good for her daughter, good for her, and good for the world.

Endor changed everything. Catherine had at first enjoyed the detailed letters and reveled in Anna's Christmas homecoming, although she fretted sometimes that her daughter was too focused on the community. Catherine was looking forward to a lovely Nova Scotia wedding, visits to Halifax, and grandchildren on weekends. Catherine did not want to trail up the Labrador coast in a bush plane for rare visits, and live her years outside her daughter's life.

These worries had seemed so minor when Anna got caught up with a man from the community. From the limited information Catherine could gather, this man was married or almost married, and in Catherine's opinion, the terrible death of one of Anna's students over Christmas had unsettled her daughter's mind, just a little. The man must be opportunistic and quite immoral and had taken advantage of Anna when she was so vulnerable.

The outcome was inevitable, of course. Anna had gotten herself in trouble, the oldest trouble there was. Since the time of Eve, women had been getting in this trouble. Catherine decided that she could never care for this Joshua, even though he was going to be the father of her first grandchild.

Anna had walked out on Terrence, a man Catherine loved and admired, and she had come home to bear her child right here, in Catherine's own house. Catherine knew she should be excited, but Anna cried in the night and did not sleep. She paced the house and turned from her meals. Catherine told Anna that the baby would be nervous if she didn't settle down, and Anna slammed her open palm on the wall and snapped at her mother, "Is that what you did to me?"

Sometimes, Catherine's heart squeezed in her chest and wouldn't unclench. That frightened her.

Anna sent a note to that man she had met in the north, declaring that he had a right to know but saying she hoped he would not write back or call.

Catherine noticed, however, that her daughter paced and waited for the mail each day.

Catherine wondered what it would be like to hold her first grandchild. She had heard that it was the most special feeling in the world.

She would shield that child with all the love that was in her being.

PHOTO MOMENTS

The letters and pictures accumulated.

Here was a wedding picture with Joshua standing proud in a shiny suit, hair combed back and slick. His mustache was more mature somehow, not the mustache of an adventurer but the mustache of a husband and father now. The seated bride had round cheeks and a thin veil drooping over her long lank hair that parted in the middle and framed her face. Her dress was white, no puffs and flounces, a simple dress that unfolded loosely over the bulge, and tucked neatly about her feet while he stood at her shoulder. They looked like an olden-days couple, faces grave and staring, beaming family clustered around. Here they were with the groom's grandmother, and now with the bride's aunt and uncle. Next, they were joined by several cousins from both sides, without and then with the grandmother and then the aunt and the uncle. Here they were with his grandmother and his grandmother's sister, and now the bridal party moved in. Here was his cousin, who was his best man, and the bride's sister, her radiant bridesmaid.

Here they were with Mattie.

And here was Mattie alone.

Mattie looked like an olden-days child, neat little dress with puffed sleeves, hem brushing below her knees, socks straight, and little patent leather shoes. A wide ribbon with a wilting bow straggled in her hair. There was a hint of over-sized baseball cap and drooping T-shirt in her stance, but she was dressed for a wedding now and clasped her flowers before her.

The packet of photos Anna received was addressed with a child's wobbly hand. "The wedding was very nice," the note inside with love from *Anânatsiak* Ida said, "and we hope you are well. We liked your play. Write sometimes. Send pictures."

Anna put the envelope in the bottom drawer, behind the socks.

Next came the baby pictures. First there was Baby Girl herself, who would not be called by name until she was baptized. There were many little crosses in the graveyard, and if it was hard to say goodbye before the name was given, once the child was named, the heartbreak would be without end. So, she was Baby Girl, and here she was by herself, now with her mother Leah, now with her father Joshua, now with both, but only a few pictures with extended family this time. Last, though, was a picture of Baby Girl in Mattie's arms; Baby Girl looked bewildered, and Mattie looked fierce, protective.

These went in the bottom drawer under the wedding photos.

M

Anna paced her childhood room and waited. She should be in Halifax. She should be working and coming home to her own apartment, not sneaking past the little office off the living room where her mother virtuously updated the books for small businesses while Anna retched and paced and wept in the night.

She should be in Halifax, detouring around Terrence's apartment, Terrence's school, and Terrence's street outreach, but walking freely, nevertheless, striding to the bus stop and always on time for work. No one there would type or scratch figures into ledgers, like her mother, dutiful and meek as Bob Cratchit. Her mother did not judge because that was against the rules, but, oh! Her mother would love to judge, to celebrate the triumph of her own virtue.

Anna had not been pleased to return to Terrence that summer.

Terrence, as conventional man, had crowded her, cutting off lifegiving oxygen to her womb. Terrence had posed as martyr, a Hosea-man taking back the whore wife for duty's sake. Spring light would never dazzle his eyes or quicken his blood. Terrence had flinched from her shirt taut across the belly, making casual reference to the child's heritage, and the child being better off in his own culture, surrounded by his people. And Joshua had felt the same way. Joshua, once a god with the salt wind fanning the sweat from his muscled shoulders, was now refurbishing his grandmother's house and fetching water and washing dishes. Anna was suffocating.

Terrence and Joshua had independently suggested that the child should be raised in Endor, by his own family.

"I am his family," Anna had shrieked at Terrence.

She had said nothing to Joshua, but she had torn his letter into seven strips before striking the match.

There were more letters from Joshua. Baby Girl, who became Miriam, seemed to be a colic-free baby who slept through the night, smiled, cooed, and did all things well. Joshua would describe the weather, the food they were eating, and Baby Girl's latest acts of cleverness. His little girl was very smart, Joshua said once, and he hoped her baby brother listened to her. There was a little smile face beside this one. Joshua was polite and methodical. He had cast off the old man and become something new.

Joshua asked her to write sometimes and take lots of pictures. There were no photos in his envelopes, but there were a few bills tucked into the folds. He still wished she would bring the baby to Endor, but if she wanted to do things her way again, then as a father, he wanted to contribute to his child's welfare.

Anna didn't want to accept Joshua's cash while Leah watered the stew and patched their clothes and shared Joshua's income with extended family members. The Kalluk family needed that money. In her heart, though, Anna knew she rejected Joshua's support out of jealousy at his generosity.

She was independent here. Joshua no longer set her free, he bound her.

She had freedom here in her mother's house, and if her mother sniffed when Anna mentioned Joshua, at least Anna had a warm, neat home to grieve and puke in. Anna resented her mother's stiff shoulders and little sighs as she touched the photo of Anna's father, but Anna could come and go and answer to herself. She pictured Terrence squaring his martyr's shoulders to raise the child of her whoring, and she was relieved to be here. She pictured Joshua and his family handing her child from embrace to embrace, exclaiming over the cleverness and the cuteness, and sometimes remembering that they should have Anna over for Easter dinner, since she had, after all, brought their child into the world. Sometimes in the night she felt Joshua turn to her, his hands caressing her and his body shifting until it was snug to hers and, oh! Whatever she had done, she had that, and it had been love, true and deep, even though Joshua was slave to convention after all.

Would her son be free of the burden of convention?

Joshua and Leah had named their daughter Miriam—Miriam, sister of Moses and Aaron, she who sang when the Red Sea surged together, casting horse and rider into the sea. The woman whose feet drummed out the victory over Pharoah, Anna decided, should have changed her name to something powerful and exultant. Miriam was a busy little name, but just the thing meek and weary Leah would choose.

M

The New Year came, and with it, the birth pangs of a new order.

Anna named her son Aaron, after Joshua's grandfather, Aaron Songujuk. Leah would not get the satisfaction of naming a future son Aaron. No, Joshua would always look at his namesake (for he was Joshua Aaron Kalluk) and his grandfather's namesake, and know that this was the son of Joshua and Anna, conceived on the Land in consecration of their loving.

Now there were pictures to send: first Aaron by himself, now Aaron with his mother, now Aaron with his grandmother, now Aaron with them both, and here with the nurse who delivered him. There was no rich framework of family defiant against the encroaching darkness; there were no laughing, tea-drinking baby passers in this house.

When Joshua arrived in late January, he was worried when there was no laughter, no gathering of family and neighbours. Catherine, however, had his immediate approval. Catherine herself was surprised to discover that she liked Joshua; he was a gentle and fatherly man, and the baby knew him immediately.

Joshua smiled and chatted at Catherine's feet while Aaron cooed, and Anna watched as through a window. Anna had a sudden impulse to scoop up baby and diaper bag and credit card and flee to the North country, maybe to her cousin in the Yukon, whom she had met once as a child. Her cousin was wild and free, and Anna would be the mother and her cousin the friend who believed in her, and there would not be this prosaic, smothering little family on the outskirts of Bridgewater, and Anna's lungs collapsing in the stagnant air.

Joshua was very pleased that the grandmother would be raising his son. He believed in her. Grandmothers were important.

When Joshua went home, Anna went to work mornings in a coffee shop, serving breakfasts to businesspeople in dull business suits, people who had no idea how to swing an axe or create a historic play or cope when a creative dramatic genius had a tire iron slammed into the base of her skull. Anna despised them all, but she was still a good waitress, and she placed the cup in precise position, the knife, the fork, and the napkin straight.

In the afternoons, Anna was available to supply teach for those who went home with a headache or had a medical appointment or a child suddenly ill. It was enough like teaching to keep her in touch with her career, but it was not Endor. It was not Tonya. It was not Mattie.

For four years, Catherine rose in the morning to raise Aaron, and she could not believe her joy. She listened for the phone, which would mean she had the afternoons, too. Oh, her grandson was a gift. His father came each summer for a visit, and he loved the soft bread with a good crisp crust and the firm cakes with a little frosting.

Catherine was bewildered when, at the end of four years, Anna started packing her books and her bedding, Aaron's treasures and his toys. She was going to teach full-time. She was going to return to her career—in a community deep in Northern Ontario.

And no, Catherine was told, conducting her bookkeeping business long distance would be too difficult.

Surely, Catherine hoped, Anna would soon see that she had broken her mother's heart. Her mother's whole purpose in the world had crumbled, and she was once more abandoned.

Chapter 6: *Horizons without Mountains*

JOSHUA'S LAMENT

The past four years had been good for Joshua Kalluk and his growing family. He had acquired his own lot and built a warm, modern bungalow for him and Leah, their daughter Miriam (who was almost ready for school!), and now the new baby, Dinah. There was a special section off the kitchen for his grandmother, *Anânatsiak* Lisetta, who was delighted to have paneled walls, easy-to-wash floors, running water, and a sweeping view of the harbour. How she loved to phone her friends and tell them when their loved ones' boats or snow machines were returning.

Joshua was well-pleased with his wife, Leah; she was skilled in the home and strong where it mattered. She could raise a smile in his heart when he was irritable or critical. She was quiet though, when he paced the floor and stared toward the mountains, for Leah knew Joshua thought of Anna then. Those were the times she drew her mouth down and sewed.

Sometimes, Joshua worried. After Dinah had been born, Leah had been different for a while. She had sat by the stove or by the window with tears trickling down her cheeks. All the women in the family had told Joshua that this happened sometimes. One or more of them would often sit with Leah, sewing and being present, or making meals and taking her out for visits and fresh air. The women had told Joshua he must be patient, and then he had been anxious, for he had thought he already was patient.

His beloved first daughter Miriam loved her new sister Dinah very much, but at times, she would kick at her chair leg and demand to see her brother Aaron, whom she had never met. She taped all Aaron's pictures to her bedroom wall; then she lugged her baby sister Dinah into the bedroom and lectured her with stories of each picture.

"When you are a big girl," Miriam had told little Dinah, who stared bewildered at the colours on the wall, "you and me will go way, way down there and find our brother. And we're gonna grab him and run all the way home. 'Cause we're his home, not her."

Joshua and Leah had exchanged wide-eyed glances. The idea had not come from either of them. Yet, the idea was in the world.

Now Joshua was newly troubled, for Anna had decided to move all the way to Northern Ontario, far from her culture and far from his.

She would be far from family, and family was at the heart of Joshua's world. Family was not always friendly, and family sometimes fought, but family was always friends. Family hurt one another, cried over one another, hugged one another, and forgave one another and started over. Family stood together and walked together and saw one another strong again.

Family shared their hurts. Anna had acted like she cared about Inuk family ways, walking and smiling among them. Then she had turned her back on them; she had scooped up her hurts and pushed them down deep. She carried them alone and that made a bitter and lonely heart.

Joshua had gone to see his son Aaron before Anna left. Aaron was a strong boy, a good and helpful boy, but he did not seem to be a happy boy. He had eaten the ice cream Joshua had bought for him at the park place, taking slow little licks until it was gone. Then he had looked up and said, *"Nakummek,"* but he said it like an English word—flat, not singing. Aaron had never wrestled in the dust with his cousins or tumbled down on the fir boughs at the *iKaluk* camp after a long day fishing and playing in the spring light. He had never gone campfire to campfire to sip from an auntie's tea mug and hear stories and people singing out his name, so happy to see him.

Aaron's grandmother Catherine was a loving person, but Aaron seemed to be the only one who honoured that love. Joshua was proud that his son looked after his grandmother.

Anna always seemed to be watching, pulling the love to herself, worrying when it turned to another. That would make the child nervous and uncertain. How would he be calm and confident and become strong on the Land?

Anna was all about Anna. Anna did not even seem to like it when her mother did something nice for her or Aaron. It must be Anna who did the nice thing. Joshua worried about how this was affecting his son. When he tried to talk to Anna about that, she said she was tired or went for a walk or picked up a book.

She had loved being on the Land in Endor; she had been alive and happy and giving.

Anna was a shadow now. She had not married her man; she had walked away when Joshua had asked where her fiancé was. Anna's mother had said things hadn't worked out, but when Joshua offered to speak to Anna's man, Catherine had said that probably wouldn't be a good idea. When Joshua suggested that Aaron could come to him and Leah, for some men were not comfortable with their wife's other children, Catherine had said that would probably do more harm than good.

When Leah had been so sad after the birth of Dinah, family had watched over her and seen her through. Family was about warm hearts and a safe and happy place for a child to grow.

Now Anna was taking Aaron away. There would not even be a grandmother to help. What if Anna got tired or sick? What if she got angry?

Who would speak for Joshua's son then?

ANNA IN GALILEE

Anna did not expect to see grass when she stepped from the train at the end of their journey. She expected it would be like the other stops along the way, the train lurching and halting and then the silence. Far down the train, a baggage door would rasp open, and she could hear voices calling from the doorway. There were muffled thumps and clanks as bundles dropped to the ground. An all-terrain vehicle would start up, and then she would see it winding away into an overgrown track, disappearing into the spruce and poplar. Children's legs would dangle with practiced ease from the little trailer behind the all-terrain vehicle. Then the family diorama would be swallowed into the silence that lay on the way to this new north, a north with no mountains.

But here, in the town, there was a station, and a platform extending along the tracks. The dust rose from the edge of the road that led past the school and scattered buildings—a hardware store, a liquor store, a police station, and a church beyond them. The road was oiled and almost paved.

And the grass was lush and thick with flies.

A woman stood near the station door, leaning against the wall. She wore faded jeans, a brown hooded sweater, and neat sneakers. Her long, thick hair framed her face and tumbled over the hood on her back. A little TV tray perched beside her, piled high with rough cylinders of tinfoil, like fat and opulent cigars. People crowded close, proffering coins. "Buy her scone," a woman urged, unwrapping the foil and sinking her teeth into a bannock log. "The best," she mumbled, holding the log to reveal its steaming sausage centre. "See? She got black bean sauce in this one, and some with cheese. She looks after her daughter's kids, you see," she added, raising the scone to her mouth again.

And so, Anna juggled purse and satchel against her hip and gripped her son's little hand as he stretched for the pair of husky dogs emerging from the baggage car. She wrenched a cluster of change from a pocket and held it out. "Two of those, please," she said.

The woman neatly plucked loonies and quarters from the pile. "He wants the hot dog scone," she said, extending a smaller tinfoil log to Aaron with a smile. "Half price, special guests. You want cheese or black bean sauce?" she asked Anna.

Anna chattered about cheese, and the woman smiled, neat white teeth showing for a moment. "You must be the teacher. Sandra is looking for you. *Wachaye*, little man," she addressed the boy.

"*Mamâktuk, nakummek.*" He smiled, already deep into his scone dog.

"*Nakummek!*" she exclaimed. "Not 'Nishnabe, then? North? Inuit? Our peoples were trading partners," she said to Anna. She brushed a gentle hand over the boy's hair, then seized Anna's elbow, drawing her close. Her gaze locked on Anna, and she nodded.

"Welcome, Ms. Caine," the old woman murmured. "My name is Reah. This is a good place for you and your boy. But," she sighed, "this is not the right place for him, because he needs to build the memories that will see him strong. He will still have a good life here; this fall, he will build towers in junior kindergarten with my granddaughter, and you will work with my daughter. All good, yes.

"But it is not the right place; your eyes are not on us. You will not find what you are seeking here."

Anna turned her gaze to the train and stared at the baggage car. She knew this woman; she had met her on the wharf that first day in Endor. What was the woman doing here, in jeans and a hoodie, no skirt or headscarf now?

The scone woman continued. "You will be lonely, lonely all your days, for mountains and cutting northern air, and the man who brought you to them." She chuckled. "It is easy to see! Your son is Inuk, Labrador T-shirt, mountains there. Ah! You think I am a mysterious 'Nishnabe woman, reading the future. No. But I can read a T-shirt. And I know a broken heart when I see one. Yes," she affirmed. "I know."

"OK, well, he's married," Anna muttered, "and I don't see—"

"So, live across town," the woman named Reah declared. "And your boy could play after school with his siblings and his cousins. You could see him, and his father could see him, and they would all grow up sheltered in their stories. Lots of people do that, so why not you?"

"It's really not—" Anna tried to interject.

"My business, I know." Reah grinned. "Hey, maybe this is like that Galilee place in the Bible. You know? Where Jesus tells them to go and wait till he tells them what to do next?

"But maybe it's more Galilee for me, because Galilee was home, like this place is my home." She gave Anna's elbow a little shake and whispered, "I came home from residential school. Eh? Not everybody was so lucky as me. But sometimes, I remember, and it hurts to be alive those times. Do you know about the residential schools?"

"Yes." Anna nodded, looking toward the tracks now. "Yes. It was appalling. Outrageous."

The woman released Anna's arm and stepped back. "I want to tell you something. I want to tell you the saddest thing, and it might not shock you, but it will break your heart and haunt you all the days of your life."

Anna took Aaron's hand and sidled toward the baggage car. "You are not ready?" the woman called after her. "No? I will wait. And one day, you will hear this story. I did not have your choice, Anna Caine. I have carried that story since I was eight years old."

Aaron tugged free and trotted back to the scone lady. He stood before her and lowered his gaze, and her hand caressed his hair once more. "I crushed it down," she whispered, her eyes far past him. "I crushed it down and crushed it down, and not all my children and grandchildren are strong, because no eight-year-old should see and hear the things I have seen and heard. They call me in the night, but I am healing now; I stand in the light the Creator shines over and around and through me. I hear them in the night, and they are calling for justice. But most of all, they are crying for love."

She smiled down at Aaron. "I will be your friend, and I will walk with you while you are here, and all the days that come afterward. I will find you on the wind.

"I am fifty-two, just fifty-two. You think I am an old, old lady? Well, that is what happens when eight-year-olds are crushed.

"Now give your mother this scone. It is a welcome gift. With black bean sauce this time. Those are my best."

Thus, Anna and Aaron arrived at the end of the train line, and here came the promised Sandra to see them through the confusion of getting their car from the chain car, piling their luggage in, and driving out to their family housing unit.

Here was Aaron, scone dog done, alternately wiping his little palms on his new shorts and slapping the flies that probed his legs. "I like that lady," he said.

Anna looked and she looked, but the scone lady had vanished in the crowd.

MOUNTAIN SKETCHES

Indeed, it was a good place to raise a child. The leaves dappled yellow as the autumn progressed, scattering along the riverbanks, clogging in the eddies, packing against the shore, then washing away in the easy tide on the river. Winters were snapping with cold, and they could drive across the river in the starlit nights, the ice rigid and thick beneath their tires. Snow mounded and heaped and then began the thaw. Now the roads were quagmires, and the ice road was flooded; the ice began breaking up and surging from far upriver, huge chunks charging down the current, battering and gouging the shores. Now and then, the ice chunks piled and packed across the river for days; sometimes, huge walls of ice loomed on the shore near the houses. Next came the sparkling blue of open water and the grass and leaves quickening and the flies quickening too, and through it all, the seasons of the school with literary themes for Anna and roughly coloured turkeys and pumpkins and reindeer and hearts and bunnies and Mother's Day flowers created and stuck to the refrigerator by Aaron.

There were pictures for Father and Grandmother Catherine, and a special Christmas card for Joshua's grandmother, Aaron's *Anânatsiasuak* Lisetta—for however that woman felt about Anna overturning their lives, her great-grandson was a blessing, and Lisetta yearned to hold him close. For now, she tucked his card on her bedside table among her sewing work and photos and Miriam's artwork from her school. Now Joshua's son would not be lonely, she explained. Now the boy had his place in their family.

Suddenly, it was the first summer driving home, with Aaron singing with the Smurfs and bouncing on the seat and wanting to camp, not go to a hotel. Anna longed to take him on a real camping trip, like she used to do in Endor, but she did not know how. Real camping was not a game. One did not swagger off into the bush with only a hatchet and a pack of matches in nostalgia for a bygone era. Real camping took a lot of planning and a lot of people to tell the stories—before, during, and after.

There was the heartbreaking reunion of Grandmother Catherine and Grandson Aaron, reminding Anna that her freedom came at the sacrifice of her mother's heart. And Joshua's heart. And the hearts of all the Kalluks and Songujuks and Amaroks who yearned to know Aaron.

Anna could have taken her northern allowance and gone to Labrador, but then she would have had to witness the many painful goodbyes—first in Endor, and then in Bridgewater—and her guilt over Grandmother Catherine's lonely summer.

Anna thought of staying every season in Ontario and never looking back.

It might be better, though, to find a place with mountains. Aaron had never seen mountains, yet he always scanned the horizon, looking puzzled. He drew them in his father's pictures: blue water squiggles, black overturned U's. Daddy's house.

Anna witnessed the ten awkward days when Joshua came to visit his son, with Joshua beaming gratitude at Catherine every meal. There were picnics and park days in her southern wilderness, which overflowed with trailers and generators, and Joshua suggested that they should go camping in the lake country. But the ticks were so dense, and Joshua would probably snare a rabbit or shoot a deer for their supper or trim fir boughs for a bed. He would want to light a fire, and the helicopter and wardens would come. Anna suggested they didn't have enough time.

Catherine heard Joshua's stifled sobs the night before he left, and she leaned her ear to his bedroom door and asked if he was all right. Joshua called through the door that he was missing his daughters, back in Endor.

"Bring them next time," Catherine urged.

"Then they will miss their mother," Joshua replied.

It came to Catherine that she and Joshua were alike; they both longed for the unbroken, continuous presence of family, not the scattered and lonely reality they both experienced. She swung open the door to Joshua's room. "Bring their mother too," she declared.

Joshua stared at the floor. "Thank you. But I am not sure," he said. "I am not sure that would be a very good thing, in the end."

Aaron was quiet after his father left. He ate his meals, he sat still beside Anna while she read, he went to swimming lessons, and he did not complain about outings to parks and museums and lakes. Still, Anna felt like she was playing mother, and her own mother seemed a wooden parody of grandmother, jerking through the motions and eyeing the calendar.

Soon it was time to drive west, and there were more quiet tears in the night.

This was the cycle for eight years. Later on, there were riding lessons in the summer, kayaking in the fall when they returned to Ontario, snowmobiling in winter, basketball for Aaron, and drama clubs for Anna. There was Aaron's friendship with Reah, the Scone Lady, through all their seasons; Aaron would sit at the woman's side, his head tipped and his eyes following her hands as she wove her stories and breathed them to life. Sometimes these stories taught history, and sometimes they taught science, but always Aaron felt close to the earth. Sometimes, he pressed his ear to the ground, and yes, he felt the pulse of creation. Other times, he stood on the muskeg's edge and heard the buzz and chirr of the Land and yearned to go there.

M

At the end of the third year of Ontario, Anna, Aaron, and Catherine all flew to Goose Bay, where Joshua's wife Leah was about to give birth to her first son. This would be Leah's fifth child, for the two miscarriages following the birth of Dinah were her special children in heaven. Sometimes, while preparing for the birth of this son, Leah had cried in the night, but she had known that she must think only of the two children who were present, and her son who was about to join them. Today, she was serene in her hospital bed with little Sonny Boy, who would be called Simeon but not until his baptism, while her daughters scrambled onto the sheets and touched the baby's face, and Joshua stood straight and tall, his eyes glowing as he smiled at his wife.

Yes, she was wife: true wife, full wife, and beloved wife. Now here came Joshua with Aaron clutching his hand; Aaron, straight and strong like his father; Aaron, with the eyes and smile of his father. Aaron placed a finger on the baby's foot, but he was afraid, Leah could see; he was not used to babies. Her Miriam, meanwhile, had been carrying babies since she was four, and she was teaching Dinah already. The true, full, beloved wife Leah could be generous in her heart, and she wished that Aaron could come to them, to be happy and unafraid and fill their house with light.

Now Miriam received the baby into her arms, her face beatific, her eyes shining. She turned with great caution and lifted the baby to Aaron, who stared in horror. "This is your big brother Aaron," she announced to the baby. "You got to mind him."

"Take him," she said to Aaron. "He likes you to hold him."

Joshua slid in behind Aaron, guiding his arms into position, shadowing him, tense, because Aaron was not of Endor, and babies were strange to him.

"You should come with us," Miriam declared. "Then our whole family will be together."

Joshua shrugged and shot an apologetic glance at Leah and was grateful that Anna had not insisted on monitoring this encounter, her mother Catherine wisely recommending coffee in the cafeteria, so they wouldn't be crowded.

"That is a good thought, Miriam," Leah murmured, "but she is a mother too."

"You're the mother," Miriam insisted, pouting.

Aaron was lost in his little brother's eyes, or perhaps he hid his noticing.

Dinah clapped her hands. "I like Aaron. I like Sonny Boy."

Catherine slipped in alone, and Leah was relieved, for she could not shake the feeling she had had on the day she had given Anna the slippers, the ones with the beadwork dancing over the fabric. Catherine had a set of receiving blankets and a rattle for Sonny Boy, who would be Simeon, and a gentle hug for Leah.

Perhaps, Leah decided, it was easier to be friends with people who have not shattered the hearts of your dear ones or known raw passion with them. Perhaps by the time you became a grandmother, you simply were grateful for all love, witnessed and experienced.

Grandmothers could embrace relationships with the openness of a child. Dinah said, as she hugged Catherine goodbye, "I got two grammas now, *An'siasuak* an' you."

M

Aaron drew better mountains as the years slipped past. They became rounded and shaded, with wisps of clouds and a distant gull, and he began at Christmas to ask about a trip to Labrador in the summer. That was hard, Anna pointed out, because they would only have seven weeks home, and what about Grandmother

Catherine? *"What about Aaron's father? What about his siblings?"* Grandmother Catherine countered. *"There is room for all of us in Aaron's heart and in his life."*

Thus, for one more summer, Joshua visited Aaron in Bridgewater before the construction season began in Endor, and then for three summers, he met Aaron in Goose Bay and took him back to Endor.

There was supposed to be a fourth Endor summer. That was the summer Anna decided to come home because her mother Catherine was not well; Anna would be callous in the extreme to abandon her now, and Anna was a dutiful mother and daughter. When your mother's heart is weakening, you bring the grandchild home to stay. And although she had carved out a life at the end of the train line, she had been lonely there every day. Perhaps she would be able to carve a life here too, but that was just an instinct now, a vague hope.

Aaron had not been happy in Ontario. He had been quiet and dutiful, but there had been an emptiness, a listening, in him. It was time to move on to their next permanent destination.

Anna had been happy in Ontario but also homesick. She had made true friends like the Scone Lady, Reah. Every time she saw the horizon, though, she had felt the absence of mountains, and the laugh that lifted across the water, rich in the joy of life itself.

She remained homesick for both homes but was unable to claim either.

FROM ANNA

I am leaving in summer.
Dusty trees droop on the edge of things.
Mosquitoes cluster over the crowded platform.
The grass is flattened by many feet.
This is not a postcard but
This, too, is the North.

My son stands to the side.
The boy is lean and tall, now
His father's son.
Shades of mountains surround him now.
His eyes look past his mother these days.
He is listening, always alert, these days.
I know who he is listening for.

∧

She is suddenly there,
A little stooped now
But her hair long and thick on her neck,
Her wrinkled face shining.
"I am coming to Cochrane with you,

Then Toronto with my daughter."
She laughs, hitching her satchel to her shoulder.
She is forever Reah, and she flows like water.
We are swept onto the train, losing each other
Among families packing the cars with pillows, blankets, bags, and toys,
Artifacts for a journey South.

She is in the dining car
As we shudder over Moose River.
"Going back," she says.
She stirs sugar into her coffee.
"Sometimes it's hard,
But then it's all right."
She sips and nods, brightens.
"See those houses? And that bench?
There, by the tracks.
We used to watch the train there,
All along there.
That was after residential school."
She nods, eyes on the trees slipping by.
"I was eight then.
I was very lonely."
She leans toward the window, pointing.
"There. That little river?
Always lots of sturgeon there."
The little river winds away.
Spruce trees lean on the banks.
Poplars bow over the water.
It is gone.
"I was lonely there. We were afraid.
You heard the stories. It was like that."
She settles in the stiff chair.
"Houses, maybe twelve families
On that little river,
And so many sturgeon."

There are no houses now, no sturgeon.

"Children died there," she murmurs.
I know.
I am informed and suitably outraged when I am informed.
I have heard.

The train sways and clicks through the spruce and birches.
Evening is closing into night.
The dining car is sharp under the lights.
In the corner they play cards.
A family of five squeezes ketchup over fries.
And we drink coffee
As she guards my passage.

She leans forward again.
"I was ten when I left.
They could not hold me there.
But they held me, here." She taps her temple.
"Every step.
They held me.
It was hard for me.
Hard for my children.
Hard for my grandchildren.
They never saw residential school,
But it took them.
It reached like a claw through my heart, and it took them.

"Children died there," she says again.
"And now I will tell you that saddest story,
The one that will haunt you all the days of your life.
You still are not ready?
But you must be ready.
I need you to bear it. Please."
She leans forward, her eyes look past my shoulder.

My son's hand touches hers.
He knows.
"They died in the night," she whispers.
"They died of loneliness.
In the silence, something tore, and I think
That was the Creator's heart breaking.
They turned. And they died.
They died of broken hearts."
Her eyes are on me now,
Dark and calm,
Dry of all the tears shed and unshed.
She carries all the children
Touched and still touched
By that time.
Her shed and unshed tears
Burn in my eyes
And my future is so easy,
Just a little waiting,
Until the next adventure.
I will never hear children die in the night of broken hearts
For all my nights.

Her entire life is crowded with empty eyes and
A flash of shining water thick with sturgeon.
I leave her in the night by the station,
Gathering son and luggage and kayak and car,
I rush into my future.

"You got my email," she calls.
And I leave her,
A little stooped
Still smiling
All the children tight to her heart
A flash of sturgeon on a hot morning
Rising behind her.

THE PASSING OF
CATHERINE

Catherine deserves a moment. She was not an earth mover or a reformer or speaker of words of power. She was a woman who loved: dedicated to her husband, gracious to her daughter Anna in her search, and devoted to her grandson Aaron. Catherine had, perhaps, great things to say and important works to do, but the living of her quiet life itself was great and important.

Some say she was disappointed in her daughter, but that was not so. She loved her daughter, even as she was bewildered by her.

She accepted her daughter's restlessness, for at times she, too, was restless. She did not know how to talk about this, and so she cooked nourishing meals, puttered in her garden, and swept and dusted, soft as a shadow. How could she explain to others that somewhere inside she wished she could go to Endor and learn to work sealskin with the grandmothers, and some days when she looked at her garden, she too yearned to go ripping across the ice with the wind numbing around her eyes? Her husband had been the love of her life, and every moment without him was so dull, but if he were here, together they would pack snowshoes and mitts and descend on the Kalluk-Songujuk-Amarok family, laughing and proclaiming they were there for the winter.

Instead, she kept the books in neat columns of figures, typing the data into the spreadsheets. Catherine Meredith Caine did meticulous work.

And when her heart muscle decided to allow a little rupture and a little blockage and a little damage, she found she slowed a little. Now and then, she was short of breath. At times, the twist was sharp, other times a slow, steady pull. Catherine schooled herself to think of other things.

Sometimes, Catherine imagined reading in the sun porch, her grandson, forever seven, listening at her feet. Both would smile in their innocence, a little naïve, life splendid in the stories sprawling out before them. Then Anna Jennifer Caine would intrude in the background, tense, guarding her stage and the movements of all the actors upon it. It was, after all, Anna's play.

In Anna's play, Catherine reflected, *Joshua knelt as loyal lover, arms extended, eyes on Anna. Aaron was a statue fixed in position, caught in the motion of turning to his mother, the fulfillment of his mother's fancy. Catherine herself was a prop, without voice or emotion, a mannequin tilting on a chair, in shadow.*

Anna in light would thread a path among them, never touching, for it was her stage, her play, and they were there at her sufferance.

It was, Catherine decided, *a depressing play, with a mood of anxiety pervading.*

So, Catherine read in her mind to a child, forever seven with smile always glowing, in counterpoint to that scene. She knew that Anna did not enjoy her play but was entangled by it and could not exit.

Catherine lived right and ate right. She was moderately active, and her rheumatoid arthritis was mild. She had had meningitis at fifteen, but she had recovered. She had coped with stress before, during, and since her husband's illness, but there were no mitigating factors like diabetes or obesity. She put one foot forward and then drew the other up to it. She bore her grief; she did not surrender to it.

Her heart had ached in many ways these past eight winters. The last weeks of summer, however, had always been hardest for Catherine, as all days tumbled faster and faster until Travel Day arrived.

The silence had crowded against her head, buzzing in her ears, on Travel Day. It had pressed down on her chest while her heart pushed back, fighting for space.

The doctor had done a lot of talking about internalizing stress. Somehow it sounded like Catherine had allowed her brain to rampage through her body. Her dark mind had been attacking her heart.

There was no outstanding family history, just her grandfather, and he had been in the War. And her aunt, but she had been old, hadn't she?

Catherine had not been in the war, and she was not old. She recognized no justification for a heart condition. She would live her life, and the condition would go away.

Aaron was coming home to his grandmother-home. Catherine knew he longed for his father's home. He would sit with her and tell story after story of the skill of his father, the cleverness of sister Miriam, the warmth of little sister Dinah, and the emerging talents of little brother Simeon. And Auntie Leah was always smiling for him. Like Grandmother Catherine. Smiling and kind.

Joshua's grandmother Lisetta had been discovered sleeping late one morning the summer before, but she had in fact been dead, not sleeping, and Aaron had cried for her and told his grandmother stories of her as she rocked him. And Catherine thanked God that Aaron's great-grandmother had died in summer, not in the loneliness of Aaron's winters with his mother who loved him but as a memory, sometimes, more than a real child.

Aaron was Anna's Joshua-token, and it pulled Catherine's heart to realize that Anna loved, but her love was static.

Now, Anna and Aaron were coming home, and Anna seemed warmer this time. She remained somewhat distant and stiff, perhaps, but some of her old compassion was stirring. Anna had not been passionate about teaching or people in a long time.

The stiffness had begun with Tonya found lying on the road between the church and the school, blood coagulated at the base of her skull and staining the snow. It had grown with the Joshua affair and deepened with his fatherhood visits. There was a little light in Anna's eyes now, when Aaron talked of Reah, his forever Scone Lady. *She knows things*, Anna said. *She knows all things.*

Then came the morning of a new scene, one never witnessed before in the little family. Anna stood rigid as her arm went around her son's shoulders the morning in early July when they found Grandmother Catherine reclining in her rocking chair, alone in her sun porch. Catherine's eyes were closed, and a little drool trailed from the corner of her mouth. Her hands were rubbery, cold. She seemed to have come out to her sun porch in the night. She had sat down, a storybook on her lap, and she had died, asleep or awake, the police were not sure.

Then Joshua came, and he and Aaron vented the tears that burned in Anna's eyes but would not release. They were noisy in their grief, not like Anna. When the tears finally drained the wound, they were calm.

Anna clenched her fists as Aaron and Joshua put all Catherine's pictures on the fridge and on the walls and talked about each. Anna stared at the picture of seven-year-old Aaron with Grandmother Catherine, sharing laughter over a book in the sun porch. In her mind, she saw a laughing Tonya holding up her little Bobby, now fourteen and a hockey player who might not make the NHL if he kept smoking weed, and beside her, the Scone Lady Reah of the calming waters who cradled all the broken hearts of that school in Fort Albany. There were tears burning for all of them and for her mother, but Anna had forgotten how to cry, and if she started, she would not remember how to stop, and she, too, would be lost. She disciplined her heart and started to form hamburgers for their supper.

She pushed back the image of Mattie, floppy bow and flower girl dress, a hint of scuffed sneakers and oversized baseball cap in her stance. A little girl of Endor who looked after her grandmother.

Anna's life drifted on a grey wasteland, but she decided that she was being strong for Aaron. Joshua had said that Anna was cold, like ice, and asked did she not love her mother and her son? Why, he asked, was her heart filled with hate? Did she neglect her son to punish him? She knew that this was Joshua's grief speaking; he could not really despise her mothering skills, or he would have done something long ago. This was not the fifties, and mothers who were truly negligent did lose their children in the courts. She was, she affirmed, a good mother being strong. She was not full of hate; she was filled with discipline and strength.

In her own way, Anna had been loyal to Joshua, never taking another man, never seeking another father for her son. She had not cared for sex that time in Halifax student days when she had closed her eyes in shame and lain still until her classmate finished with her body. With Joshua, sex had not been about debt and mastery; it had been sacred and beautiful, their bodies coupling and merging and soaring beyond the universe itself.

Now that time was over, but when she looked at her son, she remembered that he was conceived in a moment of truth, and even though that time was gone, and Joshua as she had known him was gone, the memory was burned into her soul. The father-man who visited Aaron was a shadow, not her Joshua, and that made the visits bearable.

She would not look at her mother's pictures and weep for Tonya or her mother or the lost children or herself. She would walk forward, hurting but strong.

Now, she could have the freedom to be home and the freedom to be, but she was desperately lonely for the woman Catherine, whom she loved and cared for but did not really know. They had never argued or yelled or stormed out of rooms; they had tiptoed around each other with Aaron in the middle, quiet and dutiful, afraid to offend.

So, she put her arm around Aaron and explained that, of course, he would miss his grandmother; they both would. Aaron pressed to her side and was silent.

But with Joshua, Aaron could howl out the loneliness that was in him, for the woman who had lifted them all with her lack of fire and her silence. His grandmother was like the Scone Lady, rich in love, and maybe, Aaron decided, someone had broken her heart, too.

"Can I come for Christmas?" he asked his father.

MATTIE'S NEW DREAM

"This is the third one," Leah murmured, dabbing the split skin on Mattie's lip. "You cannot stay with him. I think maybe soon you will not be able to have children if this keeps up."

Mattie flashed a grin, then grimaced as the skin on her lip tightened. "What can I say, eh? My man is one rough dude. Maybe we're both a little rough," she added, her eyes glinting now.

Leah wrung out the cloth over the small basin and closed her eyes. "No," she said. "You aren't. He doesn't care about you. He goes on the homebrew for days, and it makes him mean. He hurts you. He beats you. He puts you down so bad. And when he gets you pregnant, he doesn't change. He doesn't care about your baby. Some men are bad like that, but when the baby is coming, they stop all that. But he keeps on being mean. Ugly things, hurting you inside and out. Hurting your mind, hurting your body.

"You used to always help your *Anânatsiak*, you and Joshua. Hey? When you were a little girl? Always going wooding with Joshua. And helping with little Bobby, raising him for your cousin Tonya. Now your *Anânatsiak* is cold in the night, scared sometimes, when Bobby is running with his friends. Joshua tries with Bobby, but he needs more. You drinking and off with that one you call boyfriend, it's not right, Mattie. Remember the play? With Ms. Caine? You were doctor of laws, and you really could be. You are smart, Mattie."

Mattie's eyes narrowed as she fumbled out her pack and lit a cigarette. "Screw the play. And screw Ms. Caine. Don't you defend her—you know Joshua is down there having sex with her."

Leah lowered her eyes. "Joshua goes to see his son. Anna Caine is nothing to him now. He worries. It is like she does not know she has a son. We want the boy to come here."

Mattie blew a stream of smoke over her shoulder. "Oh, yeah. Bring him to Endor. Perfect spot to raise a kid.

"And if I were sticking around, I would tell him to stay away from the path after dark. That's where they killed our cousin. That's where they raped me. And do not tell me it takes two to go to bed 'cause there was three of them and no bed, and I was a kid, and at least Jay looks out for me. Little Miss Holy Bitch Wife, don't you judge me."

"I don't," Leah said. "But I wish you would go back to school. Lots of people your age go back and finish."

"Screw that." Mattie ground out the cigarette against a saucer on the table. "And screw Endor. Everyone judging me." She sighed. "I always wanted to go to St. John's and live. Like, go to school. I was thinking archaeology. I guess now it'd be waitressing or the streets. But Jay wants to stay here anyway."

Leah leaned forward. "Go back to school. There's night school now. Get funding. Be an archaeologist. What about social worker? You have such good feelings in your heart. Jay . . . he's mean. He bosses you." She paused. "You let him run you."

Mattie rolled her shoulders back and reached for the cigarette pack again. "Leah, dear, sweet little Leah. Bet you turn off the lights and close your eyes. It's a hard world out there. Jay is not the worst of it, and he's sorry, you know, when he does things. Yeah, we fight, and we get crazy sometimes, but it's a hard world, and we got each other's backs."

"You said you were leaving him when you came through that door," Leah reminded her.

"Yeah? Well, now I'm done with that. And done with you."

Mattie shuffled toward the door, wincing as she moved. She turned, her toughened face now a little dreamy.

"He says we got something special."

AARON'S HIDDEN YEARS

Aaron asked to return to Endor with his father that summer when the funeral was past, the cards and casseroles packed away, and the photos listless on the walls. The late July days pressed down on Aaron; the dust sifted through his running shoes, and the flowers wilted on Grandmother Catherine's grave. The silence thickened and pushed against his shoulders, tightened at his temples. His mother hovered with arms extended but never quite encircling. They were not Grandmother Catherine's arms. They were not Leah's. Theirs were mother arms, arms that enwrapped him and pulled him close. Anna's arms hesitated; it was like they did not believe that they had the right to hold him.

And this, he knew, was not his mother's fault. He felt the tension that pulsed from her, the need to laugh and cry and pull him close until his world was whole. His mother was awkward in her role, struggling to feel her character but restrained, afraid to do it wrong.

This came to him as images, not thoughts—Aaron in hockey equipment, shuffling stiff across the ice, seeing the careless freedom of his teammates' bodies rolling past him, their movements oiled and fluid. Their sticks swung down to the ice in a graceful arc; there was a clack as the puck shot forward. Aaron's stick chopped at the puck, and the puck faltered to the side.

That was like his mother, he decided. She was clumsy when it came to hugs.

His father's hugs were real. Sometimes he would do that great laugh, and people would turn on the street, faces staring and a little worried. They did not understand an Inuk laugh: When something delighted you, you just tipped your face to the sky and celebrated with a good laugh.

Aaron tried to laugh like that sometimes. It did not work in the schoolyard, and it did not work on the street for him. Perhaps you had to be out on the harbour or the hills or really, really feel you were.

He loved his mother. He was an obedient son who did his homework, read the books chosen for him, watched the appropriate movies according to his age, did basketball drills in the yard with neat and quiet friends, played a few video games but for short durations, completed camp rituals with proper attention, and ate vegetables and salad without protest.

In Endor, he was also an obedient son, but he laughed at the table, scrambled in the hills with his sister Miriam, teased Leah into hugs and laughter, and drove his father's speedboat when he was nine. Miriam had been wild about that and had tried to push him out of the boat, so he had held her in a headlock until she said sorry. Miriam and Aaron had both been laughing so loud that it had been hard to hear the "sorry," and their father had scowled and lectured them, but his eyes had been shining. Their father had driven them home while they had sat in the middle seat, arms around each other. "Friends," Miriam had declared. "Friends forever, best and best."

Once, when he had been ten, he had noticed an older girl, a hard girl, maybe just finished being a teenager. She had sat on the church steps, elbows on spread knees, nursing a cigarette down to the filter. She had swayed a little. "Aaron, Aaron," she had slurred. "Little cousin, baby boy. Your mommy was our cousin's teacher, hey? Tonya, you know? Our Tonya *loved* your mom, but then she died. Yeah, our cousin died. Gone. And your mom went running after your dad till she got you; then she took right off. Yep. She left us. Never looked down, and me runnin' and bawlin' after the plane. Cold woman, your mommy."

Miriam had stepped in front of Aaron, fists planted on her hips. "That's just drunk talk, you. You don't talk like that. Gee, hurt my brother's feelings. None of it his fault."

Miriam had grabbed Aaron's hand and hauled him down the road toward the new house. "She don't mean it," Miriam had hissed. "She got a bad luck, and she says anything comes in her head."

To Aaron, it had sounded like a real story, one he was supposed to know but could not quite recognize. He had been glad to get home, to his father-home, and Leah hugging him, Leah laughing because they were grimy from head to toe.

Aaron loved his mother, and she always hung over him on Christmas morning, studying his stance, watching to see if his face was wreathed in smiles; she waited, her mouth a tight line. She was just like Aaron on skates—NHL star in his mind, teetering through the motions in real life.

ANNA'S WANDERING YEARS

Aaron began Grade 7 in Bridgewater, living in his grandmother's house with his mother. Grandmother Catherine's house had been stripped of her trinkets and photographs; Anna kept one photo of her parents on the mantel in the living room, and the rest were packed away. There was new bedding, new furniture covers. Anna bought new dishes, in a clunky, functional style, and packed away Catherine's delicate pattern.

There were times of basketball and riding lessons, school bus rides, and Anna finding regular work as a supply teacher.

Aaron wanted an Endor Christmas, and Joshua started planning it in September. Anna was pleased that Aaron would finally have a proper busy family Christmas, cast in the mould of Christmas itself. He would be inundated with love and tradition and packed houses instead of the quiet meal for two without even Grandmother Catherine in attendance. Anna regretted that Aaron had not experienced the chaos under the tree with a pile of siblings and cousins. That was the Christmas she had yearned for as a child; yet she had given her son the Christmases of her own childhood.

Nevertheless, over the Christmas holiday, she counted down the days until Aaron's return. Then, on New Year's Eve, Joshua called. How would Anna feel about Aaron staying for a while, maybe till Easter? Lots of traditions for Easter, remember? And maybe spring? Do a little hunting? Maybe fish? But it was up to her, of course. But Aaron was suddenly on the phone saying it was just this once, and he really wanted to; it was just this once, and then she would have the whole summer with him, not just some. Please, Mom?

Anna saw the long, dark winter spiraling forward and only her in it. She also saw the long, dark winter spiraling forward and Aaron jerking through the motions wooden and subdued.

So, of course, she agreed, and Joshua came back on the line and asked if Anna wanted to come up. She could teach in Endor when someone got sick, and they would fix up a little piece of the house for her to have her privacy.

Anna could not imagine how he thought that she or Leah would want that. Anna did not want to perch on the periphery of the Kalluk family, surrounded by their compatibility. And so, she thanked him, and said to thank Leah but that she thought Aaron would be all right.

In February, when the quiet had dipped beneath silence and become a buzz in her ears, she took a long-term occasional contract in a fly-in community west of the scone lady Reah's town. There was oil in the soil and mould in the walls, but she taught math, and she made it alive. Anna coughed sometimes, and she was lonely sometimes, bur she played volleyball with the seniors in the evening and went cross-country skiing on Saturday afternoons with the junior division. She threw herself into her new life in a new way because then she would not feel the hole in the room where her son should be.

She was keeping busy. She was making do. Until June, when she returned to her mother's house, where all would be right again.

When summer came, her son returned, tall and tanned, with muscles in his arms. He laughed more at first, and they had long walks and talks along the river as they had in the past. Then he told her about the cabin they were building up north in the fall.

"You make it sound like you are going to be there," Anna said.

Aaron pushed his hands deep into his pockets and walked on ahead.

And thus, in late August, they packed the car and closed the house again. Anna delivered Aaron to the airport and turned west.

M

At first, her cousin in Whitehorse was delighted to see her childhood pen pal, and they shared evenings tipping back beers and reminiscing about childhood aspirations. In time, her cousin wearied of Anna's tears and rambling, of peeling her from the table and depositing her on the couch, of working long hours and coming home to cook supper while Anna sat absorbed in a book. She was thinking of pursuing her masters in English, Anna explained. Then she decided that waitressing would give her life experience, and eventually, she was waitressing afternoons and evenings in one of the bars. There she met the bartender David, and in the winter, to her cousin's relief, they set up house together in the trailer park behind the bar. Anna had slowed down the alcohol consumption, as it really had not agreed with her, but the long, self-analytic rambles continued. David told her to get over it, and then the rambles stopped.

With David, there was no secret ecstasy, no suppressed gasps of pleasure to avoid offending roommates; there was regular, unimaginative sex, and Anna really didn't mind. When, however, she came home from work late one spring evening, feet dragging and head aching, and found David with an off-shift waitress engaged in irregular and highly imaginative sex with rather explicit ecstasy, Anna moved back to her cousin's couch.

And didn't self-analyze out loud anymore.

Anne left Whitehorse at the end of May to prepare her mother's house for her summer with Aaron. She was now an experienced bar waitress with a relationship in her past—not a placid engagement, not a hidden passion, just a plain, old-fashioned affair.

She did not think she cared to have another one. David was not a man that a woman should miss, although, being Anna, she felt she should.

M

Anna Caine had not really cared for Whitehorse, although she had liked the view of Grey Mountain rising over the sprawl and subdivisions. Perhaps she had been looking for those rolling rounded mountains spilling along a harbour and the laughter of farewells as family left the camps.

Perhaps she could have gone to Labrador then, but she needed the words, and she did not have those yet.

The Whitehorse year marked the beginning of Anna's wandering years, the years that would prepare her for that last winter of all, the year when the world was ending, and Anna Caine became beautiful again.

Some would see it that way.

MATTIE'S PROMISE

Mattie ran her palm over the Formica tabletop in her little apartment in St. John's. My God, little Mattie Amarok had arrived. She stared at her hands—neat nails, clear nail polish. No tobacco stains, no cigarette clutched between chewed fingertips. Her gut clenched and spasmed. *A good brew will fix that*, she remembered Jay saying. *We got something special, remember.*

Not for a long time, Jay, and never again. Mattie's old boyfriend had preyed on her rage and fanned it hot, until no one had wanted Mattie Amarok around. Only Jay. Jay had looked into Mattie and had made her over as his own creation. She had drunk hard with him, hating the beating of mind and body but reveling in her strength. She, Mattie Amarok, could handle it. She had been through the fire and could take anything.

Mattie had been filled with hatred for a long, long time. First, there had been the wonderful Ms. Caine and her Christmas play and all her visits, the Ms. Caine who had forgotten her and taken over Mattie's cousin Joshua, and ultimately had abandoned Mattie there, on the airstrip. Ms. Caine had walked past her little Mattie, who had run and run after the plane, but it hadn't mattered. Mattie and her grandmother had written Ms. Caine, and sent pictures, but Ms. Caine had never written back. Not a word. Not a picture. People must know how hard that was for kids.

Mattie was sorry that she had been mean to Anna's son, Aaron, that day by the church, but he had been about the age Mattie herself had been when Anna Caine had deserted her. She had never gotten over that abandonment, and the sight of happy little Aaron had angered her.

Mattie knew she would have gotten over Ms. Caine, but when she was twelve, she had been walking along the trail below the school. There had been three shadows, three shadows without faces who had pinned her and hurt her again and again, and she had hated them. Her hate had squirmed like snakes under her skin, but most of all, while they were doing things to her, she had thought of Ms. Caine climbing onto the plane without looking back. The pain and the hatred had crawled into her bones, and she had thought about Ms. Caine, how she had never helped her Mattie at all.

The last time Jay had gotten mad, he had beaten the baby out of her body. She had been medevac'd to St. John's, bleeding from the miscarriage that had taken her baby and her fertility. Mattie had gotten her body patched up and her mind counselled and nurtured. She had been in awe when her government had said she was a candidate for upgrading. She had asked if she could study archaeology, and they had said maybe later, but they were actually thinking of social work.

And now, here she was, tucking her blouse into her skirt, carrying a new briefcase, and sporting sensible walking shoes. Body clean and mind made up. Bachelor of social work.

She looked into the mirror and tugged her blazer straight. *Look out, Ms. Caine. I'm coming to take your kids!*

Sometimes, back in Endor, when someone was leaving the camp, those left behind would all grab the sides of the *Kamutik*. The snow machine would go roaring down the ice, everyone piled against the sides of the *Kamutik* box, laughing, then one by one, they would push away to roll and laugh in the snow and then run as far as they could beside and behind the *Kamutik* because that was a good way to send off their loved ones. They were with the travellers, and they were happy to be with them, and they were brave and hopeful in their goodbyes.

Now tough Mattie Amarok was on her knees in her new apartment, skirt wrinkling as she rocked and sobbed, arms tight across her chest and gripping her shoulders. No, she didn't mean what she had said. That was wrong.

"I, Mattie Amarok," she whispered, "do solemnly vow that I will take all the children into my arms. I will heal them and make their families whole. And," she was keening now, "when someone grabs them and drags *them* into the bushes, and their faces are puffed and purple like some ugly Halloween mask, and they're torn apart inside their bodies and all through their souls, I will take them. I will take them in my arms, and I will tell them how beautiful they are, and I will heal them all and release them, safe and whole as a blessing.

"Because I know. I know."

Mattie knew that her work would not be noble like that. She knew that she would break her heart and break her heart until she was able to hold their broken hearts. She knew that she would not see that many happy endings. She knew that she would cry a lot, but she realized that this new rage, and her passion for all children, would see her strong.

Until she was finally ready to go home.

She had loved Anna Caine, and she had hated her. Now, Anna Caine did not matter to her; only the broken children mattered.

MOMENTS AND MEMORIES

The years rolled down in a pattern. Each July, Aaron came to Grandmother Catherine's house, which was now his mother's summer house. During the visit, they indulged in old camping rituals, staking out a space in the camp city of the nearby park. They canoed, kayaked, and biked. They cooked on campfires. Aaron had been living with woodstoves and firepits built on layers of spruce boughs on the ice, with functional hunting camps on the Barrens, casual fishing villages at the *iKaluk* camps, and boil-ups when wooding. Still, he played cards at the picnic table with his mother in the camping city, as she studied him, measuring. Did this camping satisfy him? Had she brought the right foods? Should they go to the house and watch movies instead? Should they canoe into the back country and study predator signs? Was she doing it right?

Each year, Joshua suggested that she should come back to Endor to teach. She would be good for the community, good for their son. Each year, Anna pointed out that she had work in First Nation communities in North Ontario, that the family parameters in Endor were well-established now, and her presence would only confuse Aaron and all the family.

She knew there would be open and welcoming smiles for her; the People were kind, and they would bury their bewilderment deep. They would never speak their hurt or shame her. Therein lay Anna's shame.

Mattie had grown up hard, she heard. Tonya's little Bobby was a troubled young man.

Aaron would tense each time his father suggested that Anna return to Endor, and relax as the discussion concluded with his father shaking his head and his mother looking away. His parents did better long distance, Aaron decided, or he did better with them long distance. Aaron had his mother-home moments, and then his father-home-panorama-of-family. That way was comfortable. If the settings overlapped, he knew, he would lose both worlds.

There was one memorable Christmas when nostalgia overtook Anna, during her second year in a fly-in community two hours north of Thunder Bay. Anna flew by Beechcraft to Thunder Bay, wound her way to Goose Bay via Toronto and Halifax, then mounted the Twin Otter for the North Coast. All in less than three days.

Anna had booked a room in the local hotel, and at first, this went very well. There were meals and wooding trips and celebrations, and Leah presided with grace and dignity while keeping one eye on the calendar.

The septic line freeze-up at the hotel was plain bad luck.

The raw sewage spilling back onto the hotel floor was aesthetically deficient and unsanitary.

The hotel closed, and Anna Caine found herself perched in the Kalluk living room, her bags stuffed behind the couch and relatives pouring through the house all day. She attempted to help with the sweeping and vegetable chopping while Leah slipped along behind, doing quick tucks with broom and mop, smoothing the clumsy efforts of Anna Caine. Miriam, now a teenager, glowered, her sister Dinah pointed out the missed grit on the floor or gouges on potatoes with enthusiasm, and the youngest child, Simeon, demanded stories from the teacher.

It was only for three days, but then the blizzard descended.

The blizzard itself only lasted three days, although these were very long days for Anna Caine, sleeping in the living room of Joshua and Leah Kalluk. The two recovery days, with the power and airlines being restored, were also long. Anna was stranded an additional two days because many people were by now waiting for the plane, and there were also all her other connections to rebook. It was, as she was told often and with an undertone of reproach, the holiday season. Everyone had to make the best of it.

In North Ontario, Anna caught a ride from the airstrip directly to the school, where the administration observed that she had certainly taken a long vacation.

That was her only Endor Christmas.

Nostalgic imaginings were sometimes preferable to direct encounters.

The next winter, she taught in the same community in Northern Ontario, and a returning student, Marta, came to her attention. Marta was not Tonya, but her intensity was familiar. Marta, like Tonya, had known hardship. Marta, too, had dreams.

MARTA'S NATIVITY PLAY
FOR THE STREETS

To Ms. Caine:

You got lots of good ideas, and no offense, but you don't know what it's like. Me, I know. My sister used to go live back of that mall, that one in the west, when she was using. She was always cold, Ms. Caine, and arms thin as the needle she was poking in her veins. Pumping poison into her blood. Drinking it in.

They found her one morning in December. She was propped against the garbage boxes, and her eyes all filmed up, her teeth right through her lip. She was looking, she was seeing, I know. And she wasn't seeing or hearing no angels on high. No nice inn keepers with friendly little stables with clean hay and no shit. She was frozen to the ground in her own pee and blood and shit. Propped up there, staring at nothing now, Christmas morning and lots of pretty trees and roasting turkeys all bullshit. I want a Christmas play that's dirty. The way it really was. Homeless and refugees and babies born in the nastiest part of town. Yes, they grow up to save us all, but nobody wants them, and they poke them with thorns and pound nails into them and stick them with a sword after they're dead. Just like us, Ms. Caine. The residential school was how long ago? And we're still feeling those nails. Those thorns and swords. So why not shoot up on Christmas morning and see Jesus, walking in the alley, and I swear to God, he was the first one of us they crucified. Maybe we remind them of Jesus, not the missionary Jesus but the real one—giving out fish and bannock, healing people and hey, we got the tech, so let's practice on him, and then let's get those Indigenous people.

You want hope, Ms. Caine? Here is hope. Here is my play about Mary the Homeless Madonna of Winnipeg. And people are going to rise up and see a miracle, because maybe there is a miracle, maybe sometime. Because if I put a miracle in, then maybe someday I can believe it. But not right now. This is a fantasy play right now. I hope it is real someday.

Hope you like it.
From: Marta

M

Anna sat for a long time with the pages of Marta Raymond's play before her, but it was Tonya's face, not Marta's, that rose before her. *Did you remember my little cousin Mattie and my grandmother?* she was asking. *Did you watch over my son? And did you ever write your new friends, Reah and all the others you walked away from and never touched again? And what about my cousin Joshua? Did you ever understand him? Did you ever try? And now there is Marta. I guess you will put her behind you, too, when you walk away. So many lost and forgotten people, Ms. Caine. You absorbed their inner feelings, and their love, and then you tossed them aside.*

Anna pushed back from her desk and paced. Marta had written a play of hope and longing dragged from the depths of a grieving soul—for her sister, dead on the streets one cold December dawn not so long ago, honoured in a play with raging drug dealer innkeepers, teenage runaways fleeing violence, Mary a rape victim, Joseph her loyal childhood friend, street kid carolers who were angels in disguise, for perhaps that was the only form angels could take on the streets of Winnipeg, and withdrawal-trembling former nurses who delivered babies that changed the world—it was raw, it was horrific, but so it must have been in Bethlehem, no flowing robes and freshly brushed, compliant donkeys—just danger and fear and the stench of despair.

Marta Raymond had looked into the depths of her sister's death and pleaded for a hope that could one day be real. Marta burned with a longing to heal her world, caught in glimpses of poetry and this play she had written for Grade 12 English. It was a true Christmas play, and Anna thought consciously for the first time in years of Terrence. Terrence would have loved the play, and he would have said it breathed hope into a landscape of despair.

M

"Have you thought about theatre?" Anna Caine asked Marta Raymond that spring, as they strolled along one of the dusty side roads on the way to the airstrip.

Marta glanced at the woman walking beside her. "Well, yeah. That play? Wasn't that theatre?"

"You could become a playwright, a director. I mean, you saw into the heart of everything with *A Winnipeg Nativity*. And you brought the cast to life. Your Mary, the tears were real as she held the baby to the sky, like a prayer."

"It was a prayer," muttered the girl, scuffing at the dusty tufts of grass. "She just got it, right there on stage, everyone watching, and she just suddenly was like—*This is what it means to be the Madonna woman: alone; every step of the way, you are alone.*"

"Are you alone?"

"Hell, yeah. Marta Raymond, Madonna of the Lost. I go to Winnipeg, how long before you meet me by the mall, looking for change? I get that fancy theatre course, and I'll be so loved the first week. *Jeez, we could have a real live Native in our group; aren't we just the coolest most cultured bitches going?*"

"And then I'll be invisible. *Good riddance, Madonna, full of grace, hail and go to hell.*"

"Drama people all cool, all about those stage lights."

"But you would be studying set design, direction."

"*Native girl might get drunk, better not call her; don't tell her about our little party. Take a picture with her in the cafeteria, nice and safe. Wow, aren't we open-minded?*"

"You could find your own circle. You could go to the Indigenous counselling services, meet people there."

"Yeah, *Native girl go hide. Don't come out till you're white-washed.*"

Anna stopped and turned to Marta, hands on her hips. "You're your own worst enemy, you know that?"

Marta slid a cigarette pack from her hip pocket, thumbed it open and selected one. "Says the woman without her son, without her man, without her home. Like an alien, studying everything but not part of anything. You know? *Oh, look,*" she said in a high voice, "*look at me, saving the world, one loser at a time; my own life is screwed, but that's OK.*"

"That is so unfair. I don't think like that."

Marta grinned, cupping the cigarette as she snapped the lighter. "Nevertheless. Never-the-less, Ms. Anna Caine, I am going straight to the top my way. Right here. This is gonna be my stage. The flames are gonna start here, right in the heart of every kid, and fan out to set the world on fire. This town is our stage, and we are gonna dance the world down.

"Because I am going to be a teacher.

"I am going to T. Bay and then I am coming home. Great things are gonna happen here.

"Not one of these kids is going to freeze to the ground in their piss and puke and blood. Secretly, they are all angels. And I am going to release that secret on the whole world."

It occurred to Anna that, if she had had this passion for teaching, she might have made a difference, somewhere.

She decided, however, to move on. She was lonely here, and young people like Marta were so complicated.

It would be Sarah, the woman who eventually married Terrence, who found the envelope containing the play, years later when all was done. It would be her who would insist that it have a place in the stories, in tribute to Marta and her People, and to her husband's vision.

THE PERSISTENCE
OF MOUNTAINS

Anna's teaching years became a series of contracts in fly-in communities: flying in from Sioux Lookout or Thunder Bay, spending winters in the community and summers at her mother's old place, soaking every nurturing moment when Aaron came down in July. She could have moved to Endor and been a full part of Aaron's life, but the idea of meeting Joshua and Leah in the store or on the street, or sitting at parent-teacher meetings with them, was disturbing. Joshua might drop by her apartment to lecture her and find fault with her parenting, and that would upset her most of all.

She did not have to face the lack of passion in Joshua's eyes, the gentle but smug smile of Joshua's wife, and the exuberance and natural joy of Aaron's siblings. The family would work and play around her, and she would be invisible. She had done the right thing.

Still, she missed the years not lived, even though it was easier in some ways to yearn for them and cry in the night.

Anna did fly from Thunder Bay to Toronto, Halifax, Goose Bay, and finally Endor, to attend her son's high school graduation. As she watched Aaron, now grown, striding into the gym, she realized that he had become a man without her bearing witness to his life.

Aaron's sister Miriam was graduating too, but she did not look at Anna once. Miriam was having her graduation, and her smiles and attention were on those she loved.

Miriam enrolled in the education program in St. John's, and Aaron selected civil engineering technology in Corner Brook. Through that period, Anna worked in Northern Quebec, and although she could have flown to Endor via Kuujjuaq, she did not. When he finished his program, Aaron took a job in mining research out on the Bay, and a year later, Miriam became the Grade 5 teacher in Endor. Anna settled in a community along the northern Trans-Canada route in Ontario for a few years and discovered a quiet joy in remedial math and literacy.

She made few friends, and her thoughts turned often to home.

When she tried to picture home, she always saw low, rolling mountains rising along the horizon.

She did not look for friends and felt sometimes that all her friends were behind her, in a time when they laughed and dreamed great dreams, in the presence of mountains.

ROADS TO THE SKY

Anna Caine, always arriving, made plans to put her life in order. She was greying, and her energy was lagging; it was time to settle down. She considered settling in the house that had been her mother's house, and to thus be nearer her son and his life. She set her eye instead on a small rural property removed from the town. Nearby, there was a seasonal area with chalet-style cottages scattered along a lakefront. On the gravel road that ran past the property, there were snug hunting camps tucked into the woodlots. At this time, Aaron announced that he was going to British Columbia to further his engineering studies, explaining that he had always wanted to spend time on the West Coast. His father, Aaron claimed, understood this need to go out in the world as a young man.

Anna had not been consulted, but if she had been, she knew she would have urged him to set specific goals and a time limit, so that he too did not suddenly discover that his years were used up and he was alone.

Aaron yearned to be someone unique for a while, Anna suspected. Someone without a past—not the son of Joshua, who was anchored in his People's history, a force on the Land and a name made, or the son of Anna, the wandering teacher without roots or place. Aaron needed to ask the questions, and for a moment, not be the answers everyone made for him.

Aaron could not explain to his mother that, although Endor was home, sometimes home squeezed him, and he wanted to peel it away like a tight jacket.

He did not know how to explain that a distorted jumble of noise burned in his ears and all around him, and far away, a cool voice was beckoning.

Aaron did know that he might have been an explorer had he been born in another time.

ᴧ

It was natural, therefore, for Anna to take a contract in rural western Quebec, in a small community tucked between a river and tall, wooded hills. There she stayed until Aaron completed his studies. There was peace there, and in her secret thoughts, Anna called the hills the Road to the Sky.

Now when Aaron completed his studies, he came home to Endor. The adventure had been good, but he did not remain in the west for his graduation. As in Corner Brook, he had his certificate mailed. Anna suspected that his high school ceremony had been enough of graduations for him.

Aaron stopped to visit his mother in Nova Scotia. She had not tired of the Road to the Sky, but she had tired of her colleagues in Quebec, and as sensitivity to the minor quirks of co-workers was a sign of burnout, she was taking a year off. Anna had brought with her the dog Petra.

ᴧ

She had met the dog Petra on the Road to the Sky while she was snowshoeing along the power line deep in the hills, swinging along the snowmobile trail made by trappers. Petra was a young husky, possibly two years old, standing motionless behind the pine branches. Her face was classic Siberian husky, but her legs were a little short, and her eyes were brown. There were secrets in those eyes and that stance, the body caught in the moment between action and inaction, a Renaissance sculpture with eyes on Anna and the horizon all at once. The dog minced forward, lowering her head as she drew close. This was not the lowering of a challenge, but an acknowledgement, and Anna stood, hands at her sides.

"You're like me," Anna whispered. "Somewhere out there is the life I was meant to be living. You know? I know what it looks like, but when I get up and say I'm going to start, I do something else."

The dog slunk nearer, crouching.

"You and me. Hiding in the pines. Life passing us by." She lowered herself to squat on the snow near the dog, who sidled closer, sniffing near her snowshoes.

"I bet you had puppies." The dog gave a quick lick near the side of Anna's extended hand. Anna settled, twisting at her pack. The dog sprang back, poised to run. "No. No. It's OK. I have food in here, that's all." Anna tugged the zipper on the pack and extracted a wax paper package. "Look. Yes. You know what this is? Yes. It's bannock. I make it Labrador style, though. They call it *panitsiak* there. You know? Yes. I had a friend, and his great aunt taught me, and then he and I fell in love, or I fell in love, and our babies grow up and leave us, don't they? I was lucky. I had mine for twelve years. I bet you didn't have two months. No. Everyone loves us; then they love the babies more, and they forget us."

She spread her fingers along the dog's rib cage. "My god, you're so beautiful. Do you have a home, girl? You do, don't you? Yes. Who wouldn't want you, eh?"

"You talk to dogs, do you?"

Anna stumbled to her feet, staggering a little with her snowshoes flapping.

The man wore a green parka, hood pushed back and toque riding back from his forehead, his expression inscrutable behind the dark sunglasses. He carried a gun loosely under one arm. "That's my cousin's dog. He went back to Longlac and left me his dog. 'I don't want no dog,' I told him. 'Moving,' he told me. 'Your dog now.' So, I got a dog, and it's a good dog, but I don't really want a dog. You want a dog?"

Anna shrugged. "I never thought."

"Yeah, I figured as much. But I tell you this: You been like a shadow here, always ready for school, always doing things right, but never smile, never part of things. Politically correct, but like you're scared not to be.

"I come along, and here you are, talking all out to the dog. Like she's your therapist or something. And her listening all out. I think she's your dog."

"Oh. I don't have any of the stuff, like collars and dishes, and food. I've never had a dog."

"Time to start. Dog chose you; that happens sometimes. It might be important, I think."

"What do you want for her?"

The man shrugged. "Just take her. She wants a home, I don't want a dog, and you two are a good match. I'll take a piece of bannock, though. Oh. Her name is Petra."

Petra.

A rock.

"Is she really my dog? When I go home in the spring, she comes with me to stay?"

"Sure. You'll be good together." He lifted the packet of bannock she held out to him. *"Meegwetch.* See you on the trail some time, I guess."

Then he was swinging along the trail, his snowshoes swishing as he swung each out and about the other.

No matter how hard she tried, Anna's snowshoes always clacked together.

M

Anna, Aaron, and the dog Petra spent a month working on the small property Anna had finally purchased on the pothole-ridden gravel road, the one tucked in the woods with the lake community a few miles off. This was to be her retirement home. She would live there, supply teach locally, and take short-term contracts with Band-operated schools.

She would not stay long enough to grow weary of colleagues or get homesick. She had roots now, was no more a wanderer; she had a place for Aaron to call home. There was a cozy room tucked off the living room, and they painted it and floored it and furnished it with bed and dresser. They placed photos on the shelf beside the window: Joshua and Aaron on the Barrens with rifles and fur-trimmed hoods and goggles; Aaron with his father and Leah and his three siblings, his face alight; Aaron and Anna and Catherine, stiff and teeth in line; Anna and Aaron, rigid beside each other at the lake; Aaron grave with high school diploma as his father beams by one shoulder and his mother hunches by the other.

Anna looked at the photos and pictured herself in Endor—growing old there, with grandchildren dropping in, and her aged mother serene in the living-room window, beloved by all.

She whispered these things to Petra in the night, and Petra lay with head and shoulders up, grumbling her own stories low in her throat.

Then Aaron returned to Endor to work and live, and Anna and the dog shared the silence of the new house for a year of burnout recovery.

LEAH: LOW FIRE
BURNING BRIGHT

On a perfect, windless morning in November of the following year, Joshua Kalluk was going to drive his wife to the airstrip for the medical flight to Goose Bay, for routine tests at the hospital there. Of course, Leah would also go Christmas shopping for her expanding family.

Daybreak found Joshua and Leah lingering over tea and hot breakfast in the quiet of their new home high in the hills above the harbour. The early ice gleamed, the eastern sky lightened to the new day, and in the living room, logs crackled in the wood heater. The house was emptier these days; their eldest daughter Miriam and her husband and their little Beth had a sweet bungalow near the school, and their youngest, Simeon, had started college in St. John's. However, there was still their middle child Dinah, laughing and easygoing, with her little girl Tonya and her new baby. Dinah did not seem inclined to marriage and career like her sister, but she was a hard worker, and her children were happy.

There was also Joshua's son Aaron, quiet and content here in his stepmother's house. Leah had made a home for Aaron, and Joshua knew this. Aaron was now building his own small house on the corner of their lot; one day there would be grandchildren running between their houses.

Little Leah Piguk Kalluk was now fifty-four and the mother of this great household. And her husband still turned to her, and her only, with a young man's eagerness because that was how it was when soulmates bonded.

Joshua caressed the hand he had known all his life, drew it close to his cheek, and kissed it. "I will miss you," he said.

"Three days." She met his eyes.

"Weather permitting," he acknowledged, his arms reaching around her and drawing her close. "Do you forgive me?" he murmured.

Her eyes widened, and she smiled. "Did you do something?"

Joshua ran one finger along her jawline. "You know what I mean. For her. And that time."

Leah shrugged. "We were all young. We were all learning. Now we are here. It is all good, my Joshua."

He kissed her then and drove her to the airstrip on the snowmobile as the November morning unfolded, the air clear and still. Joshua's heart tightened as the plane shuddered down the airstrip, engine rising to a thin roar as it skipped faster and faster over the gravel. Had they done the flight checks? Would the plane suddenly stall and pitch into the sea or the rocks just when he was learning that each day with Leah was a blessing, that her peacefulness was worth more than any passion with Anna Caine?

Joshua wanted to say all these things to Leah, and he vowed to do that as soon as she came home. They would grow old together, hand in hand, smiling over the harbour while their grandchildren scrambled in and out, and they would guard each other's passing.

M

The plane flew without incident or turbulence to Goose Bay, where the medical van delivered Leah to the hospital so that she could register and prepare for her scan. She had two days before her return flight, and all the kids and grandkids and cousins and aunts to get little gifts for. Most of all, she wanted to find a new scope for Joshua's rifle. This was a surprise, and she smiled, anticipating the light in his eyes.

The ice storm came down that night, and in the morning, the streets were smooth and slick. Oh, but the next day, the weather would be clear and calm for the flight home, so this morning, Leah must take a taxi from the hostel and have a little shopping spree. She should not walk, for she might fall, and the taxi would be careful.

Alas, Martin Code had not been careful. He had been strumming his guitar, and sipping whiskey with friends until early morning, but for some reason had decided that he had to get home at ten a.m. He was still belting out that last song, and he did not notice his speed. When he spun out of control and smashed his truck into the side of the taxi, he did not see the face pressed against the window or the blood on the woman's temple, and there were sirens, and the woman was being strapped to a stretcher, and it was like a medical emergency show.

And then he knew nothing.

When the ice had melted on the roads and airways, and the planes flew again, Joshua Kalluk came down from Endor and was at Leah's side when she awakened from the coma. "Who will look after my Joshua?" she whispered, as he sobbed like a child on his knees beside her. She cradled his head, seeing his long years stretching away, gazing over the harbour, and no one to give or receive a secret smile. And then, she settled. Her breathing slowed, and Joshua listened as her heartbeat weakened and faltered, and then he pressed his ear to the silence.

His calm and soothing helpmeet was gone from him, and he was left kneeling in an empty room, all the unsaid words twisting in his heart.

He wished and he wished that he could follow her. He wept until he was empty of tears, and then he called Miriam.

MATTIE'S RETURN

Mattie Amarok pulled the thick sweater over her head and tugged it down against her hips. Home still felt colder after her years in St. John's, but although she might feel the cold in her bones, being outside the circle of the virus was not a bad thing at all.

A few years earlier, Mattie Amarok had come home to be a family counsellor in Endor. Mattie could walk down the road with pride—no cigarette between her lips, no belly tight with raw homebrew. Sometimes she still felt the clutch and pull within her body, but she had learned that the feeling would pass. Delay the fulfillment, and delay it again, and then get on with life.

Mattie pressed her forehead to the windowpane and stared over the harbour. This place was supposed to be home, but home should have laughter and a grandmother's arms somewhere in its corners. After Mattie had left, her grandmother had lived alone with her great-grandson Bobby, who had grown up wild and finally taken off down the coast. Home then had become her grandmother huddled alone in a corner, remembering plays and songs, refusing to go to Joshua and Leah, and them checking daily until the day they took her to hospital. Home was shadows and faces and voices, but it was the echo of laughter that made Mattie cry.

In the year after Leah's death, Mattie's cousin Joshua had developed a tumour that burrowed behind his eyes, and he had chosen a harsh course of chemo to scourge the cancer out of his body. He had beaten that cancer, right there in the hospital in St. John's, but Mattie knew it had been the dark mountain spirits of his homeland that he had been fighting; he had fought them down until their power over him was gone.

And, Mattie decided, he had fought them for Leah. Theirs had been a love story to remember.

There had been talk that Anna Caine would come to St. John's for the chemo, but she had been going to Quebec or some other far-off place. Aaron and his sister Miriam had been there. Mattie had sat with them a few times, but when she had seen the still, brittle body encased in tubes and sinking into the mattress, she had thought of dazzling snow and a lithe young man scolding the teacher down from the slopes, and had heard his laughter echoing over the *iKaluk* camp under the huge Labrador sky in a time when grandmothers were young, and all children were safe.

And then she had felt the old rage rising in her blood and known it was not time for home yet.

Mattie had been relieved that Anna Caine had not come to Joshua; men in those situations needed women like his departed wife Leah—strong, calm women, women of balance. It was better to be alone than have Anna Caine tipping and turning the balance and making a mess.

Mattie knew that Anna was not a bad woman, but sometimes, Mattie was still that little girl sobbing in the willows while the plane flew away.

M

Joshua had come to see Mattie when she had first moved home, scraping his boots on the mat before flinging open the door. "Mattie! Little cousin Mattie!" he had exclaimed. "You come home at last. St. John's is not like Labrador, eh?"

Mattie had pushed the kettle forward on the woodstove. "I'm here for a bit," she had said. "Feels a little strange, I guess."

Joshua had dug into his pocket and produced a thick envelope. "Pictures," he had announced, waving it. "Lots of pictures of your old friend Ms. Caine."

Mattie had turned back to the stove. "Yeah, I heard you went there. And you were with her for your PET scan that time before? What, you guys getting together or something?"

Joshua had studied Mattie's stiff shoulders. "She is Aaron's mother," he had said. "There was no one else that PET scan time. Family here was busy; family in St. John's was busy, and," he had added softly, "you never answered my messages."

Mattie had examined a speck on the countertop. "Maybe," Joshua had continued, "you are ready now? To face it down? To get strong?"

Mattie had felt the familiar pull and clutch in her muscles. Oh, to feel the brew pulsing, pushing out the tightness, pouring down her throat, baptizing her soul.

"I got pictures," he had said, "but it was a quiet few days. A very lonely woman, your friend Ms. Caine. Lives in the woods, two dogs. Nice husky, and then this big yellow one, always jumping. Always in your face. Always drooling.

"So, I made her a fence for them. No trouble. And she got no wood stove, you know?"

"What? She lives in the woods and no wood stove? What's she do in winter?"

"Electric," Joshua had explained, bewildered. "What's she going to do when all the power fails, and she is cold? And it's lonely, with no woodstove."

"I'm thinking," Mattie had said, "that it's a good thing Aaron came home and got to grow up with you and Leah. His mother was like a travel companion; you guys gave him roots."

"Maybe," Joshua had said, "you need to live now, not then. Do you want to look at pictures now?"

"Sorry," Mattie had said.

Joshua had scooped the envelope back into his jacket pocket. "No one else came, you know? PET scan time? She came. So, I made her a fence. I did not betray my wife. I did not betray you. The virus is down, so I took a trip. She's gone now, Anna, gone west, I think. Got a teaching contract back there again. Dogs too."

"She leaves everyone, you know. She left her mother behind when all that woman wanted was to see her grandson. I think something maybe happened to Anna Caine when she was a kid. She acts all friendly; then she takes off. Never good with goodbyes."

"Like you?" Joshua had asked.

"Never," Mattie had told him, "ever say I am like her. You do not know. Never, eh?"

She still regretted seeing the slumped shoulders as Joshua walked down the path, regretted the unseen pictures deep in his parka pocket.

∧

At the time of that PET scan, Mattie recalled, people had just been getting used to that first virus. The spring before, everyone had been terrified. They had stayed in their houses. They hadn't visited. They had hardly gone to the store. They had stifled every cough and sneeze, and if their noses felt plugged, they had sat still and waited for the fever and clogged lungs and suffocation. The government had been full of ideas, but things had kept changing. That PET scan fall when Anna went to St. John's with Joshua, things had been pretty good, but that winter they had gotten bad again. The summer had not been too serious, and in August, Joshua had gone to build Anna's fence, and Mattie had come home. Later that fall, though, things had gotten very bad, followed by the winter, when everyone everywhere seemed to have the virus, and people were just too tired to notice, and although it was everywhere, they just stumbled through the days and pretended they were going to be all right. That had gone on for another year, Mattie thought, but the years had begun to run together in her mind. Had there really only been five virus years? Or had the virus always been with them?

The fall after that had not been so bad, but this past winter, there had been yet another new type of the virus, and it had been everywhere. In this new and terrifying time, nothing had worked. They had lined up for vaccines, then more vaccines, but this new virus had seemed like it was laughing at all the vaccines. To Mattie, it was like they were going out to hunt a polar bear with a little stick; they would whack it on the nose, and then the bear would eat them. They hadn't gotten supplies, lots of times, and the people that had been fussing the Easter before, because they only had ten people to eat their big Easter ham, had been so glad to open the cupboard and find a box of dried soup packets. Oh, they were feasting now. The supply chains, Mattie recalled, had been totally screwed last winter.

Anna Caine had come home to stay after that winter. Maybe, Mattie decided, Ms. Caine could snare rabbits in her woods, stew them up with a little wild carrot. Anna Caine always had been lucky.

Joshua, though, had not been so lucky this fall; his usual CT scan showed the tumour had returned and spread through his body. Mattie had gone down to the plane to shake her cousin's hand when he was leaving for St. John's; she'd had a bad feeling this time. She had shaken Joshua's hand and told him that she would look at the pictures with him when he got home. Joshua had looked puzzled, but had shaken her hand, with a firm, well-wishing Inuk handshake. Joshua's daughter Miriam had been at the airstrip, and she had said that Anna Caine was going to be the medical escort in St. John's. Virus numbers, Miriam had observed, were down on the Coast, but there were some deadly cases in St. John's. Her father would be careful and would not bring the virus home to his People. Anna Caine would go back to the woods afterward, and she was always all right, Miriam had concluded.

Mattie didn't hate Anna Caine anymore, but the woman was like a lump of wet coal pressing against her heart, and she hoped Joshua would come home without his own heart getting hurt again.

Mattie studied the colours on the mountains across the harbour—the deep rusted tans where the light touched the rounded summits, the jagged greys of the shadowed cliffs. She knew her cousin. When Joshua's time came, he would lie in the churchyard, right here in Endor beside his own true Leah, who had bathed the blood from Mattie's face even as Mattie had jeered.

Watch yourself, Anna Caine, Mattie whispered. *You don't mess in people's lives, disappear, and then show up at the last minute and expect everyone to cheer. You walk beside them, there, and you guard their hearts.*

Like Leah. Like me.

Someday, I am going to be Leah to someone.

JOURNEY IN THE PRESENT

Anna Caine is beginning her medical escort duties. She shivers in the damp wind as she stares into the St. John's terminal. Regulations dictate that those who are not waiting to board planes remain outside. She has waited outdoors for two hours, and now the people from Joshua's flight are trickling down from the arrivals lounge. Although Leah has been gone nearly ten years, as Joshua shuffles down the walkway, Anna sees Leah is with him. Leah is the calm presence that Joshua smiles for as he pushes forward.

Here is Anna's lithe young lover, the shining man who covered her there in the spring sun, caught in the ecstasy of their joining. Did she ever learn his favourite colour? What was his favourite memory growing up? Leah would know.

Anna does not.

My God, he is old.

He still has that ratty grey hair twisted in a scraggly braid, those stray wisps wilting on his chin. The shoulders are more stooped than before; the waist has settled. There is a hint of amusement in the dark eyes, but they do not gaze deep into her being as they did after lovemaking. For the first time, Anna realizes that her memories of Joshua are of lovemaking, or the yearning for lovemaking, and she has never thought to surprise him with a pair of boots or mitts or perhaps a rifle scope. She has cooked meals for him in Nova Scotia, meals like lasagna with salad, which he praised, but she knows that Leah would have prepared seal meat stewed with carrots and potatoes, and he would have been strong then.

In this moment, she wants to summon Catherine and Leah and hug them close and thank them for loving Joshua and bringing light to his son. Now, Anna's moment has arrived; it is her time to be light bearer.

Her face relaxes in a smile, and she opens her arms. "I am glad to be here, my friend," Anna says as she embraces Joshua.

His eyes widen, and he stiffens for a moment. Then he relaxes. His arms envelop her in a quick squeeze; they are still wiry, still strong. "We need to call the van," he says.

She sighs. She hopes this means he is glad to see her too. Joshua would say she should know this already, but it would be nice to hear.

M

The hotel room is spacious, though very functional. Corners are sharp, with hints of grey in the flat cream. Furniture has clean edges, easy to wipe down in Virus Times, all metallic rims and shiny veneer. Curtains and bedding are stiff, but that is because they are new. They are about five washings away from limp and threadbare. Feet will walk on the carpet leaving no trace; there is no cushion, no fluff. It is bare, and all particles will be sucked up by the hotel vacuum. She suspects the room is still vibrating with virus particles embedded in the air, in the walls, in everything.

Anna tightens her mask snug to her cheekbones, puffs air, and feels for possible leakage. She extracts her 80 percent alcohol sanitizer and a cloth wipe from her daypack and starts to scrub down the surfaces. Joshua tosses his mask face-up on the desk and starts piling clothes into the drawers. "You goin' to poison us," he mutters.

Anna straightens and stares. "You are immuno-compromised," she announces. "You have to be careful." She splashes sanitizer on the cloth and goes to work on the phone.

"I got to live," he sighs, scooping deodorant, toothpaste, toothbrush, tape measure (tape measure?), and deck of cards into the top drawer. Tins of tuna, corned beef, and soup follow. "You can't spend your whole time scared."

Anna's jaw tightens. Joshua's cancer is terminal this time, so perhaps he is feeling fatalistic today. Anna, however, wants to resist the virus in any way she can. She and Joshua will not give each other the disease, and they will not die in this hotel room while the dog Petra waits on the neighbour's step, eyes on the road. The task has fallen to Anna Caine to look after Joshua in this end time. Anna truly wants to walk with him through these days and forget all the lost years in between, but not if he is going to fuss about everything she does.

Maybe, though, he is right. They should invest the time in living, not quibbling over cleaning a phone.

On the Land, Joshua's eyes are always open. He watches for the crevasse, for the dark shadow of thin ice, and for the bear that follows him, but he watches, too, for the sun that glistens on the far cliff wall, the light in the eyes of his companions. He watches, and he is ready, but he knows that if you surrender to fear, then you might fail to notice a tall slab of shadowed ice, the one that absorbs the light. It will shift and disappear, and you will be so busy worrying that you will not see it happen, and so when the bear comes around and climbs over the rocks behind you, you will be thinking "what if" right up to the moment that it takes you.

M

Anna dreamed the night before that she was sleeping, unable to move in her bed, but her bed was in a forest clearing. As she lay paralyzed on that bed, a black bear ambled into the clearing. Its head lowered, and it growled low in its throat as it clambered onto the bed, and its great jaws closed around her head. Her arm lay paralyzed, though she was willing it with all her might to reach over the side and seize the loaded rifle that lay beside the bed on the grass in the clearing. She would swing the gun into position, in one fluid movement, and fire into the bear that was covering her, but her arm would not move, and teeth were piercing her temples and cheek when she awakened.

She touched her hand to her cheek and felt the sharp pain penetrating her face, but she was unscathed. She slept again, and this time when the bear came into the clearing and growled low in its throat, she raised her arms, which were not paralyzed anymore, and she patted the mattress beside her. The bear scrambled onto the bed and nestled close to her side, and she stroked its neck, and they both slept.

She thought perhaps this dream meant something about not resisting and everything falling into place, but she didn't like either dream, and she hated the way both dreams clung to her long after she was awake.

M

Here on their first evening in St. John's, Anna pores over the appointment agendas and contact numbers while Joshua thumbs the remote, staring through the bewildering array of news shows, nature programs, detective and forensic mysteries, and comedies from the last century but no current hockey game. Finally, he settles on the scrolling programming menu and sits back, studying it.

The September evening is cooling, and dusk has arrived. Anna is hungry, but Joshua says he is not, and he continues to study the scrolling list, occasionally stabbing the remote to watch for a few minutes before returning to the satellite TV menu. Anna texts her neighbour, who informs her that both dogs have settled in well; they are looking for Mom but still eating their supper. The dogs adore her neighbour Natasha, a gentle woman who gathers all animals in her arms. If Natasha dreamed about a bear, she would get up and feed it a large bowl of kibble, and it would follow her everywhere. Anna knows the dogs will be happy with her neighbour, but as the twelve days slide away, Petra will look for Anna, and she will wonder. Anna explained last night, but Petra just whuffed and curled at the foot of the bed. Anna talks to her dogs, and the talking comforts her.

Her neighbour Natasha has interesting news. When she walked the dogs up to Anna's place, they discovered Hobo in Anna's garden, crunching down the Jerusalem artichoke stalks. Hobo was a rogue Flemish Giant rabbit, released or run away, who drifted from place to place like the dog in their childhood TV show. Their Hobo, though, did not perform heroic deeds that they knew of. He'd disappeared a few weeks before, probably taken by coyotes. Natasha and Anna, however, had decided that Hobo had joined a warren of snowshoe hares, and there he ruled in splendour. Now, here he was, alive and whole and with no warren in tow. The dogs chased him into the woods, but the husky Petra did not hunt him down. Natasha says that this is because Petra now regards Hobo as family, but more likely, Anna decides, Petra is waiting for a better opportunity.

The garden has been watered, and as urged, Natasha has selected a few small squash. (All of Anna's squash are small.) The dogs are exercised and nestled on the couch with Natasha's husband, Adam, Hobo is alive and well, and all is good in the woods.

At eight-thirty, Joshua snaps the remote and reaches for his mask. He stuffs his feet into his sneakers, and strides to the door. "Supper," he announces, turning to Anna. "Hurry up."

Anna scrambles up, phone in hand. "Too much time on that phone," Joshua says.

Leah would smile and ignore him, or make some calm remark about television being so soothing for people when they are a little tired like that. Anna wants to smack the remote out of his hand or hide it, and she wonders if this is an admissible feeling when people are finally discovering love.

His eyes did light up when he saw her at the airport.

Back in Endor Times, to see him was to anticipate making love. In Bridgewater, she had endured the shadow-Joshua, and she had not wanted to make love. Now, she is ready for the maturity of loving companionship, unfettered by desire or bitterness. She still senses that this will be a very long two weeks.

M

Anna awakens to her alarm at six a.m. The van will pick them up for bloodwork at eight-thirty, and she should summon Joshua by seven. It is calming to see his cheek pressed to the pillow across the room; she does not dwell on the fact that, at least five times, the body under those sheets made children with the humble Leah. It is a body that parodies long-ago youthful emotions and dreams, not a body that raises desire. She wants to hug him, to cradle his head to her breast, and tell him that the chemo will slow the cancer, and they will have time for good dreams, dreams of maturity, dreams of a future, holding each other.

If only Miriam and Leah and the entire clan, living and dead, were not watching.

In the time before Joshua wakes up, there is time to recreate the mornings of her life. There are the mornings of her father's illness, the stiffness of her mother's shoulders whenever Anna enters the room. There are the Saturday morning floor hockey games with Terrence's street outreach, followed by tutoring and basketball, calming cups of tea across the table, and the sun streaming over the little table while they both study. Safe. Companionable. A future of faculty functions and report cards and children growing up and away, and they would walk arm in arm along the Northwest Arm and smile together. There is a place for Anna in these mornings.

There are the Endor mornings of coffee and last checks on lesson plans, of teaching that is raw but real with young people pushing forward to honour their history and guard their future, and then the *iKaluk* camp mornings of long cups of tea and waiting along the bay. Oh, she could have gotten a new contract and raised Aaron down the road, with him running back and forth between his parents' houses, and she would have witnessed his life from the edges of Joshua and Leah's marriage.

There are the river mornings in that first community at the end of the tracks. Anna could have raised Aaron there. She could have grown old there and consolidated a circle of friends. She could have sent for her mother, who could have lived with them and joined the church and made friends and lived long. A sudden pang sears across her heart, and she sees her mother on many, many August mornings, waving down the road, smile tight to her face, shoulders stiff against her neck. Her mother turns to listen to the ticking of the kitchen clock and the hum of the refrigerator, and she strains to find Aaron's laughter.

When Aaron returned to Endor, Anna could have followed. She could have made a little home and a circle of friends, but instead, she has recreated her life many times, finding a rhythm that always goes stale.

The mornings of her life lie strewn across a wasteland, hints of life unlived and unfulfilled, and now here is Joshua, and she feels like she has awakened to him dying of cancer in the next bed all the mornings of her life. All the scattered mornings can never be redeemed or retrieved, but they have come to this morning, the one that has been from the beginning and will continue forever. Yet she is still as lonely as she has been every morning of her life.

She and Joshua created Aaron, and she has images of Aaron, but each image becomes a reproach in her mind.

Joshua awakens. "You should check the van. See when it's coming," he says.

M

The appointments blur together: There is bloodwork the first day, and Joshua is weighed. His weight is down eight pounds, and he is concerned. Gravies must be poured over potatoes; desserts must be added to the budget. She puts these on her voucher so that he will stay within his meal allowance, and he tells her she should eat more. Next, they are whisked off to a meeting with Joshua's doctor, who sweeps into the room with power. She and Joshua lock eyes, and Anna sits on the sidelines, taking notes for Miriam. Chemo might be important, but Anna senses that the intense affirmation of life radiating from this woman is what will tip the balance. This doctor recognizes the solitary quality of Joshua's struggle, but she is down there in the current with him, and whether he lives or dies, she will never allow him to be defeated.

Joshua and Anna tour the hardware stores the first afternoon because new tools are necessary, Joshua explains. Although he has many tools, studying them is comforting, Anna soon sees. It is comforting to him, but boring to her, yet she cannot take her eyes off him because the mall complex is huge, and Joshua tends to leave for new sites without notice. Twice Anna loses him, and she knows that, although he is still strong, the cancer is invading his brain, and he does not always find his way.

The second day, the chemo treatment begins. Anna has not been in the chemo centre before, and she huddles over her phone in the waiting room, losing card game after card game. Joshua, on the other hand, touches sleeves and exchanges smiles with all staff that pass them; he is an old friend, a comrade in arms, a regular. It is like a family reunion, whereas Anna had been expecting a wake. The nurse finally steps through the doors and announces that they are ready for Joshua. She raises her eyebrows when she sees Anna, and Joshua introduces her as Aaron's mother. Yes, the nurse remembers the winter of Aaron. And he is back in Endor now? Working on a government project? Good for him. You must both be very proud.

Anna follows Joshua and the nurse through the swinging doors. For a moment, she freezes. She has expected a hallway and a little cubicle. Instead, there are great chairs, looming under the windows in both directions as far as the eye can see. There is a row of beds along the opposite wall. Beds and chairs are full. And this is one hour. Each hour, someone new sits or lies there. And then the next day, the ritual will be re-enacted with more new people.

There are so many. Where is God, Anna wants to know, that there are so many?

Again, her thoughts turn to Terrence. Terrence would know. He would say that his Lord and Saviour sits with each one, each hour, each day, from the beginning to the end of time. That God does not give people cancer because he has a different plan or wants another angel. That his God grieves with and for humanity until and beyond the fulfillment of history, and that the needles pierce

Him, and the chemicals burn in Him, until history is fulfilled, and the universe is one.

Or words to that effect. Terrence was not your average minister. She thinks of Terrence and misses him in that moment.

On the nearest bed perches a woman, arranging her knitting. The nurse approaches and slips the bag into the rack; she works out the tubing and gives the woman two pills. The woman swallows the pills with a shot of water, lies back, and watches as the massive needle is inserted into her arm. Her calm smile never falters, not even when the nurse adjusts the bag and tucks a blanket around the woman's legs and departs with a smile of her own.

Joshua is led to a chair. He settles with confidence, his arm relaxed on the armrest. The nurse indicates a chair for Anna, and then her focus is on Joshua, checking his temperature, his pulse, and his blood pressure. The nurse chats with Joshua about symptoms, and he mentions a numbness that occurs sometimes in his right leg. This is new, he explains. No, it is not there now. Just yesterday, in the hardware store.

The nurse turns to Anna, who tries not to look bewildered. She knows nothing about this, yet she is the one charged with monitoring him. She clears her throat and purses her lips, nodding. She is not surprised that the nurse's brow furrows; Anna does not know herself what she means to convey.

The nurse explains that they will start in a few moments. Half an hour slides by. Anna texts Aaron, texts her neighbour, plays cards on her phone. The on-call doctor arrives and reviews the chart and the symptoms, and after a phone consult with Joshua's cancer doctor, nods. The nurse presents the two pills and then returns with the clear bag. She sets up the bag, arranges the tubing, and inserts the needle. Joshua stares straight ahead, unflinching, and he and Anna sit side by side, staring at their phones as the fluid soaks into his body.

Afterward there are directions for anti-nausea pills and steroid pills and cautions to report any recurrence of the numbness. This last part is directed at Anna; the nurse and Joshua both stare at her as the nurse repeats the importance of this. Anna would like to tell the nurse to tell Joshua to confide in her, but she knows that this would not help.

The next few days are quiet but stressful, as Joshua is tired and chilled. The thermostat is cranked up in the hotel room, and Anna paces outside in the late September heat while Joshua dozes. It is Anna who must explain to relatives and friends that Joshua needs to rest, and that although he is only here for a few days and should be enjoying the city, he also has chemo, and that is not always pleasant. He wards off nausea but has no appetite. He is irritable and forgets his pills. He orders large meals, hacks at them with knife and fork, and then places his napkin over them. Anna suggests they share a plate, and he is angry. The restaurant staff do not seem to mind; they are used to patients in this hotel.

On the fourth day, Joshua announces that they will go to the hardware store because he wants to look at wood stoves. Thus, there is respite until the next bloodwork and the next chemo, and then they are packing.

On the last day, Joshua receives his next list of appointments. They will be going home Friday and leave two Mondays later for St. John's again. She is coming, right? He will tell Miriam to notify the people who book the flights and hotel and van.

Anna sees him onto his plane, every moment expecting they will be banned from flying by an elevated temperature, a sudden change in regulations, or plain bad luck. She will never see her little house again. Or her neighbour Natasha and her dogs. Instead, Anna will grow old and die here in St. John's, at Joshua's side, in the spacious and functional hotel room.

Passionate mating in the spring sun is one thing; love is another. Love seems to involve waiting in silence, like a Leah would. Like Leah did.

Joshua disappears through the gate, chatting with the flight attendant who will escort him to his seat. He does not look back.

Anna tightens her mask, gathers up her daypack, and hikes the length of the terminal to wait for her flight. People with tickets can wait in the terminal. People without tickets wait outside.

The virus is intermittent this fall so far, but when it strikes, it is lethal. And there is still no working vaccine for this one. Yet, Anna will travel again and again, because that is what escorts do.

M

Natasha and Anna sit on the deck, the late September sun warm on their legs. The grass is mowed, the garden is watered, and the dogs are content in the shade. Her golden Joy has sped around the yard, collecting the balls they have thrown, gathering them in a small cluster. When they approached to claim one of the balls, Joy grabbed it and fumbled to include a second, racing to the far corner of the yard to shape a new collection. Petra meanwhile shuffled along the garden edge, sniffing, muttering low, and rushing Joy when she veered too close.

Natasha assures Anna that she will be glad to have the dogs again the following week, that Anna is not to worry about dogs or gardens or anything. That is what neighbours do. Natasha has raised three sons and innumerable dogs; she has thick golden curls greying with dignity and a body sturdy from hard work. Her husband, Adam, is a handy man and a gentle man. They are the kind of neighbours who see you through the good days and the bad days; they are good friends, but Anna knows surprisingly little about them.

There are virus cases in Halifax, Natasha observes, and more coming each day. But Anna is probably fine at the airport. You can't wrap yourself in cotton wool, but you do have to be careful.

Wouldn't it be nice for Joshua to come over for a little visit when his chemo is done? Natasha suggests. He'd be as safe here as anywhere, and he would probably like a little break. They had enjoyed meeting him that time, when he did the fence, and her husband would enjoy helping him with a few projects. Yes, he would be a shadow of his former self, no doubt, but it would be a nice change for him.

Anna knows that Joshua would tolerate the woods, but his heart would beat stronger with the salt wind of the Labrador coast fanning his face. Anna smiles anyway, and says she sure hopes he will come.

To say no, that she wants to disappear into the Torngat Mountains with him, does not sound sociable or welcoming. She pictures Joshua on the deck, sipping a cup of tea, deciding which trees to claim for firewood, and planning a seal hunt, while the others discuss taking a speed boat around the lake, just to drive and look at the rocks and trees and to wave at people sitting on their deck chairs. Joshua would want to pack a loaded gun and binoculars and would probably shoot a duck and get her in trouble on several levels.

Joshua is not a man to sit on the deck and make small talk, unless he is carving or working on a small engine or studying a blueprint.

Joshua stalks along the shore, Anna at his side or a little behind him.

While Miriam stands in the window, fists clenched.

Anna edits that frame: Joshua strides along the shore with Anna, his help-meet, proud beside her hunter carpenter. The church screens the churchyard;

she will not see the cemetery from the shore. And they will be out of Miriam's line of vision on this part of the shore.

On that last day in St. John's, Joshua had said that Miriam and Aaron would be coming home from school for Christmas. Sometimes, the times ran together for him now.

Only when he was tired.

Anna would cook hearty meals and make sure Joshua rested. They would walk the shore, and when they reached his speedboat, they would work side by side, sanding and patching. People on the road would smile and wave.

Their time had come, and Anna would bring it into being.

The long years of wandering would just be preparation for this greatest love.

Others find something new; they too carve out a fresh life at the end of things. Their stories would be shadows to the light of the story of Anna and Joshua.

People are dying daily from the virus.

The September sun beats down on a parched earth, and rain, when it comes, streams over the impermeable ground to flood rivers and basements. Even here in the gentle woodlands, anger burns hot on the roads, and Natasha and Anna have started to lock their doors. Although this is the end time that aging brings, Anna suspects that it is also the End of Things, and perhaps, the Millennialists were on track after all.

Anna will take what she can while she can.

If only Joshua were less moody and unpredictable.

He is dying; it is to be expected.

She will not accept that.

They will have a beautiful ending, and he will smile as they walk along a distant Northern shore, her hand in his.

"It would be a nice treat for him, coming here," says Natasha.

Chapter 12: Working the Rapids

FROM ANNA

I come at last to the place I am meant to be.
  I have walked away from many in my journey. I have wandered through a maze, never looking back to study the landmarks that would guide me home. Always I am sure I have found the way, but I cannot see the mountains that are in my soul, and I move on.

I could have brought my mother to Endor. My son could have run among all his houses and all his parents and grandparents and known he was so loved. And Terrence could have been there, yes, a minister or a teacher or both, or maybe, as Joshua once said, a hunting minister. I could have brought about all these things, but I did not.

Yet would that have made all our lives better?

I look back, and I look in all directions at once, and always, I am lost.

Now, I will plummet from the sky at the end of all things, and the People will be very happy to see me, but they will still be hurt.

I think now of Deborah, the Elder who first welcomed me to Endor. She did not have much English, so how did she speak to me that day? And why did I never look for her, or ask for her, or bring her fish from the iKaluk camp as one does for an Elder? And why, when I am examining my life, is it her voice that rises, and why do I put my words into her mouth? Why do I claim the judgment comes from her when I am judging myself? She must be gone these many years. Yet, I hear her plainly in my moments alone; she locks her arm in mine and stretches up to place her lips close to my ear.

"We were not your dolls, Anna Caine," she murmurs, "but you dressed us up and placed us on a shelf while you admired your handiwork. And when you tired of us, you tossed us into the toybox and walked away.

"We welcomed you, and you gathered us and played with us; you took pictures of us and labeled the pictures. Then you abandoned us. Yet we would welcome you again.

"Your son came home, and you could have come with him. You could have grown old here, down the road, your grandchildren placing stockings under your Advent tree, and you passing me on the road with a friendly smile. . ..

"But that is not enough for you. You want to be Leah and weep in Joshua's arms while he comforts you. Leah is dead now, passed on, sleeping in the churchyard. Maybe you could honour her just a little, for the children she raised, for the affection she held for your son, for her patience and unconditional love—that would be nice, Anna Caine.

"You look for meaning, but meaning simply is. It is present in the rhythm of each day, in each moment.

"I have seen you, all your life, and I know you.

"You were in that community along the river, there in the wilderness, when the virus reached its worst. Do you remember the little trailers they placed beside the river way back at the beginning? You wanted to take pictures, didn't you, but who dares take pictures of a people's final despair?

"Many of our communities had those trailers, but we never thought we would use them, not really. They were a safeguard, just in case, for one day.

"Do you know how it was for our communities, relaxing our guard as the virus became softer, making us cough but not filling our lungs and choking us into hopelessness? And how it came back for us in the last winter, hammering into us, until we were raging with fever and our lungs were thick, and it was even killing our children, our very future?

"The day we dreaded had come."

The voice of the Elder Deborah is soft against my ear, but each word pierces me.

"And we went to the trailers, Anna Caine, in the end. When the first cough came, or the sore throat, or the headache, that is where we went.

"Oh, we went willingly, because this was what we did to keep our loved ones safe, but there, in the rampage of fever, we could not remember their faces, and our children cried in the night for us, and we did not know them.

"We went to the trailers, because we loved, Anna Caine.

FROM ANNA

"And we prayed we would not see our loved ones because that would mean they were coming there to die too. Keep them away, accept our sacrifice, let them be safe.

"You gave up teaching that year. Yes, it was time you retired, as you said. You went to the woods where you could breathe, grow vegetables, snare rabbits perhaps. You walked away, even as we were walking to the little trailers, so our loved ones would see another day.

"Honour Joshua," Deborah urges me, tugging my arm a little and stepping back, "by loyalty to his ways and his people. He is a good man, a strong man, and he must go North. See him to the gateway, but do not try to follow. This is his story, not yours. See him to the gateway and mourn him as we will. His kind is passing from the world. Stand with us, and honour him."

Deborah must be dead, yet she hovers on the edges of my conscience, the voice of all my life, the voice of all my fear. I square my shoulders now, and I cast off her reproach.

I cast off all the possibilities of my past.

I am many stories, and perhaps they will come to one story, here at the end of our world, when Joshua and I go home.

I will not stand aside, not this time.

I set my face to go North.

GATEWAY EMERGING

The Monday of the second trip, Petra nudges Anna awake long before the alarm, while the younger dog, Joy, is still snuggled in a contented ball against Anna's back. Petra stares into Anna's face, then emits a little whuff, her front paws shuffling in a little dance. She turns and paces to the head of the stairs, where she looks back, ears forward and eyes on Anna. Anna tugs on shorts and sweater, scuffing feet into sandals. She wobbles down the stairs in the early light, with Petra swaggering ahead, and Joy pattering behind them.

When Anna opens the door, Petra jogs to the gate and stares, head lowered. Anna knows that Petra yearns to roam the bush as she did when she was young. Joy will range along the woods road and return to Anna's call; Petra will not heed whistles or pleas. If Anna opens the gate, Petra will vanish for hours. The hunting season is beginning; the dog can be shot by any random hunter. The body of Petra, her confidante and guide, might lie in an unknown corner of the woodland, and Anna would never know where.

Anna tugs on boots, finds her cap, and snaps Petra on a long lead. They walk the logging trails for an hour. There are coyote tracks and fresh scat in the early morning; a quickening in the rutted earth is a small snake dashing away. In three hours, Anna must pack the car and prepare for the trip to St. John's, but this moment is hers.

And in this moment, she sees herself with Joshua, walking the shoreline hand in hand, the village smiling for this is as it should be.

On the hill behind the church, there is a cemetery, where Leah waits.

Joshua will not go to the cemetery. He and Anna Caine will go North and keep going, until their time is fulfilled.

He was going to make furniture, and she was going to write children's books. That part was just a dream, the hazy dream of youth.

This time it is real, as dreams of maturity are.

She shuts her mind to the image of Petra, eyes on the road, waiting for her return.

Anna does not want Joshua to come here. She does not want him to stay in St. John's. It is only as they are vanishing into the North together that she will hear that great laugh, the one that rings from mountain to mountain across the harbour.

M

The voice on the airport loudspeaker bleats about the state of emergency. Anna draws her mask up, sips from the Styrofoam cup, tugs the mask tight to her chin, and checks the snugness along the bridge of her nose. She manoeuvres around a group of five, tightly clustered, masks slack on their chins as they laugh and share chips from a bag. She hopes they are a family unit, as she steps well away and holds her breath, not sure if this will save her.

Cases are escalating in the city. People are not panicking yet, not like last winter, but the steady climb in the caseload is unnerving. There have been variants in the past that were not so severe. This one, though, is lethal; Anna knows it will creep and creep, and suddenly the shelves will be empty, the ambulances will not come, and there will be no one to claim the dead. She yanks the mask up and takes another quick swallow of coffee. She and Joshua will be in St. John's for Thanksgiving; she prays that no joyful family gatherings are planned, for assuredly immediately afterward, Joshua will have a mild cough, and then the disease will burn through his chemo-battered body.

Joshua builds snow houses and fills them with light. He may die sleeping in his snow house, his time finished, or die fighting down the power of a storm. He must not die in a shadowed ward, ventilator hissing, with no salt wind, no spruce boughs, and no sun dazzling on the snow.

No one should die like that, she knows, but to lose *him* like that would be the worst part of his dying.

For Anna.

Because Joshua would no longer know.

Leah slipped away in a hospital bed, crushed when Martin Code and his truck spun sideways into her taxi. She did not get to die at home, of old age, surrounded by all her family and her treasures.

Yet would that be a happy death? Is there one?

Would dying in one another's arms, eyes on each other like they do in those stirring apocalyptic dramas, really be better?

Anna and Joshua will avoid family gatherings and thus avoid their contagion.

And brush a random stranger in the corridor of the hospital, or breathe the air of a laughing, pestilence-ridden family of five in the airport, and die anyway.

This is not how an escort thinks.

The escort is there as a support, a physical and emotional support. So, the escort should not go off visiting and shopping. The escort should not plan intimate futures or fantasize death scenarios. The escort is present to the patient.

This escort will walk hand in hand with Joshua into the North. This escort believes that they are on the brink of a very wonderful future.

Unless it is interrupted by a quick, staccato cough.

∧

Anna discovers patience on this trip. She discovers patience because Joshua follows his own free will and argument does not prevail. Perhaps it is not truly patience, but Anna feels a certain peace, an acceptance of the pattern of things, and she falls into its rhythm. Joshua resists the pills, turns up the heat, dashes without warning for the restaurant to order massive, wasted meals, and flits through the satellite menu again and again because there is really nothing to watch. Sometimes he and Anna stare unseeing at documentaries on tropical fish or rainforests; they follow Arctic wildlife documentaries for a few moments. They weary of the academic analysis, and soon the menu is rolling by again.

Anna learns to set the room temperature a little high to avoid the sudden plunges into sweltering heat when Joshua grows cold. She types notes for Miriam and takes short walks while Joshua rests. Anna believes there have been no further episodes of numbness, but she is not sure because Joshua is angry when she asks him, and he claims she thinks he is a cripple. He has cancer, not a bad leg, he insists. She checks with Miriam who says there have been no episodes and wants to know what Anna's agenda is. The cancer centre nurse asks if

Anna is sure, and then lets it go. *Why do they think there is something wrong with my leg?* Joshua whispers to Anna. The cancer and the chemo are claiming him, one memory, one thought, at a time. Not every day, but this day, and she must get through this day.

Anna gets up early each morning and climbs among the brush and rocks in the hills behind the hotel. It is not a relaxing walk, but the air is fresh.

Thanksgiving evening there is a full moon. Joshua and Anna have a late supper with a cousin on the outskirts of the city, and when they return to the hotel, Joshua wanders the parking lot, eyes on the stark clouds coiling around the full moon. The pavement is stiff under their running shoes, and the chill breeze burns their cheeks. Joshua paces, and Anna knows that he is in Endor, and the moon is rising over the mountains across the harbour, and there he will be alive, and the twists in his memory will fall away. Joshua will walk in the presence of his mountains, drawing all good things to him.

Anna Caine will walk beside him there, home, home at last.

She edits Miriam and her sister Dinah from that scene. Yet Anna hears the muttering of Miriam and the laughter of Dinah anyway.

∧∧

The function of the chemo this time, the doctor explains, is to slow the spread. And it will only be beneficial if it is not further stressing his body. The end might be delayed a few months, but in the meantime, this round of chemo is weakening him in many ways. It comes down to more time or quality of time, and this is a terrible choice, but nevertheless, it is Joshua's to make.

Joshua's response is immediate. "I will do one more round," he declares, "and then it is time for me to go North. I will see Hebron again."

His great laugh echoes off the walls, wheezing just a little but reverberating anyway. "One more round and then closing time."

The doctor frowns as the hot tears spurt from Anna's eyes and drip down her face, soaking into her mask. "This is Joshua's time, Joshua's choice," the doctor reproaches her.

Anna is nodding, her head bobbing as she blinks and dabs at her eyes. It *is* Joshua's time, and she could have settled in Endor and grown old down the road, but she has travelled the world and missed his presence every minute that she was living her bold and independent life, but she is Anna Caine, and here at the end of things, this is *her* time, too, and she will walk with him until they both step off the edge of the world.

Taimattuk! That is the way it is! This is their time, come at last.

FACING SOUTH

Anna sits with Natasha on the deck in the late October afternoon, overlooking Anna's garden with its little fence. Petra paces along the wire mesh, eyeing Joy, who sniffs at the persistent few blossoms clinging to a yellowing squash vine.

Natasha's husband, Adam, is at home, cleaning their generator for the winter ahead. The winter storms are increasing each year in force and frequency. There are flooded roads, snow-blocked roads, and roads with trees across them. Power outages of several days' duration are expected now throughout the winter and spring. Natasha and Adam have a wood stove as well, and Natasha worries about Anna wintering here with no wood stove or generator. Adam would be happy to install her wood stove; he knows the standards, and he is good with his hands. His work will easily pass inspection. Then they will all rest easy.

It would be wonderful if Joshua could spend the winter here, Natasha feels, and have a nice break. It just seems impossible that Joshua can be facing cancer like that; he sounds very active.

Anna does not attempt to describe Joshua's mood swings, the dark afternoons with the exhaustion and confusion that accompany the chemo. She witnessed Joshua's clumsiness when he set up the tent in his cousin's yard; Joshua, who could set up a prospector tent blindfolded in the long ago springs up the Bay, wrestled with the disjointed parts in confusion.

The hardest part was when he left the leaning poles and slack ropes and walked to the edge of the yard and sat on a rock, staring out at the distant harbour of St. John's. "I would like to go seal hunting," he said. "It looks good out there."

On that day, the chemo and the cancer were twisting him; he knew this, for he became quiet and would not speak or move.

Anna had wanted more than anything for him to hold her, to tell her all would be well.

But that should be the work of the escort.

The escort will leave her little home in the woods soon and first go to St. John's, where they will have the one last round. Then she will go North with him.

Joshua must go North as Joshua Kalluk; he will be thunder on the Land.

M

Hobo the Flemish Giant is shuffling among the raspberry canes near the driveway, his sleek grey body with the white saddle incongruous among the curling leaves and dry grass. Petra tenses, head low and nostrils quivering, as Anna guides her to the car for this last twelve-day escort time, the endgame chemo time. Petra does not recognize pet rabbits, only prey rabbits, and this one would be such a worthy prize. Joy prances free, gamboling over to welcome Hobo, who springs for the sheltering undergrowth and evades Joy's attempts to herd him back. Joy clambers into the car beside Petra, ears pricked up and face alert; there is luggage in the back and that means a visit to Natasha's house, with games of ball and extra snacks for persistent dogs.

Hobo drops in and out of their lives, and Anna wanders if he does indeed reign in state over a warren of untamed rabbits, a pirate lord come to port for a quick visit.

Hobo is just a rabbit, Anna reminds herself, who comes and goes as rabbits do, and she needs to focus on her journey. Natasha does not know that Anna is going to Endor when she finishes in St. John's this time, that the dogs will be there all fall, and well into the winter, and possibly forever. Natasha and her husband will have Anna's little house in the woods to look after, and perhaps they will come there for a change sometimes.

Anna is stepping into her future, yet Petra sniffs Anna's fingers, gives them a quick lick, and strolls away to check the cat's dish. That surprises Anna because Petra should know that Anna is leaving her.

Petra holds all her secrets and is her confidante, yet Anna is walking away. Anna is ashamed, but then she forces that door in her heart shut. This is Joshua's time.

Joy will find contentment whatever the future holds, but Petra will watch, and her heart will break.

This is Joshua's time. Be strong.

The goodbyes are quick and cheerful for Anna will have just enough time to park and get to the terminal before the cut-off time.

"Oh, I hope they don't shut things down again," Natasha says as Anna buckles her seatbelt.

"They can't," Anna replies, settling in her seat. "People would rather take a chance at this point. They just don't want to live in fear anymore. People are getting sick no matter what they do, so they just want to be careful and go on living."

"Well, that won't make it go away," Natasha declares. "So, you be careful and get back safe, and maybe Joshua can come for a visit and get some rest here for a bit. That would be nice. A little time to relax for you two. And no virus out here."

Anna does not think that Joshua will come here again. Her wooded hideaway is manufactured wilderness, not the raw, timeless energy of Joshua's homeland. It is suffocating for someone like him.

And there is virus everywhere. The woods are not exempt. A passerby will cough out the car window, maybe one little sneeze, and the end will begin.

She and Joshua will walk a distant shore, and they will meet no one.

There will be no virus, no judgment.

Just a little time.

ʌ

Joshua is often brooding, this last round of chemo. It is something of a miracle that they have avoided storms, coming and going, and have not had to reschedule due to weather all fall.

The storm season is almost upon them, but first, Anna decides, she and Joshua will reach Endor. Then they will travel North by speedboat, making a cold and dangerous journey along the rough shore. Perhaps they can wait for the ice to form and travel by snowmobile, but that is unlikely, for as the earth warms, the ice comes later and later each year. It will not be strong before the end of January, and even then, cracks and thin spots will be hidden under a film of snow.

In the evenings as Joshua picks at his supper, mauls it with knife and fork, and then discards it, he tells the story of the journey that he will make. As always, Aaron, his eldest son, will accompany him. Aaron can easily get time from work because this, too, is important work. There are many kinds of work, remember. Taking an Elder home is an honourable task; they will give Aaron time, no problem. Could Anna go instead of Aaron? Well. She doesn't know the way. She might get cold. This is her world here, the city, and she is very good at it. Anna is a very good escort, and gets him to all his appointments, and does all the things an escort needs to do. Joshua is very pleased with all she has done. But that is not the same as travelling into the mountains. That will take two. Him and his son Aaron. And maybe his younger son, Simeon, as extra driver. Not his daughters, no. They are not ready. Aaron is the one who knows. Besides, Joshua must concentrate, and he cannot be worrying about Anna. No, this is not like going wooding up the ponds; Anna does not know what it means. They cannot be waiting for her and fussing over her. She can go sometime with the tourists if she wants to see his mountains. This is not a sightseeing trip. Of course, he likes her. She is the mother of Aaron and his friend and escort, but a friend should understand this trip he is going to make.

A friend would not ruin it for him because they insist on coming.

That is a child's way.

"Aaron will bring me back," he says, "and then I will lie in the churchyard beside my wife. And I will be at peace in all my worlds.

"Love is not something we make, something we do. Sometimes, it is just the way we are. The way we live."

Anna takes notes at the appointments and sends these to Miriam, and Anna hears all that Joshua says, but she continues to see a couple walking the shore in the presence of mountains on a windswept afternoon.

∧

Joshua broods in the evenings and sleeps in the afternoons, but at his appointments, he is another being—cheerful, even flirtatious with the nurses. When the doctor says they can continue the chemo if he wants, or he can go North if he wants, Joshua laughs and says she knows what he will do. Why does his doctor ask? Does she think he wants to dangle from an intravenous tube in a dark hospital all winter, when he could be packing Advent stockings for all the grandchildren, even first-born Beth, who is almost thirteen, and then heading North? Will it be dangerous up there? Yes. But they will stop if the weather comes down. They will even turn back if they must. Because the most important thing is to face North. They will face North, and they will listen to the Land. Then they will return, and he will be strong until the day he dies.

Anna? She is his friend and his escort, but this is not a journey for her. This, here, this is her journey.

The doctor is a strong woman, a straight and forceful woman, and surely cancer flees from her when she strides into the room. Still, her embrace is gentle as she murmurs, "You honour us all, Joshua."

And he is strong in the chemo, although he is tired and cold and confused and sometimes angry afterward, and when he rises from the chair after the last session, he catches himself, holding the arm of the chair until the weakness passes, and then he walks out through the door, brushing fists with each nurse as he passes. "Its power is gone," he affirms.

A muffled bong announces an email from his daughter Miriam.

> *Anna: There is a major storm in Goose Bay and all up the coast. They will be sending you new tickets and itineraries. You will be in St. John's for the weekend, and they will try to fly Joshua back on Monday. You should stay with him; he should not be alone.*

Joshua's face drops. "I don't want to stay in St. John's four more days. Talk to Miriam. You got a ticket for Halifax for the morning. Tell her to ask them: Can I go to Nova Scotia for a few days instead? I'll pay that part. St. John's to Halifax to Goose Bay. Then they send me home from Goose Bay, next Wednesday or maybe Friday. You wanted time, for us? This can be our us-time. So, we say goodbye, like we been practising all our lives."

This is not what Anna wanted. Suddenly, though, the idea appeals to her. They will have real time together, not frozen time like when he came to see Aaron, not awkward time like when he built the fence. This will be healing time, bonding time, journey preparation time.

Then she will go North with him, his weakness and confusion and her lack of skill and her bad knee notwithstanding.

The young dog Joy will be ecstatic to have time with someone new. Perhaps she will even remember Joshua. Petra, Anna realizes, had already known.

If they go straight from the airport to the woods, they will stay safe. It is in the city itself that the hospitals are already filling.

Joshua will be well for now, and they will set the stage for their great journey. Here comes their future after all.

She makes sure that Miriam understands that this is Joshua's wish, Joshua's dream and hope.

Miriam's response is as expected:

> *Anna: No one here objects. We all want my father to have his wishes respected at this time. I trust that you are helping with the tickets, since my father is not that wealthy. Keep him safe and be careful on the roads.*
> *Regards,*
> *Miriam Kalluk-Peterson*

HOMECOMING OF SORTS

Natasha had delivered the dogs to the house after she received Anna's text from the airport, and they are staring from the living room window as Anna pulls into the driveway. They know the sound of her all-wheel drive on the gravel road and press faces to the window, panting and alert. Joshua scrutinizes the patches of lawn and afterthoughts of garden that cover the open front yard, then smiles at the wire mesh fence that neatly frames the back half of the property, enclosing the lawn and the bordering trees.

"It lasted well," he says. "Not much frost here; poles are not too bad. Easy to fix."

A few poles are indeed listing just a little; Anna had not noticed.

The little house is cozy with its white clapboards and greenish-grey shingles; behind it lies the lawn, bordered by second-growth woods that allow a partial view of the sunrise. Her home on the flats is warm and inviting, neat but a little rugged, the sloping back yard providing good drainage. It is a good place to wait out whatever plagues and weather systems bombard the world.

"No wood stove yet," Joshua observes. "You need one, here."

Anna likes her stove-less living room, her fire-free peace. She does not want to drag in dust and bark and ticks and probably fungal spores for them to inhale. A wood stove is also a major investment. Anna cannot do major investments; although people assume she has unlimited finances, she is broke at this point of her life.

"Maybe a small generator," she says.

"You need a wood stove," he insists. "Let's find one, online."

Anna's internet connection is not stable. They will watch wheels spin on the screen, and they will go mad until they leave on Wednesday. They should be sipping tea instead, from her snug kitchen nook overlooking the deck and garden and the woods below, while the November wind, raw and cold, rattles the panes. Bannock will sizzle in the pan, and Joshua will smile because Anna is kind and happy, not the stiff Anna of his olden-times visits.

Joshua shakes the gate, squinting a little. "I will tighten that," he says.

Anna smiles. This is the direction their narrative should take: Her carpenter close friend will putter and work on the fence while she prepares nourishing stews. He will sigh with satisfaction when he comes to their table, and she will ladle ample portions. They will reminisce about Endor times and Bridgewater times and make plans for the journey North. He is strong today, vigorous and clear.

At the door, he turns. "Aaron is not coming out?" he says.

"He is in Endor, working," she reminds him.

His face clouds as he processes this, and then he forces a small chuckle. "Oh, yeah. Of course. I was thinking of something else."

The dogs are there to meet him. Petra paces past him and nuzzles Anna's palm. Joy flings herself into Joshua's arms, and he pushes her down. "That dog still not trained?" he mutters. Joy sits back for a moment and then launches herself at Anna, wriggling in her arms, lolling tongue flinging droplets of saliva across the front of her jacket. She scrambles after Petra next, nipping at her shoulder in passing before galloping around the yard and bounding back.

Joshua sighs. "I need to rest a bit," he says, shrugging off his jacket and prodding his sneakers from his feet. He stares at the vase of dried leaves and late wildflowers adorning the kitchen table, a welcome token from Natasha. "Dead leaves in the house?" he asks.

"We do them here, for the fall," Anna explains, and Joshua nods, his eyes on the leaves. "Natasha made that to welcome you," she adds.

"Ah." He nods. "Yes, that is a good idea." He heads for the room off the kitchen, the one he used last time, and pulls back the covers. "Just a short nap," he tells her.

In a few moments, he is sound asleep, the weathered face half-sunk in the pillow.

Anna tiptoes around the house, distributing luggage, hanging jackets over chairs, hauling meat and vegetables from the freezer. The dogs are scratching at the door, and now Petra bounces up and down, her face still serious, announcing her pleasure as only Petra can. Joy creeps to the bedroom door and studies the sleeping figure. "Leave him, Joy," Anna murmurs, and Joy bounds back to her to sit, wriggling in anticipation of a treat.

Anna drags her luggage upstairs and deposits it in the little sitting room at the top of the stairs before entering her bedroom. Joshua will not join her here, for they are friends now, allies facing the end together. They will not surrender to passion for there is no passion now. Making love with Joshua would be like exploring old photo albums, dabbling in the sweetness of what had been; she will not cloud this sacred time with sex.

Moreover, it makes her think of Leah.

And she doubts he feels much like sex, in the aftermath of chemo.

Thus, the first day, the Friday, slips by as Joshua sleeps and Anna browns meat with onion and pepper for their stew. She could let the meat mixture simmer while she chops carrots and turnips and cabbage and scoops them in, letting the flavours seep together in a rich broth; instead, she dumps in frozen vegetables from a bag, because it has been a long twelve days. She sets the mixture to simmer and prepares the *panitsiak*. She finds tinned milk and sugar for his tea and lays the table.

It is dark outside when he shuffles from the bedroom, yawning. His eyes widen as he surveys the contents of his bowl. "Broccoli?" He shrugs. "Yeah, that looks really good. Yes." He spreads margarine on the *panitsiak*. "Good. Yes. Maybe salted butter, sometimes, but this is good. Good way to do it." His lips form a smile and then he bites into the bun, nodding, and reaches for his tea. "All good."

Anna wishes and wishes she had chopped vegetables and gotten salted butter and then it would be perfect. Tomorrow they will do a real shop, but only at the local store, because it is quiet there, and he will be safe from the virus. She hopes she can keep him from the hardware stores of town. And not just because Miriam expects it.

The first day ends with Joshua's realization that he cannot go online whenever he wants. Anna's internet connection depends on the wind, the leaves, and the moisture in the air.

The evening is not a full success, but he submits to a few hands of cards before returning to sleep. Anna reads long into the night, but the words scatter in her mind.

M

Joshua is up at sunrise the next day, and when Anna arises, she finds him in the kitchen, catching up on his texts and messages in the early morning connectivity. He has also found her stove online. It is in Bridgewater, and they should get it today. Natasha's husband, Adam, has said he will be up this afternoon with his tools and give him a hand. Anna does not know how Joshua knew Adam's cell phone number, but they have already connected, and Saturday is well-planned. Anna would prefer to clear her outstanding debts before sinking into fresh debts, and there are the upcoming vet appointments that she must take responsibility for. Still, she knows that by this evening there will be a stove with a very expensive and safe pipe installed, with protection below and beside and wherever else it is needed. And wood will be purchased because she has not been cutting and curing wood against the approaching winter. Undoubtedly, they will be cutting down trees and stacking wood right up until the time they leave on Wednesday. She will have no time to build memories for the dogs she is leaving behind, and she must find room on her credit card for dog food for the winter, to be stashed in this house for Natasha as part of the surprise. Anna will go North without proper gear because after the wood stove and the dog food and the pending vet appointments and tickets, she will be well into debt. Debt will be her legacy to her son, and he will be stuck with a little house to sell but nothing else to show for his mother's brilliant career.

Well, that is just the way things are. Only an earthquake is going to stop this stove from happening.

CHANGE OF DIRECTION

Today is milder than Friday. Although dense clouds pack the sky, there is no rain, and the wind is low. Joshua's mind is clearer this day, and he oversees the first stages of the installation of the wood stove with focus and energy. Adam brings his friend to help, and Natasha brings a peach cobbler with whipped cream for a snack for the workers. The friend rolls his eyes just a little as he loops a mask around his ears, but this is second nature to Natasha and Adam. Natasha and Anna sort out a new location for the two bookcases they displace, and they all contribute to managing the sawdust and mess that go with any renovation.

During the second hour, Joshua measures and remeasures and then stands staring at the tape measure. "I can't see that," he remarks, passing the tape measure to Adam, who takes over the measurements without question or comment. Anna wonders if the world would be a kinder place if someone always stepped forward to do the measurements when the other said they could not see, if they lived the moment with grace and dignity, without judgment, without rank. The way two friends put in a stove.

Joshua turns away at the end of the second hour, walks to his bedroom, and is soon asleep. He does not seem to mind Joy, who cuddles at his feet watching, or Petra, who paces the floor and moans sometimes.

He awakes, and they all enjoy the peach cobbler that Natasha brought, with good strong Labrador-style tea. It is irresistible.

Then Joshua watches the final steps in the installation.

By supper time, the gleaming wood stove is snug in its corner, measurements are checked, and all agree that the work is completed to standards. Pretty close, anyway. Then they laugh, and Adam declares it is perfectly to standard. Yes, Anna will get her insurance certificate. Anna has purchased a small load of wood, which Adam has delivered and neatly strapped down under a tarp, where hornets and snakes will nest the next summer.

They make a small fire in the early evening, assuring Anna that the inspector will not mind since there is nothing wrong with their work, and a grey November night needs a fire. Anna waits for the sparks to ignite the chimney or the roof and is not comforted.

She is well past broke now.

But Joshua has had a wonderful day.

On Wednesday, she is going North with him anyway.

M

The next three days glide by with woodlot work and long naps for Joshua, dog walks, and easy-to-cook, one-pot, nourishing meals for Anna. She explains to Natasha that she will be accompanying Joshua to the Labrador coast for his safety; she does not mention the secret ticket from St. John's to Goose Bay that she purchased last week and then exchanged for her Halifax to Goose Bay flight. She makes it sound like routine escort duty, but Petra tenses and Natasha notices that, and Anna knows that Natasha has figured out Anna's plan. It is in the way Natasha caresses Petra's ruff, the way she draws Joy close; it is in Petra's lowered tail, in the way Joy wriggles to probe Natasha's cheek with her nose.

Anna closes that door in her heart tighter; she will not look back now.

Joshua is more tired than before, the last evening, but he packs and repacks, getting ready for the morning. The storm that hit Labrador is well past, and conditions all along the coast are excellent. He might even get home tomorrow night. Anna is coming? Does Miriam know? The office will not be paying her way. How is she affording this? She has miles to use? What does that mean? Oh. Like coupons. The way to Goose Bay is different and new for him, coming from Halifax? Ah. That does make sense. And Anna can maybe see her son? Is he coming to Goose Bay then? That would be good.

Anyway, his head aches, Joshua tells her, and he is tired. No, it is not the virus. He has a condition, remember? And the air is different here. That is all.

M

The headache is still there in the morning, and it is worse. Anna takes his temperature, and there is no fever. Joshua says it might be from the type of wood they burn here. That and the heaviness in the air down here. He feels fine, and she should stop waving that thermometer in his face.

At Natasha's place, the dogs spring from the car and bolt for the kitchen, leaving Anna standing by the car. Natasha understands about the headache; Adam has had one off and on for a week, sometimes with a little fever. But she and Adam have both been testing, and they are always negative. Don't worry; Joshua will be negative, too, and once he gets home, he will feel right again. Well. She holds out her arms, but they never hug, because that is the way of things now. Anna extends her arm, passing Natasha cash for dog expenses in a plastic Ziploc bag. It is heavier, she explains, in case they need it for emergency vet trips. She will tell Natasha about the dog food stashed in the upstairs closet another time.

At that moment, blood spurts from Joshua's nose and splatters down his jacket, and he crumples to the ground.

M

The next three weeks are long and filled with emails and calls between Miriam and Anna. Miriam is very worried about her father and wishes Anna had not overworked him and exposed him to that flu bug the neighbours gave him. Joshua's immune system is very weak, and a minor flu in this Adam person could be a major, life-threatening event for Joshua. Because Anna was not careful, Miriam's father has been confined to hospital in Nova Scotia for three full days, routinely exposed to the virus while deprived of family and friends and all who love him. He has lain there, friendless, in the grim ward, monitored by strangers who do not know Endor or Hebron. They have pumped fluids into his bloodstream and monitored his heart, his temperature, and his breathing. Oh, they have understood the danger to him, and they have been vigilant. Yes, Miriam knows the hospital means well, and they know his medical history, but that does not mean they know his personal history. Miriam says they talk to him like a child; they patronize him. They do not know or care that his grandfather nearly died with the Spanish flu, but he beat it. He lived long and well, and he raised Joshua, her father, to be a power on the Land. Her father Joshua Kalluk is legend, unbeatable as thunder. He is a builder and a husband and a father and a survivor.

They see only a frail body, its surface powers faded. His People would remind him of who he is; they would bring forth his strength.

Miriam is relieved that his fever, though persistent, has remained low, and the aches in head and body have been made manageable. However, her father is weakened and must remain in Nova Scotia for two weeks convalescing in this backwoods cabin among strangers.

Anna does not point out that she lives in a neat little clapboard-covered, cottage-style home with an upstairs, half an hour from the hospital. She does not say that neighbours have sent soups and stews and good wishes, and she refrains from saying that she is not a stranger. Miriam, on a practical level, knows these things. Her People's history, however, is fueling her fears, and she speaks to break past them.

Miriam keeps the history of all those exiled to lonely wards far from home; she carries every heartbreaking story and the despair in their families left behind. She holds the pain of Northern history in her very soul: that to be sent South is to be isolated and abandoned, and all the tragedy and loneliness pulls at her heart.

Now the worst has happened, for even though Joshua is now strong enough to come home, he cannot. Now, the virus is spiraling out of control in the cities and in the countryside, and for the first time in several years, the borders have closed. Tight. This is lockdown such as has not been seen in several years, and this time, no one is complaining. Yet. Everyone is too afraid to complain. For now.

The supply chains are disrupted, and they will be living on salt beef and turnips from the store in Endor. Pray that the *iKaluk* pack the winter lakes, that the *ukalik* and *aKiggik* will be fat and slow. Pray that the herds return, and the ban on hunting them is lifted. This is survival time returned.

The great lockdown might extend to Christmas. Joshua might miss Christmas—his Great Christmas, his Goodbye Christmas. *Watch over him, Anna Caine,* Miriam warns her. *Keep talking to your government. There must be a law that says he must not die far from home, in a strange land. He must walk in our mountains one last time, and then he will sleep in the cemetery beside my mother, in peace.*

Anna does not speak, for it would require not only the blessing but the personal escort of the Son of God himself to see Joshua through the crossing. All journeys must be overseen by one of the select few entrusted to escort travellers; only those with political power or essential skills can obtain such services: world leaders, medical teams under orders, and probably a few CEOs in secret. There is no allowance for *nipangittuk Inuit* coming home to die. That part is like the old lockdown.

Anna also does not speak because Miriam would never accept that, when Joshua comes at last to his mountains, it will be Anna Caine at his side.

Anna secures the doors and watches passing cars. Lockdowns like this are necessary, but they strike deep at the heart. The novelty of lockdown passes quickly; people grow weary. They begin to brood. It is human nature to resist rigidity.

The anger cannot be far off.

Meanwhile, Petra and Joy range along the road in early mornings with Anna, sporting orange streamers and vests; there have never been so many hunters in the woods.

Joshua purchases a coil of snaring wire at the local hardware store. The snowshoe hares are healthy yet still abundant. Anna suspects there will be few left by spring.

RABBITS AND COYOTES

By December, Joshua is on his feet and stronger, and Anna thinks his complexion is less sallow than when he arrived. He cuts down saplings and saws them into lengths and stacks them on the leeside of the shed. They will dry there and serve for her firewood next year, he says. He insists on cutting the dead trees below the yard; these, he claims, can be used now. Anna thinks of termites and fungus spores but does not comment. He rests most of the afternoons and studies magazines and catalogues from the hardware store by the fire each evening. He expresses surprise that Anna has no television, and sometimes mutters about the cell phone service and internet fluctuations, but she feels he is somewhat at peace.

Anna decides to go to town one morning, and admonishes Joshua to keep the gate closed; the hunting season is winding down, but the dogs must not disturb the last hunters, who are still allowed muzzle-loading rifles this late. Joshua is baffled by this, not by the muzzle loaders, although he does wonder why they choose these, but by the restrictions on the dogs. It is natural for dogs to run free; the hunters know the difference between a dog and a deer, don't they? It is not allowed here, Anna explains. Joshua shrugs and sighs. So many rules, he says.

Joshua is not always attentive, so she banks the fire, places fresh water for the dogs by the front gate, checks the latch on the gate, and departs.

It is a crisp and sparkling early December morning, and she will only be gone a few hours. Joshua has nearly finished in the woodlot and is unlikely to harm himself with a crosscut saw. His lunch needs only a brief reheating in the micro-wave. (She bought one the second week, as it seemed inevitable.) All should go as planned. Joshua would like to come along, but she worries about the virus. She tightens her mask and sanitizes regularly, but Joshua tends to stuff his mask in his pocket between uses and sanitize when he thinks of it. He likes to stop in hardware stores and roam the aisles. Anna likes to zip in, seize her purchases, pay, and hurry out. When possible, she arranges a pick-up order with the stores. Today she will run into the post office to mail a late Advent parcel to Endor, collect their grocery order at the store, and duck into the pharmacy for Joshua's prescriptions. A quick trip for virus times.

When she returns in the early afternoon, Joshua is smiling. He is pleased to see lots of good foods from the store. He will be making their supper tonight, he informs her, and has already started. Anna inhales the aromas of simmering meat and onion and feels the calm of country living. Yes, their lives are merging. Joshua is growing strong. He is not even resting today, and that is new.

Anna packs away the groceries and heads out along the road with the dogs while Joshua works over the cutting board, dicing carrots, cubing turnip, and peeling potatoes. They will eat early, a late lunch for her and an early supper for him. The daylight is so brief in December, but they will enjoy a leisurely hot meal while it is still light, and she will clean up and sweep while he rests. They are a mature couple, comfortable with the rhythm of their merged lives.

The stew is rich and hearty, the broth worked through the chunks of veg-etable, the potatoes soft but not mushy. The chicken is succulent; it draws clean from the bone, tender and gamy.

Where did he get the chicken? Anna brought chicken, but this one was cooking when she arrived. Is it a free-range gift from Natasha and Adam? It tastes a little wild, not like chicken from the store.

"Your *ukalik* here, they are starting to get white, but only a little, not like North," Joshua is saying.

Anna scrutinizes the bone in front of her. "This is rabbit?" she says.

Joshua grins. "From our own snare line, down in the bush. Your husky likes a taste, but the yellow one, she won't eat rabbit."

Petra sits by Joshua, her eyes intent on his plate. Joy huddles in a chair in the living room, ears drooping.

Anna stares. "You snared this rabbit? Don't you need a license?"

Joshua returns her stare. "In your own backyard? Well. I will get a license tomorrow if you want. But Adam says you don't need one. Just a stamp. This one was nice and fat, not wasting him, no. And just turning white for winter. All along his back. Not like home, where the white grows in little by little, all over the *ukalik*. This one has a clean white patch, and the rest is all grey."

Joshua sinks his teeth into the rabbit thigh, meat easing from the bone. "Nice pelt. Still in the shed. You can make mitts, maybe."

The tender meat surges up from her stomach, blocking her throat, pressing for release.

"I left something in the car." Anna mumbles the words through her mouthful, then clamps her lips tight, heaving and swallowing as she rushes out the door.

Beside the shed, she pukes out the tender meat that was once a living leg, bounding free through the woodlands and across the garden.

In the shed, the glossy pelt drapes limp over the back of a chair, the head hanging down, one eye loose and bloodshot. Hobo must have struggled mightily for his life. It is the ears, limp and forlorn, that break the spell, and the tears come.

Anna will not tell Natasha this story. She will say that it looks like Hobo moved on, not ready to settle, just like his namesake. Gone to his warren for the winter, perhaps. Not cooking among the vegetables on her stove.

Oh, Hobo. Anna will not tell Joshua, for his heart will break if he thinks he has hurt Natasha's grandchildren, who made a great favourite of Hobo. If they tell him about their Hobo, Anna will say it is a pet they keep at their own house.

The pelt will go missing. She will recommend that Joshua tack it to the shed wall in the evening when there are no flies. Or grandchildren. The pelt will be gone in the morning, and Anna will say that the coyotes are very active this season. They often came out at daybreak, before the dogs are up to give the alarm.

She will bury Hobo's precious remains way out along the logging road and put up a little cross.

Anna vomits again. Then she returns to the house and says that she caught her hand in the car door, and that is why she took so long. She has been crying with the pain. She suggests ice cream for dessert.

If only Adam hadn't had a headache, if only she had resisted the stove. And now the waiting time is here in earnest.

COUGARS AND AXES

The hunting season is winding down, but Anna remains cautious and walks the road with the dogs on a long tandem leash. It is still early morning, and the sun hangs above the horizon, with traces of leaves shivering on the poplar that press close to the road. Soon, they will walk free, Joy and Petra darting among the pines and hemlocks and poplar along the logging road.

As they draw near the entrance to the logging road, Petra stiffens, ears up and nostrils raised to the slight breeze. Her eyes are half-closed and following a movement in the bush, something Anna cannot see. It could be a porcupine, but Petra is alert and tense, not straining after it. Joy presses to Petra's side, head low. Perhaps it is a weasel, something less familiar to her; Petra would lunge for a porcupine or rabbit or partridge; she would wail and strain for a deer.

Maybe it is a bear, or a coyote pack hunting late.

Anna gazes down the logging road as they walk past. Down the slope where deer cross, there is a light brown movement. Something is padding across the road, light dappling around it. Deer do not pad. It must be a black bear, a brown-coated one, padding along the deer trail, seeking.

It is padding, but it is a jog-padding. It is moving low. It is skulking, half-crouching, cat-like.

There are not supposed to be Eastern cougars in the province. It should be a bear, being stealthy, moving low, jogging like a large cat.

She is sure she saw a cougar once while driving her car far down the back roads, although Natural Resources told her it was a coyote. One time, though, a summer resident from Europe commented on the presence of "lady lions" way down on the point. Cougars might not be recognized by the province, but everyone has a story or knows a story and this animal is jogging parallel to the road along the deer trail that comes out on an old farm below her property.

The dogs follow with their eyes and are silent at her side.

When Anna gets home, she tells Joshua that there is a cougar in the woods, and he must stay in the yard. It might spring on him in the woodlot; it is not safe out there.

"Like a big wildcat, like a mountain lion? Cat like that?" he says. "No. Bear. There are bear tracks down in the swamp. I saw them near the snares yesterday. But older. Dry. Maybe four days. Getting ready for winter—watch for them."

Anna's eyes widen and the woods seem close and pressing. Branches snap and leaves rustle. "You should have said something," she says.

Joshua shrugs. "Bears in the woods, bears on the ice. You watch. You stay ready. But you hide in the house and maybe the house gets hit by lightning. You can't hide, eh?"

Those tracks in the swamp would be bear tracks. Joshua would know. But that was not a bear this morning. A strange predator is stalking the bush. When she goes to town, Joshua must come with her. He can sit in the car, and she will change masks and sanitize before she gets back in the car. They can walk in the park in the town, stepping around the flowerbeds and shrubbery. She will pace the perimeter of the yard in the evening, her headlamp at full power, her walking stick in hand.

No. She will carry an axe.

Joshua keeps a large sharp axe in the shed, but she cannot store that in the little house. One of them will step on it; there will be split knees and bloody paws. No, she has a small axe, one from long ago camping days with Aaron, and she keeps it tucked in a corner, between the bookcases, dulled blade to the wall.

Perhaps when she surveys the yard with her headlamp, she will catch the glint of baleful yellow eyes in its beam.

And then run like hell for the house, stumbling over dogs on the way.

Dusk comes early, and she takes the dogs out for a game of fetch in the yard. As usual, Petra stares at the ball and then stalks away, while Joy snatches it up and capers about, tossing back her head and gnawing the ball, taunting Anna to throw another. The game gets monotonous, but it exercises the dogs, and Anna is not going outside the fence. The clothes hang on the line about twenty metres from the fence, but Anna is not going to be cut off and run down, laundry tumbling and then screams dying to moans as ripping sounds begin.

"You leave the clothes all night?" Joshua asks. "They're getting wet again, lots of dew, all mouldy by morning."

At that moment, Joy rushes the fence, her bark echoing off the trees. Petra jumps in front of her, nipping at her face and cutting her off.

"Owls," says Joshua, opening the gate and slipping through. He clicks the gate closed and saunters to the clothesline. "These will need all day again, and still be damp."

Anna casts a quick glance toward the woods and dashes for the house while Joshua stuffs clothespins in his pocket and starts cramming towels, T-shirts, and sweatshirts under his arm. He drapes the jeans over his shoulder and turns. His eyes widen and he stares.

Anna is at the gate, clutching her little axe in both hands. She scans the edge of the woods with her headlamp, prepared to catch yellow eyes glowing. Now both dogs start barking. A wailing and muttering begins deep in the swamp. Coyotes.

No. When the dogs pause to draw breath, the sound drifts up to her unfiltered, and it is the call of a barred owl. But Petra had nipped Joy into silence, so the cougar must be out there, too. It must have ranged back from the old farm to circle her lot and scheme.

"You do your three-sixties for owl?" Joshua asks. "We usually turn in circle like that for polar bear, they sneak up on you."

"A cougar will stalk you," Anna insists. "It's out there, pacing around, watching."

Joshua pushes past the dogs and into the yard. "Glad when they go free," he comments. "Always in the way like that."

Joy is silent now, trembling, and Petra's nose is raised to the breeze. "Something in the bush, for sure," Joshua agrees. "But how come you think cougar? Never any signs."

He bundles the damp laundry into Anna's arms and takes the axe, testing the blade.

"Dull," he observes. "Maybe you could use a hammer? All you do with this is make him mad."

The laugh that used to echo over the harbour is muffled by the surrounding woods, but it is good to hear it at any level again. Anna remembers that when he laughed in the town on the sidewalks and the parking lots, she was embarrassed; she wants those years back, to take his hand and walk right past the starers, meeting their eyes with a cold stare of her own. *They* were not of Endor. She is not of Endor either, but she could be. She will be.

Joshua hefts the axe and listens to the night. The owls have gone quiet, and there is not even a breeze to stir the branches.

Finally, he nods. "I do not think it is your cat," he says. "But tomorrow, we will look at the place where you saw something and check for tracks. This land is new to me; it is hard to read it. But I think your cat would take our snares. It would not leave such a fine *ukalik*."

No, Hobo was not taken by coyotes or cougars. No, she and Joshua ate him.

∧∧

In the morning, there are scrapes and edges left by deer hooves on the trail. Joshua finds rubbings in the dry earth made by a large, padded foot, but there is no shape, no clear definition, just a scuff. Petra sniffs deeply but is silent. Joy crowds beside her and Petra growls, but it is a warning only for Joy. Joshua follows the path into the woods, crouching low. There are deer droppings, some of them fresh, and little press points in the leaves, but no predator tracks, not in this cover. A tuft of grass is flattened here, and there a few grizzled hairs that could only be bear. But Anna knows what she saw, and it was not the movement of a bear.

"Every time you tell me," Joshua reflects, "it gets more and more like a cat. I think you are turning a bear into this cougar, with your mind."

Anna tightens her grip on her axe, for she has brought it with them. When the time comes, she will swing with authority, legs set and shoulders squared. "I know what I saw," she says. "It just didn't leave signs. The ground is too hard."

"Everything leaves signs," he replies. "They just don't leave them everywhere."

Anna has texted Natasha several times to warn her that there is a cougar nearby, and Natasha has finally texted back to say that usually the cougars stick to the back country. So, there are cougars living there, not just roaming through? Oh, yes, but they stay to themselves. However, she will keep a close eye on her chickens, just the same.

Adam keeps a pellet gun, because he and Natasha live near the garbage boxes and the rats sometimes gather there. He explains that it is only a question of time before the rats find their way to the neighbouring houses. He and Joshua make occasional forays to the garbage boxes for target practice, but a pellet gun will not solve the cougar problem.

Adam's friend Liam, however, has a .30-06 on hand from his deer hunting days, and when the huge dark shape is seen bounding inside his own chicken fence in the December dusk a few days later, Liam pulls out his old ammo and takes aim. He is fined for discharging a firearm in proximity to the road, and with shooting a protected animal.

"How the hell can a cougar be protected if they insist there aren't any?" Liam demands. "How can there be a law against shooting something that doesn't exist?"

It is explained to Liam that this protected cougar has strayed into this area, and his gun is confiscated anyway.

Joshua is bewildered by the way the laws unfold here, and by the subtlety of the cougar that slipped past him. Anna is relieved, but also allows a moment of vindication. She has protected her home, after all.

Joshua is not pleased that she continues to carry the axe, anyway.

GREAT CHRISTMASES

December darkens and Christmas approaches. There is a dust of snow the week before Christmas, which lightens the landscape, but Joshua's heart is far north, where there have been many storms already. Missing First Advent has been hard for him. There is always a stocking for each grandchild, from Miriam's twelve-year-old Beth down to Dinah's youngest. The stockings lie all in a row, and there are even surprises under the tree for the adults and teenagers of the family. This year Joshua had to send a parcel in the mail, mailed late because of his hospital episode, and it is still in Goose Bay. The little ones will not understand, Joshua says. He sighs in the evenings and looks at the pictures he carries with him.

Anna knows that Joshua sighs because he is not bearing witness to the celebrations that should mark his last days. The wood stove might be comfortable here, but this is not his world. He is suspended here, and his last days are taking place without him.

That is hard. And there is nothing to be done.

Now there is a Christmas parcel added to the mail waiting in Goose Bay, because the lockdown continues, tight and merciless. Anna yearns for the days when the biggest concern was vaccination mandates—who would need them and what they could do with them. Now the virus has bred out of control; it has a will of its own and a thirst to survive, and it is fierce. Humanity will in the end be like a population of rabbits; the disease will burn through them, and a handful will survive. All that separates them from the rabbits is the hope that, if they all hide, then death will pass over and burn out with no fuel.

Because no one wants to be one of the dead rabbits rotting on the roadside with flies swarming over its eyes.

There are fevers and flooded lungs; people who survive are weakened in mind and body. No one jokes about having a senior moment anymore because enough people are trapped in such moments for life now.

And there is anger growing out there, anger because we were good, so it should have ended, but it hasn't. There is anger because we have missed so many times.

There is only sorrow in Joshua, a deep, abiding sadness that he is not there to make his goodbye rich and kind for his family. He might die here with Anna and the dogs, and they are kind, but his family will grieve for him as one of the many People who have died in strange lands among strange ways.

On Christmas Eve, they cut a small tree from the woods below the house and place it in the front window. Joy and Petra hover close as Anna strings lights and a few ornaments on it. There are no grandchildren to leave stockings for the morning, but there are a few cards on the bookcase. There are no gifts yet from Labrador, but they receive small gifts from each other—a Labrador scarf and pin for her, a sweatshirt from the local pharmacy for him. They must plan for their future, because Joshua now accepts that Anna will come as far as Goose Bay. They have to save money, but there is room for this frivolity because it is, after all, Christmas.

On Christmas afternoon, she finds Joshua brooding in the fading light, watching the road from the front window.

"Miriam didn't come," he says. "Always her, her husband, the kids, every Christmas afternoon and stay for supper. Busy, I guess."

"Did you call?" Anna asks, not sure how to handle this moment.

Joshua startles, shakes his head, and turns to their little tree. "Sometimes it all runs together," he mutters. "Maybe soon I won't know them. Maybe I forget them, forget my name, forget everything. Forget how to breathe, maybe."

He shakes his head again. "My son Aaron," he says. "I remember his mother. She went away, you know. Far away. Took him with her till he found his way home."

He is silent then, contemplating the few snowflakes that are falling. His eyes clear, then widen. He lowers his head and runs a fist below each eye. He stares at the floor. "Oh," he says after a long pause. "You have a nice place, good and warm. You are a good person, a good teacher." He offers a quick smile.

Anna steps up behind him and wraps her arms around his waist. She presses to him, jerking her head close to rest one cheek between his shoulder blades. He stiffens, and she presses tighter.

She works around until she is facing him, and her hands now press the small of his back, and her cheek lies against his heart. He raises one hand and gives her back a brief pat. Then he lays his palms on her shoulders and steps back. His eyes meet hers, and they are warm though puzzled. "You are Anna Caine," he murmurs. "We were young, those times."

He leans down and his lips brush hers. "Thank you," he says. Then he walks to his room and closes the door, leaving her by the tree in the front window, an old woman with a young woman's longing. The sky is darkening, and she thinks of her mother and her Christmases alone, her grandchild and daughter far away at the last train stop, and they never invited her, and she would have loved to come. *I understand you now, Mother.*

She wonders if Joshua will wait for Leah in the last days.

WINTER IN A NEW WORLD

January brings raging storms that rip down power lines. The weather systems have grown in strength and frequency over the years. The summers are hotter and drier, the earth bakes, and then the moisture pools on the surface in the storms of fall and winter. Anna is now grateful for the wisdom of the wood stove with its half-cured or dead wood; she can tolerate rabbit, which is a regular meat now that the story of pelt-stealing coyotes has been told, and Hobo's bones and fur and ears are neatly buried along the logging road. She only hopes these are not his wild descendants, but they need the protein, and the stores are low on meats.

In February, the storms come as rain, and the marsh along the way to the main road is soon brimming with water. The water spills over onto the gravel following the second storm. Anna does not think that the water is deep, but Joshua declares that she does not know what lies beneath the surface. The gravel is soft; it does not freeze well in this climate. There is a current there, getting strong, and that will cut a channel in the wet gravel. Even where there isn't a channel, the ruts will be deep and sticky. Does she really want to drive blind through the water, with channels and deep ruts beating up her all-wheel drive? Maybe it is so soft and deep that they will bog down, and then if it freezes, they won't have any car to go around the long way. There is an alternate, longer route, higher and drier. Patience and a little extra time will see them to town in safety. Her way, they won't have a car to go anywhere.

Adam drops by one evening to warn them about the road. He stands by his car and calls down the driveway, for he remembers each day that Joshua has missed his Great Christmas because Adam had a small headache when they put in the stove. There is a four-by-four truck blocking the road to the village, he informs them. Up to the hubcaps. And the mess is starting to freeze. People will probably be taking the long way until spring.

At these times, she exults in Joshua the carpenter and hunter and fisherman, strong on his Land, strong on her land too, and she yearns to hold him and press her body to his. This is her Joshua, who reads the ice, who reads all the roads, is great on the Land, is wise among the mountains, and knows the passages.

She will not try to hold him again, though. He is right. They were young, those times, and this is a friendship walk, not a lovers' walk.

Then why do they call it com-passion?

M

The hospital in St. John's has arranged for routine bloodwork and CT scan in Bridgewater. In these troubled times, the medical staff stretch resources, imaginations, and endurance to support their patients. Anna is relieved that they do not have to go to Halifax; although there are outbreaks everywhere, they have marginally less chance of exposure in the smaller centre. Also, they will have fewer angry people, less traffic, and fewer left turns on clogged streets. They will be back in the little house in the woods sooner.

Joshua does not want to go for his CT scan or bloodwork; he argues (with Anna) that he feels fine, and that these are not needed. She points out that his cancer doctor arranged this, so they would know exactly what is going on. Joshua says it does not matter; he will go home and go North. Anna can come to Goose Bay, but she cannot go to Endor. He can handle that part on his own, and the fewer people there are, the safer they will be. Endor has stayed safe during this latest outbreak of virus, and he must keep it that way. He will stay out at Aaron's cabin for a couple of weeks, just to be sure. Anna will go back home.

Once again, emails and calls are exchanged. Miriam would like for Anna to respect her father's wishes but feels she should explain the importance of these tests to him. Miriam consults with the cancer doctor, who reminds them that this is Joshua's journey. Anna cherishes a dream in which the results come back, and the cancer has simply disappeared. These things do happen. But they will not know that without the tests. She would like the tests to prove the miracle she weaves into her plans. Joshua has not had an episode of confusion in weeks, just occasional minor bouts, and those are surely the after-effects of the chemo.

Anna and Joshua will go North, and they will live on the Land. She will write marvellous plays, in which people triumph against all odds, and Joshua will build furniture and cabinets for the people of St. John's. During the summer, the coastal boat will bring visiting family to them and deliver Joshua's cabinets and furniture to southern markets They will fade into old, old age, side by side, maybe spending the harshest part of winter in town with family.

She will witness Aaron raising a family. She will have grandchildren with Joshua.

That is her plan.

Joshua has another plan: They will go to Goose Bay in March; Anna will escort him, and then go back to her place. He will take the hospital plane to Endor and spend a couple of weeks at Aaron's cabin. Then he will prepare for Easter with his family. When Easter Week with all its games and traditions has been observed, when the grandchildren have been spoiled in all the loving ways, and he has walked the town enough, he and Aaron will load the *Kamutik* for one last journey up the coast and into the mountains. They will go as far as they can, maybe even to his Hebron home if the ice and weather are good, and Aaron will drive because Joshua sometimes forgets now, and when they have looked upon the old ways once more, he will return to Endor and wait.

When his time comes, they will put him in the churchyard beside Leah. They will all be at peace.

Anna does not remind him that there will be pain, gripping, relentless pain, and they will all feel the release of his passing because it will be dementia and weakness and incontinence and rage. Joshua knows, but this special journey is what he will remember, deep in the madness.

She cherishes the little dream of their old, old age, the cancer vanished into the ether, but on other days, she imagines pressing a blanket to his face as he sleeps out on the Barrens, so he will die without horror, without pain. He will be the Thunderer, and she will tell herself that he died on the hunt, his faithful-at-last woman bearing witness to his passing.

Anna Caine has changed the ending of her own story many times; she will rewrite Joshua's story without hesitation.

THE NARROW PORTAL

In March, Joshua and Anna find themselves in Halifax, seeking clearance for the journey North. They wait in an auditorium, metal chairs set in rows with two-metre aisles. At intervals, a new set of digits flashes in red above the little office shielded in Plexiglas, and someone new approaches and takes a seat. Sometimes the interview begins and ends in smiles, and the applicant departs satisfied or rejected but still smiling. Other times it ends in tears with chairs scraping and people shrieking; at times, it even begins that way. Anna decides that the Plexiglas and locked door protect the well-being of the staff on many levels; very few people are going anywhere and very few are tolerating rejection at this point. Anna worries that soon there will be protests and blockades forming outside the building. Fear is dominant right now, but when people grow weary of the fear, the fury will take over. There will be angry mobs marching into towns, disrupting church services and demanding food, just like the Beghards of the Middle Ages. Only these modern Beghards might bring disease and guns.

Joshua taps at his phone, taking advantage of the good signal to send texts and messages to the family. Anna hopes he is not telling them that he is on his way home; interprovincial travel is technically possible for regular people, but it rarely happens. Some argue that the virus is everywhere, so travel restrictions are meaningless. The goal of the current plan is to reduce movement in the hope that less movement and less interaction will mean less coughing on one another and hopefully less illness. We will be able to look back and say we tried our best.

Anna wonders about the ventilation quality in this auditorium, but there are only twenty waiting now, and they are well-spaced.

The man beside her is neat and straight, although his clothing is a little shabby, his features creased and strained. He is focused on the phone in his palm, and she wonders if he is thinking of her. She ponders the winter behind them, when they sat beside one another, parallel, never intersecting. They were polite and tolerant, but sometimes Anna wanted to scream and beat the floor with a stick of firewood until Joshua really looked at her, until his eyes shone for her, and he saw the mother of his first son, the one who gave herself to him, body and soul, in the spring sun, the one who has worshipped and hated him these almost forty years. Does he know? Does he know the cost, the despair, the unfulfilled-ness that has suffocated her creative adult years and saw her forever on the fringes of her life, unable to enter? Does he know that she has missed Aaron, with every fibre of her being, that she has yearned again and again to sit beside her own mother and pronounce a daughter's blessing, *Now I understand you, Mother,* and weep for them both? As Joshua puttered about with his axe and his crosscut saw and his damnable snare line, as he poked at his screen in the evenings and picked at his meals without a smile across the table, did he know that she was waiting for a word, one word that all this mattered, that she was not an unfortunate stopover gone bad?

Does he know that, sometimes, she thinks how simple her life would be if she had never come back here, never been the reliable escort, never known the terrible strain of these past months? Does he look within her mind and see the intrusive terrors that she resists, but that are there, nevertheless, the ones in which she finds him, eyes closed, body stiff and cold, in the woodlot, down on the snare trail of which he is so proud, or on his side in the tiny guest room, and then she fears it will happen, and the world will be empty of Joshua?

Does he know?

Perhaps he does.

Perhaps he does, but he is as trapped as she is, and he always wanted her to live in Endor, not as lover but as neighbour and friend, to see her child grow up, to teach and live among his People, to be welcome and to grow old with one long set of memories, not the tiny jerks of memory here and there, which sometimes overlap but never quite add up. He needs to be home, and then he can be well, and she can be well.

Maybe the cancer is leaving him; these things happen, so why not now? Perhaps his way is better; do not have the tests because then you can dream, and there is no way your dream can be proven false.

She studies the figure beside her, calm and spare, and in that moment, the love is there. Not the intensity and yearning for the next coupling of youthful, immature love, but the comfort of sitting side by side, knowing each guards the other's passage, the snug comfort of mature love.

She fingers their health reports and wonders how people who lived for the last two months on tinned goods, wild rabbit, and the occasional partridge that wandered into the rabbit snares can be so healthy. Perhaps it is the good fresh air of country living, and at least, they had heat in the dark months and were not mauled and gutted by a cougar.

Petra's face fills her mind. Petra stood before Natasha that last day, then raised her paws to Natasha's shoulders and looked into her eyes. *You are my home now,* Petra was communicating. For a moment Anna allows her heart to twist, and then she fights it down. She might return; she might. But Petra cannot keep giving her heart. Let Petra be with Natasha now, and let Anna walk alone when Joshua is gone.

Anna marvels that a man with cancer threading its way into his brain and choking his memory can have a heart that beats strong and a body that is straight and fit. For here he sits beside her, thin grey hair combed back in a neat braid on the back of his neck. The eyes are strained, but their expression is clear today. The salt wind is on his face already, perhaps, and he hears the call of mountains. Joshua sits straight and ready, image of Elder dignity preparing to honour the ways of his Land.

Beside him is his faithful-at-last Anna, a little shorter, the right knee stiff but still supporting her, the hair home-cut and a little shaggy but not quite grey yet, the legs still muscled, the head up and confident. The confidence is external only; inside, she is in turmoil. Each moment brings them closer to the rejection that she knows is coming, to the crushing news that Joshua will die of a broken heart, here in exile. Let the officials see how well he is when he is going home; let them understand that he will lie down and die right there, when they deny him.

People do die of broken hearts. The scone lady taught her that.

Now it is their number, and they sit on metal chairs, deftly wiped between uses, there in front of the weary-eyed staff member who crouches behind her computer screen, preparing for the pain of this encounter. Anna tries to make a smile radiate from her whole face, there behind the mask, as she holds up their health cards and their health reports.

The staff member makes note of the numbers and works her keyboard. She stares at the screen, and her eyes squint a little. Anna senses that the worker is pursing her lips. The eyes soften. "Mr. Kalluk, I see you have been through a lot. And do you think it wise to be travelling?"

Anna opens her mouth and shifts on her chair. Joshua leans forward. "I will tell you, yes, and you will know." He speaks in a soft voice and paces his words. "My English . . . is not good like yours. But yes. I have a cancer, and it is going to take my life this time. This time, I will not go forward and leave it behind."

The woman glances at her watch and moves in her seat. "You will listen, please," Joshua says, "because this is the last time we will meet. The last chance that I have. Yes, my heart is strong, my lungs all good, no fever, no virus. No. All is good. But the cancer is coming for me. It is soon. I know this thing. And I have been trapped here. Like a fox, in a snare. This is your place, and it is very good, but it is choking me. I cannot breathe. Not here. I need the air home, North, feel the wind, smell the snow. My daughters, my sons, my grandchildren, we need to meet and teach each other to be strong. Then it is peace for me, peace for them.

"Your laws say I will have to stay in Goose Bay, ten days. Then I can fly to Endor, and Endor will be safe.

"I cannot do that. I need to be on the Land. I do not have ten days for Goose Bay.

"I will come straight to Endor. I will stay two weeks at my son's cabin, instead, and never see anyone. Never let anyone close. And after two weeks, when all is good, I will go to my family. We will be together, and that will make us strong.

"Too many times," he says, his voice stronger but still gentle, "my People have died far away, in distant lands. That has hurt us all. We carry those times. We hear them, and it hurts us, and we break sometimes. But I will die among my own mountains. And when I am gone, my grandchildren will grow up whole, not all broken.

"I have no fevers, no sickness to hurt others. I ask to go home, for there, even when the cancer takes me, it will not be beating me.

"This I ask of you." He lowers his eyes now, and stares at his hands.

The eyes above the mask shine with tears. The woman nods, and turns to Anna, blinking. "And you?" The voice is husky now.

Anna leans forward. "I will go with him, to see him through his journey. I will do all the things I must do. He must not be alone."

The woman sits back and contemplates her screen for a moment. "OK. We support your claim here in principle, and more than anything, I would like to send Mr. Kalluk home. And you would escort him and stay with him at this cabin?"

"No," Joshua interjects. "She needs to stay in Goose Bay and come to her home again."

"If she is escorting you, Mr. Kalluk, then she is in for the duration." The worker gropes for a second language way to convey this. "If she is coming, she needs to come with you to Goose Bay, and then this Endor, then this cabin— but," she suddenly realizes, "then you would be in contact before the cabin. . . . And we have an obligation, to the communities. Maybe you have heard of the Spanish flu, as it was called, and the troubles of those times? How hard it was for some communities, not so far from where you want to go?"

There is tension along his jawline, but Joshua's voice is calm. "I believe so. Yes. There are those among us who were there, in Okak, and other places. It is in our heart. That is why I go to the cabin."

The woman leans forward, and her voice is gentle. "What if you bring the virus on the plane, to the passengers, to the people where you stop, and then to Endor, when you get off the plane, before you even go to the cabin? We cannot risk it. Not with this virus. I am sorry."

"We can have someone leave a snowmobile, supplies, at the airport in Goose Bay," Joshua interjects. "I know the safe ways up the coast. Someone will meet us, stay apart, bring guns."

"Guns!" the woman exclaims.

Joshua's eyes widen and he shrugs. "For polar bears."

"Oh," the woman says in a low voice. She stirs. "Very well. We want to approve situations like this because we honour our commitment to the Indigenous community."

To Anna these words ring hollow—a political platform, a noble stance, the words of someone who knows the rhetoric but not the inner history. *Let's see you in a quarantine shelter in isolation; you don't know, not like him. Not like the people living it and dying it.*

Anna does not say that aloud, because it is not the woman's fault, and she almost cried just now. Besides, they are so close.

"The problem," the woman begins, shifting in her seat again, "is that no one may travel without an approved travel escort, someone to vouch for them and stay with them and see that every protocol is followed. The fines are somewhat steep if the authorities suspect you are out of compliance. For you and for them."

Joshua nods. "It is like that on the Land," he says. "When we take someone with us, we are responsible. We must keep them from danger, keep them so no one will maybe die looking for them, rescuing them. It is a trust. It is what we do."

"Yes, well, yes." The woman clicks the mouse and turns to her printer. "We have a list. If you can get one of these people, and they are in demand, to agree to represent you, then you are going home, Mr. Kalluk."

She slides the list under the Plexiglas and taps the last name. "That one is a curious case, a professor and hospital chaplain or counselor or something like that. He only goes on a few. He is an older gentleman, so maybe snowmobiles and polar bears are a little much for him, but if anyone would take your case, it would be him. His wife and I are on a committee together. She is a pet; she tells me he has a special attachment for the north."

Anna knows this already. She is staring at the page and remembering for the third time in many years. And then, she is thinking, *Wife?*

"Hey!" Joshua is tapping the paper, smiling. "Hey! You know him. That's your friend, right? Call him. Let's talk to him. Today. Maybe Goose Bay soon!"

The staff member is stamping papers. "OK. Here are your documents. These only become valid when presented at the ticket counter by the escort. He has to come here, sign as your representative, but he knows all the drill.

"I think this is going to work for you. Sarah tells me Mr. Sutherland is getting restless, and she's pretty sure he will take another assignment soon."

TIME FOR TERRENCE

Terrence paces the reading room in the library overlooking the Northwest Arm, his sermon notes forgotten.

"I have looked, O Lord, deep and long," he murmurs. "I have revisited and relived. Each moment has been sifted and weighed, and I know, dear Father, I know that I did right when I did not follow Anna into her wilderness when she returned from her North."

He had wanted to find her, to tell her that he loved her and the seed within her, that together they would find a way, and her child would be raised a minister's son. An adopted son, uprooted from his world, and Anna's motherhood denied. Terrence is grateful that he did not follow that day, and say these things.

He knows that now he would embrace Anna and the son that came to her on her journey; he would join them and bear witness to them. He would not shut them into a little ecclesiastically pure box; he would be bold and reckless, wind in his hair, riding down the storm and laughing into the sky like that Joshua Kalluk, the man of thunder.

Terrence would stride through the streets of Endor, shake hands with that Joshua, smile and say what a good son he was raising. He would eat at Joshua's table, and walk the shore with Anna Caine. He would be friend, not cuckold or fool.

And then he would release them all with a blessing.

In his story, Terrence would have gone in early summer, for he does not find snow appealing, and his neck always swells from mosquito bites.

But he would have gone, with his head up and his hand out in greeting.

Today, no one travels, as the virus rises anew. Patients in the wards ask him, "Is this the End Time? Is it happening? Will Jesus come soon?"

They want Reverend Terrence to smile indulgently through his mask and assure them that it is indeed happening, and every tear will soon be painlessly wiped away, and they will see all their loved ones, forever and ever.

Terrence personally thinks that eternity with certain loved ones would be tedious after the first few hours. *Is the family reunion over yet? Can we please relax now?*

He would like to boom from the pulpits and hospital corridors: "Verily, this is indeed God's own plague, and all the vaccines in the world are powerless against it. Behold! He is purging the earth."

This might shock them, but Terrence suspects many would take secret pleasure in the possibility of a good purging of the earth, having a private purge list that does not include their own name.

Oh! The witty, shocking things Terrence would love to say, while his listeners' eyes grow round, and they gasp behind their flimsy masks—Anna always said he went too far with his little musings. He turns his mind back to Anna and That Time. She had changed; she had grown, but it was a wild, untamed growth, and she could not find a place anymore in his ordered world.

She said she was suffocating. She needed to move, to go, to breathe.

He did right.

But he has missed her, every day of his life from that day to this.

He has married, and he gives thanks for the grace and peace that Sarah has brought to his life. She is a wife *far beyond the price of pearls*, straight out of the Book of Proverbs. *She is clothed in strength and dignity; she can laugh at the days to come. When she opens her mouth, she does so wisely; on her tongue is kindly instruction.* (Proverbs 31: 10b, 25-26)

Sarah is indeed perfect and has made the living of Terrence's life bearable in the days since Anna. Sarah has looked into his heart and honoured its breaking. She does not offer advice on the days when he walks in his possibilities. She loves, but she is not jealous. She guards Terrence's brokenness and cradles it in her generous arms. She tends their little garden, and prepares meals that are satisfying and on time, here in their cottage on the hill overlooking the Northwest Arm. For Terrence is faculty now. He teaches courses in pastoral care and church history. He and Sarah are at peace here, meandering through their senior years in the quiet, repetitious boredom. They read together, in the evenings, and if Terrence goes out to pace the shore, Sarah is waiting when he returns.

Sarah is his dear helpmeet, his sweet friend, but Terrence cannot picture her whooping the length of the gym, floor hockey stick high, or climbing into a float plane to fly to a remote school.

He knows, too, Sarah would never fornicate on the tundra with a near stranger, although sometimes he wishes she would.

Then she would be alive, as alive as Anna Caine.

There was such fire in Anna Caine.

Terrence is in the theology school library, not the prosaic old one in the former main building, but the new one, with sweeping views and a scriptorium. A library for a visionary.

A library for looking beyond all his losses and being grateful for the view.

Now on the lower fringes of his vision, there along the water's edge, Terrence sees an older couple walking arm in arm, heads leaning close together. He and Anna were going to be like that once, content and old together.

The woman on the shore is old, but not elderly; she is still lithe, still striding. She is limping a little, favouring a knee. The man is old, but sickness old, not aging gracefully old. He is shuffling with shoulders drawn; he walks in pain. His eyes are on the water, and he points suddenly. The woman leans her head on his shoulder and smiles at something he says.

They are lovers, as he and Anna would have been.

And behold, it *is* Anna. His Anna, growing old but still strong and resilient, still receiving the world into her life.

The man walks on, laughing to the sky, the salt wind on his face. Wisps of grey hair brush his gaunt cheeks, and his hunched shoulders stiffen as Anna embraces him, her head to his chest now. And he looks past her, eyes still on the water.

Terrence comes scrambling down the stairs, legs jerking like a wooden soldier, damp palms gripping the banister. Now he is out of the building and shambling wildly down the hill. He is going to her, to Anna who was his Anna, and to that Joshua he has heard about but never met, and Terrence knows that God has put him here in the library this day so he can stumble down the hill and bless them.

He will bless them with all the love that is in his heart for he knows now, or has always known and is now ready to receive, that Anna Caine embraces the world, and that is why he loves her and every single thing and being that she loves. He will kiss the grass that she walks on; he will bow before this Joshua, this Thunderer.

Sarah will prepare a nourishing fish chowder for them all, with apple tart for dessert.

Terrence needs the fire that is Anna Caine.

This Anna has tears in her eyes. "Terrence," she says. "We are trying to get home. Can you help us?"

Instead of bowing and kissing grass, Terrence is staggering to a halt a good two metres away from them and pulling his mask tight. This reminds Anna, and she produces two fresh disposable masks from her shoulder bag, and for some reason Terrence pictures Jesus, walking on water while tying on a three-ply mask, and he laughs.

The man who is Joshua smiles. "There was a seal out there, lots of good *utsuk*."

Terrence listens to Anna's story of her and Joshua, how they got trapped here when all the borders closed in the panic. They have been to the hospital and the processing auditorium, and now she is showing Joshua the water, Anna says, because he is so lonely for water. Joshua could not get home for Christmas, and now Easter is approaching, and he is missing wild foods and journeys and family, living in exile since he came for a week but developed a fever that was not the virus, and then the borders locked hard. He is being stalked by a cancer that is stretching its tendrils into his brain. Joshua yearns to go to Endor now, and then north, and Anna will accompany him. Joshua looks away, out across the water, as Anna explains this.

Terrence sees a man in exile, but an exile who smiles instead of weeping, as he remembers.

Terrence has worked long with patients in palliative care. He knows this man is dying.

And when he looks at Anna Caine, Terrence knows that she is going to follow this man wherever he goes. And the urge to give blessing rises in Terrence's being, and he longs to place his fingers on the scars left by the cursed chemo needles, and beg to be their friend.

Terrence does not interrupt as Anna explains what he knows already: They can get travel permits on compassionate grounds with proper protocols in place, and the right person to vouch for them. Someone with impeccable credentials, who will guarantee their adherence to the protocols. One who will escort them to the end. Someone on the list.

That list includes the name of Terrence Sutherland. They said they came to see the water, but Terrence knows that they are, in fact, looking for him.

Anna has turned to him, for Joshua's sake.

Terrence will journey to Endor and release them into the wilderness. Sarah is going to tend her garden and make fish chowder, and he is going on a wild journey with the untameable Anna Caine and her beloved Joshua.

If he takes them, they will die. If he does not take them, they will die. But then they will die without an open sky and without the Creator of the Universe holding them in the palm of his hand.

Terrence will be wild and reckless. He will be like the desert ancestors marching out of Egypt with nothing but the power of God to warm their hearts and fill their bellies.

He is ready. His unclean lips are prepared to receive the purifying coal. *Here I am, send me.* (Isaiah 6:9)

But first, he and Anna and Joshua will sit down and break bread together.

SARAH, WIFE AND GUARDIAN

Terrence's wife, Sarah, has always had a warm spot for the mistress of St. Augustine, her unsung heroine of church history. Augustine does not name this woman in his *Confessions*, claiming this is to protect her reputation, but Sarah suspects he doesn't quite remember her name. Augustine records that when he sent her back to Carthage—of course, keeping her son to be raised a proper Christian like Papa—she lamented that she would never love another man. Augustine seems to take this as a tribute to his prowess or maybe his lovability, but Sarah insists that the words were uttered in relief. Kind of, *Now that I am free of him, I will be damned if I get stuck in this same trap again.* Or perhaps, she spoke as a mother: *He took my son from me. Men are all swine!*

Sarah does not think of the woman as St. Augustine's mistress, for a careful reading reveals that they were a formal couple, although not blessed by the Church as neither was Christian. Sarah claims that dumping his common-law wife to join an elite priesthood would make Augustine look like a scoundrel, and besides, legal claims might be pending. So, Augustine presented himself as a pious and devoted man who refused temptation, declared his beloved was just a mistress, scooped up her son, and seized salvation with both hands. God had never blessed their union, so he was off the hook. This is Sarah's version of church history.

Terrence has told Sarah that her reading of church history is unorthodox, but she suspects privately he is delighted. Terrence claims he married Sarah because she is not a romantic, but Sarah knows that she is the original romantic—devoted to love and to nature, to the triumph of the individual, and to the spiritual victory of cast-off common-law partners. Sarah is a pragmatic librarian in a theological library, and she is well-read.

She is also devoted to her husband because he is a hurt and hopeful man; no Augustinian arrogance here, just a man who loves all.

She guards his heart.

Especially when it comes to Anna Caine.

Sarah is familiar with the tale of Anna Caine, a somewhat simple teacher looking for security in an insecure world. Anna floated through an engagement to Terrence, who was gentle and devoted; Sarah believes Anna would have loved to dare the world but was too afraid. Something in the world must have frightened Anna, and she was in hiding, licking her wounds and building strength for her next attempt. Terrence still does not see that Anna hid behind him, readying herself for something grand.

Terrence is still a little hurt that Anna went off to a northern school for a year, had a riotous affair that set the community on its ear, came home pregnant, and then advised Terrence that their relationship was over. The father of the child was married or getting married, and Sarah suspects Anna fancied herself a strong woman who would raise her child free of the confines of marriage or fatherhood. Sarah has the impression that Anna moved in with her mother, and then abandoned her too when the child was a more manageable age.

Terrence feels he did not handle the situation well, and that he offended Anna's innocence. Sarah believes it was her pride. In her less kind moments, Sarah imagines figuratively shaking Anna until her figurative teeth rattle.

Sarah's husband is a gentle man, a scholarly man with a beautiful and dazzling love for his Creator's earth and all its inhabitants. People like that are always being hurt, and Sarah believes it is the work of people like herself to hold them together.

Sarah is happy in her marriage, and her husband's sensitive core touches her being. At the same time, on those evenings when he roams the shore and comes home all windblown and brusque, she knows that he still cares for Anna Caine and believes himself the wild and rugged lover that she might be seeking. Terrence is still in love with the core of wildness that was in Anna, and he fancies it is also in him.

Sarah is no fan of Augustine, yet she does not sympathize with his mistress-wife. Sarah does not go weeping home to Carthage. She stands her ground. She stands with Terrence because, unlike Anna Caine, she prefers gentle and whole-some love, the kind that sits side by side, in matching armchairs, one reading a passage to the other and both laughing, and when one disappears into the night and wind to play wild and rugged lover, the other smiles and is silent.

Sarah will not let anyone use Terrence like Anna used him. They will answer to Terrence's wife.

His wife is meek, yes, but she defends her own.

And now, the enigmatic Anna Caine is sitting at Sarah's table, scooping up her fish chowder and casting quick glances at the dignified and humble man beside her. He does not look coarse and sensual, as Sarah had imagined him.

TWO LEAHS, ONE RACHEL

The March evening is darkening slowly as the unlikely group huddles over fish chowder and crusty rolls. Terrence presides over his table, beaming and gracious, Sarah opposite. Her figure is rounded, soft but neat, her make-up light but tasteful, her hair swept up in a neat bun. Her skirt is plain but stylish, her sweater casual yet rich in texture. She is younger than Terrence, but older too, her mind calm and assured, knowing itself. Her table is set with matching dinnerware, solid but lightly flowered. There are linen napkins.

Anna sits beside Joshua, the roughness of the winter radiating from her. Her clothes are clean but stiff, dried on the poles upstairs. The jeans are a little baggy, the sweater is loose at the neck from wringing, the thermal socks carry the faint odour of her heavy boots. Joshua's hair has been tidied into its braid after their walk, his heavy shirt buttoned neat to the neck, his jeans belted, though a little loose. He is tidy and careful in his movements, taking the chowder in small sips, nodding his approval to his hostess.

Terrence begins to speak of the journey ahead, and Sarah lowers her spoon and dabs her mouth with the linen napkin. When she speaks, her tone is calm, measured.

"You have been travelling every month, it seems," she begins. "Each time, there is some risk. That is part of any travel.

"But this one," she continues, "is different. You are travelling into the Labrador, and my understanding is that you must convey these two to their final destination."

"He only needs to come to Goose Bay," Joshua explains.

Sarah closes her eyes for a moment, then shakes her head. "They will not see it that way. Someone will say that you will stop in a community, or meet up with people, and that you are travelling unescorted. No. If you go, my husband"—She emphasizes these last two words with a quick glance at Anna—"must accompany you. He doesn't have the right clothes for a snowmobile trip into the wilderness. And then he must stay with you in a cabin, with a gun and polar bears, for two weeks, and then on to the village where you live. Then he can fly home. So maybe a month?"

"He will bring Anna back; she'll be quarantined and ready to fly back. Just medical first," Joshua elaborates.

Sarah's lips tighten, just a little. "Yes. That will be nice."

Anna is already shaking her head. "I was thinking I could stay on, maybe work at the school some, help with the grandchildren, but go North with him and Aaron too."

"No." Joshua's tone does not encourage argument. "That is not your trip to make. You are good to offer, but this is not your time."

"It can be," she whispers, eyes lowered.

Terrence clears his throat. "I think the main thing is, we must get Joshua home. I think," he emphasizes, "that is the main consideration, and should be honoured first. Remember the disciples; when their leader said he was going to Jerusalem, they looked around and shrugged and said, 'Let us go and die with him.' They did not really understand. And perhaps you don't. But mainly, it isn't your time for this Jerusalem."

Joshua listens, leaning forward, but his eyes are staring past Terrence's shoulder. Then he nods, shrugs, and picks up his spoon again.

Anna stirs her chowder in slow circles, saying nothing. Anna, Sarah sees, will force her way on this quest although it is unfair to demand to be part of someone's final act.

A change of topic is needed. "So, Joshua," Sarah says, "I understand that you are married, and have a grown family, and now grandchildren."

"Yes," he replies. "My wife has passed now. She was a very special woman, my wife. She was Leah."

"Yes," says Sarah. "I can see she would be. I know, you see, how that feels."

Joshua's face clouds for a moment, and he nods. Perhaps he thinks Sarah is widowed, too, remarried now, but all the old sorrows still press her heart. Terrence fumbles a water glass, rights it, and mops the small spill. He never knew. Lord, he was blind, for he had never seen that, through all their years together, Sarah had seen herself as Leah, the Bible's loneliest wife. In the Bible story, Jacob loved Rachel, worked seven years for her, and assumed that she was the heavily veiled bride at his wedding. The father of the bride, meanwhile, had decided that his older daughter, Leah, would be married first. The wedding night passed in joy, until Jacob lifted the veil away in the dawn light. *When morning came, there was Leah,* it says in Genesis 29, verse 25. And everyone today feels sorry for Jacob and Rachel, but not for unloved, unwanted, humiliated Leah. In this moment, Terrence's heart breaks for his Sarah, who seems to have known always that she was poor substitute for his heart's desire, Anna.

Forgive me, Sarah, for I have sinned against you.

"I think," says Terrence, "that Anna must do here what is best for Joshua. But know, Anna, that I will be coming straight home after my duties are fulfilled, and if you do not come, then you must be very sure that you want to stay in Endor, possibly for years. I know you will be glad to spend time with your son, and I trust you are in a good relationship with all the family?"

ELUSIVE LANDMARKS

Terrence signs the paperwork at the processing auditorium and completes the final arrangements, and then for three days, all of them quarantine inside the house of Sarah and Terrence.

On the fourth day, the travellers spill out of the house, squinting a little in the spring light. The interior of the van is wiped down and sprayed; Sarah settles in the driver's seat, masked and barricaded by a plastic shield, while Terrence, Joshua, and Anna pile into the back seats, sleeping bags and snowpants and duffle bags tucked around. How threadbare their coats and how thin their mitts, but there will be bundles of winter gear and tracking devices and supplies awaiting them in Goose Bay, gathered by family and paid for by Anna, whose legacy is debt.

There is the moment at the airport when two hands press toward each other with the window glass between them, and Terrence's eyes are shining as he says goodbye to his wife. There is no smile on her face, for she sees that he is already North, far away on a rugged shore, the wild and reckless hero he has dreamed of being. In the moment of driving away, Sarah's eyes stare forward, her mind on Anna's vehicle plugging her driveway. She tries to picture Terrence smiling in the doorway, clasping her in his arms, but all she sees is the empty place at her table, and the heavy little tank that crowds her driveway and her future.

A month. A month, and she will know.

There is little joy on this day as the travellers wait in the long, bleak corridor at the airport.

They shuffle forward, and Joshua taps his phone endlessly. He is coordinating the ground crew in Goose Bay, and he looks aloof and calm, but Anna can smell the tension soaking into his armpits. To come so close and be denied—it must not, it cannot end that way. Terrence thumbs through their papers, which are now rough and dogeared, no longer smooth and fresh.

Finally, it is their turn.

They stand before the desk.

Terrence converses with the security officer, who looks bored and skeptical at the same time. The officer's lips press together, and his face twists—he will turn them away, Anna knows. They will step back into the warm Halifax morning. Joshua will not feel the raw snow wind on his face, and he will break.

There is a whump as the stamp comes down, and then another, and another. The officer leans back and hauls three packages from the table behind him.

"We put these on now," Terrence explains, distributing them.

Each packet contains a full mask and face shield, a small jar of sanitizer, boot covers, and a plastic overall, full-body.

Joshua wipes down his hands and removes his mask. His hand goes to his pocket, but Terrence indicates the waiting receptacle. Anna is grateful that Terrence insisted they all wear disposable masks this morning, or there might have been a showdown over dumping Joshua's mask, made by his daughter, in the garbage. Joshua wipes his hands again and dons the mask, then the boot covers. "I cannot wear this," he says, pushing the shield back in the packet with the overall and tucking the parcel under his arm. "Good enough."

The officer is on his feet, alert now. Joshua steps forward. The officer tucks his thumbs in his belt and intones the regulations in a flat voice, and Joshua tosses the packet on the table. "Too hot. No," he says.

The officer fumbles with his shoulder microphone, but Terrence steps in and scoops up the packet. He stands before Joshua, offering it on his open palms, and Anna sees a young man, a man with warm and hopeful eyes kneeling in the slush and water and offering a binder to a fragile young woman, and she marvels at the roads her life has taken, and yet here they are, at the beginning again.

"Please, my friend," says Terrence, " so you can go home."

And Joshua nods, first to Terrence and then to the officer, and now he is donning the vestments of the journey.

To go home. What will we risk to go home?

M

Of the flying, there is little to tell. It is a flight like any flight with its boredom and its turbulence. It ends with the clustered buildings sharp along the tarmac in the Labrador morning, the line-up, the luggage sprayed, the shields and suits and boot covers stripped and discarded, and the masks changed. Then the travellers are standing beside the *Kamutik* near the parking lot, shrugging on the heavy clothes and hauling goggles over their faces. Joshua's cousin and his friend lean against a second snow machine, which is a good ten paces away. They live in Goose Bay, and Joshua's machine and packed *Kamutik* have been sitting in this cousin's garage, sprayed and untouched for the past three days. The cousin and his friend have not come near it except to drive it here, for they have family in Endor, and they will not bring the virus to them. The machine will quarantine with Joshua's group for two weeks at Aaron's cabin. Midway on their journey, Aaron himself will meet them, with another rifle for his father, and he will shadow their journey to the cabin.

It is a chess game of virus avoidance, but every detail is in place.

Terrence looks so eager, a boy who finds himself on a pirate ship or deep in a True North adventure, as the case might be. He is puffing just a little as he fidgets with his goggles, finally pulling them off. Joshua shakes his head.

"No, my friend," he grins. "Put them on. So, we can go home."

This is as close to revelry as the travellers come this day. The wind is cold as they set out, and their blood has been thinned by the southern winter. Joshua declares his mind is clear and ready, but his body tires quickly, and he will not admit this, and so the trail blurs sometimes, and the hills are no longer familiar to him. There is a GPS system, but Joshua does not trust it. He knows the way; it is there in his being if he can just unlock it.

Two hours into their journey, the way hides itself from him.

Joshua stands on the ice, a little hunched, his mouth buried in his scarf, but Anna knows its corners turn down; the opaque goggles shield his eyes, but they will be a little lost as they trail along the shore, seeking the landmarks.

Joshua stands forlorn, a figure collapsing and lost in the March light that sparkles and makes unprotected eyes water and blur, but inside, yes, not so far inside, the Thunderer is strong, and the dark ones will not prevail against him. *He is Joshua Kalluk*, Anna pleads. *Let him walk free, just once more.*

Terrence pokes at the GPS device, but the circles and x's and lines and dashes and numbers are a jumble to him.

Anna wills Joshua strong, sees the young man pushing back the hood, the spill of thick black hair on his forehead, the goggles shielding his eyes. He will be strong and straight, and he will lift the goggles and squint over the ice, point, and the great laugh will be cast across the bay.

Anna looks back, and all the hills and inlets are a featureless blur of snow and trees and rocks and ice ridges. For the first time, it occurs to her that they are lost on a featureless icescape, and no one is coming for them, and the rifle is snug in its case, useless.

She turns in circles, seeking the pillar of ice that does not reflect the light, the greyish shadow that is the white bear that will hunt them.

"What are you doing?" hisses Terrence, hands tucked to armpits, cold already.

"Tighten your scarf to your waist to hold the heat," Anna says. "And move around some. You can't let yourself get cold."

Terrence tugs the scarf tight and yanks the mitts a little farther over his sleeves. "Yes, but what are we looking for?" he persists, shuffling a little left and right like a reluctant square dancer.

"I was thinking there might be bears in the area," Anna explains. "We need to look in all directions. Look for ice that isn't ice, I think is the idea."

"Delightful," Terrence mutters. "I don't suppose you can use the GPS?"

Anna shrugs. "I don't think he trusts it anyway."

Terrence sighs. "It should only be two days."

Anna scowls.

"Are you content now, Anna?" He hesitates. "I mean, you wanted this in a way, but maybe this is not—Anna, this must be hard for you, to see, to be here, but not to be here. . .."

Anna turns away, facing north and hoping for some forgotten idea to surface, some word or memory of conversation that will bring the flash of *This is what they meant! Yes! There it is! The way is here.*

"Just be, Anna," Terrence murmurs. "That's all any of us can do."

And it comes to Anna that this is how Terrence has lived his life. He had been her comfort and joy, and the comfort and joy for many, but who has brought comfort and joy for Terrence? He has been poured out, but how is he filled? And yet his face lifts in peace, at one with Creation, side by side, not with an institutional Christ, but with an unsophisticated and passionate wanderer, carrier of the broken-hearted, champion of the wounded. Terrence stands with a very human Christ, and in this moment, Anna loves him again and is glad that on a sudden impulse she sent him that copy of Marta Raymond's play. It deserves his acknowledgement, his blessing.

They are three lone wanderers, but today, they have each other.

She does not even consider Sarah. Sarah is the driver, the boatwoman; this is not her journey. She cannot know as they do.

No, she is not jealous of Sarah or of Leah; they are dull women with dulled vision; here, on the ice, she and Joshua and Terrence flame together on this quest.

But they are lost. And they are getting cold.

A hacking, rasping wheeze penetrates her reflection. This is what the great laugh has descended to; scarred by tubes, strained by life, it forces past Joshua's lips and trickles into the air, barely reaching her.

He points. "There," he says. "All this time waiting. Waking up now. That way."

Anna and Terrence stare into the horizon he indicates, but whatever he sees is hidden from them. The laugh pushes out again, a little farther, vibrating a little on the air. "Eyes too long south," Joshua says. "Let's go see if Aaron made a good camp."

Anna and Terrence clamber into the *Kamutik* box while Joshua slides the rifle from its case and checks the action and the load. He hauls the strap over his shoulder, and the gun is snug to his back. He pushes up the goggles for a moment, and Anna sees a gleam far back in those sunken eyes, and she knows that he will be strong again.

Terrence sees a quickening in frailty, for he has seen this many times, and his thought is less grand. Terrence simply hopes that Joshua will last to Endor.

JOSHUA'S WAY

Their journey wends over land and ice. The plastic slides stick to the snow-mobile track on dry ice; then they wallow in slush where the ice floods. Joshua is quick to bang the machine against the ice to shake the slush free before slides and wheels form a frozen jumble adhering to the track, requiring a long, slow process of chipping that might damage the underbody. Terrence is warmed as they run sometimes, pushing, and Joshua, amazingly, lopes beside the machine at times, leaning over the throttle while pushing, but not with all his strength, for then he will sweat and become chilled. Joshua knows the balance, and it comes back to him. It sinks into him, and it is good to see.

Terrence drives at one point, Joshua riding behind and balancing with the machine, and Terrence continually looking back because he cannot feel Joshua's weight behind him. But that is how it is with someone who knows how to ride. With Terrence, Joshua remarks, it would be easy to know if he fell off; when you don't feel a tree sitting behind you, then he must be gone.

They are deep into their journey when they stop that night. Aaron has made a camp for them with two tents set at a distance from each other, with two separate fires burning along the shore. The larger fire is for the travellers, so they can sit apart and warm themselves. Anna has not seen her son in three years, and they are waving across the open space, hugging their own shoulders instead of each other's, but it is only a matter of weeks now. Anna sees that Aaron was right to come to Endor, and she was right to send him, even though she did not choose to. Aaron is tall and lithe like his father, with that same thin moustache brushing his lip; he is a young Joshua, and he calls himself Kalluk, not Caine, and she no longer minds. She has missed Aaron all his life, first because he was so lonely in her world, and then because she could not find a way to be in his. Nevertheless, here she is, and they are family together now, and in Endor, they will sort out his close sister Miriam and all that lot. Then she and Joshua will go North.

For now, here they are, the family of Anna's youthful fantasy, journeying together on the ice, with faithful Terrence in tow.

Somehow, Terrence belongs. Maybe they should have all settled in Endor. They could have been neighbours. But they would not have known what they now know.

The travellers eat from their provisions, and Aaron eats from his provisions, and Terrence seems content chatting across the distance with his ex-fiancée's love child, for Terrence, like Jesus, knows no rank or social strata and loves humanity. She is proud of Terrence this day, and she wonders if Sarah appreciates him. And Aaron—he laughs with his father in their language, shifts to English to include them all, and she and Terrence are like family friends. She wonders if Aaron, in his heart, thought of Leah as mother.

And she discovers it does not matter.

Joshua is as alive as Anna has not seen him since that Great Spring. He presides over the camp of good friends and family, and all are safe in his care.

The stars glow in the darkening vault, the fires diminish to coals. Aaron mounds snow over his own campfire pit, and Joshua does the same for theirs. "Wouldn't a fire be nice?" Terrence asks. "You know, warm, and well . . . bears?"

Aaron walks a short distance and kicks the snow with his boot. There is a clanging and rattling of cans and bits of metal.

"He puts the wire all around the camp," Joshua explains, "so, when they come, we will know. But get a big fire, then sleep, then a spark, and maybe you go North with no tent, no sleeping bag."

"When?" Terrence prompts.

"If," says Aaron. "He means 'if.' It is just a second language issue."

Terrence frowns and settles into his parka, glancing left and right, and Anna looks over her shoulder more than once. They are in Joshua's backyard, which is Aaron's backyard too, and she wonders if the dog Petra is thinking of her.

∧

They depart as the light is rising the next morning, and a long and grueling journey brings them to Aaron's cabin late in the evening. By that time, Anna is sick of the sight of mountains and sun dazzling on snow, bored with breaks for tea and stretching legs and resting, fed up with Joshua's new laugh that strains to find its power, and aching in heart because she does not know her son or share happy memories with him, except of Catherine, and that is his memory. Anna is glad she did not marry Terrence because this brave new man is wearing on the soul, always puffing a little and pushing at glasses when not goggled, cheeks bulging round as he slurps, yes slurps, his tea, for perhaps this makes him the wilderness man he fancies himself. She no longer sees an all-embracing Jesus but a conceited little man playing happy camper, and she is sick of him and Joshua, and heartbroken by Aaron, and she hopes she is just tired.

After all, they have two weeks in this one-room cabin. With bunk beds on two walls, stove centre, table under front window, barred, and an outhouse listing to the side. All this time, Aaron is scrupulous in distancing himself. He does not enter the cabin even, although he must be tired and cold. He waits by his machine as Joshua does his inventory, finding various tinned goods stashed in the food locker, and a spare gun and ammunition stowed in the padlocked steel drawer under a bed. All is good, and the quarantine can begin. Aaron says their two days on the trail should count, but Joshua is adamant. They will pass two weeks in the cabin. That is what he has promised. Aaron shrugs and pulls on his mitts. He will drive home in the darkness, arriving late in the night after two long days on the trail, but he will be at work by eight a.m.

He is young.

The senior travellers group around the table, a low fire in the stove, musty parkas airing from the lines along the rafters, and there is nothing to say. Tomorrow, Joshua will pace around the low bush in snowshoes, teaching Terrence the skills of wooding and partridge hunting. Anna will tend the stove, heat the water, wash dishes and small clothing items, and sweep the rough plank floor. The next two weeks will be deadening, she knows, for her. She is in the wings for this play.

She hopes that the weather holds, so the men can spend a good day out conquering nature while she putters and does not have to listen to them. An image flickers for an instant: Golden Joy is galloping through the garden, eyes shining and tongue lolling, Hobo sprinting ahead.

We make choices. This one is the right choice.

But she is tired, and she hates her choice and everyone in it this night.

INTRODUCTION BY MATTIE

My name is Mathilda Amarok, but I have always been called Mattie. I met Ms. Caine when I was eight years old, on the road in Endor, and I took her and my grandmother berry picking. Anna Caine left in the spring, and I never saw her again till the very end of things. That was a really amazing time, those last days, and lots of people have a story they want to tell about it. So, we are each going to tell our own story, one at a time.

Sometimes, I get lost when I am thinking about Anna Caine. I think of her, and all I see is waste. She let so many years slip away from her, and she never let herself just live. She just kept running here and there, like she never made a real camp, just squatted by a fire for a minute, then ran to the next one, half a cup of tea and gone again. Our People visit lots in the camps, but we stay for a proper visit. We don't just scramble around; we are alive together. It's like Anna Caine never took the time to taste the tea or hear the words in the voices.

I didn't have an easy life, losing my mother when I was small, and people telling lies about her. I lost my beautiful cousin Tonya when I was eight, and her little boy came to live with us. Then, when I was twelve, it got really hard. Those shadow faces came. They took me into the trees, and they strapped duct tape on my mouth, and there was vomit bubbling out my nose, and I was choking, and I should not be telling you this because I can feel the tears burn, and it makes me want to hurt this body, hurt it down with alcohol and hard things like it deserves because my body took that hurt and never protected me.

I never thought before that I hurt myself all those years to punish my body for letting me hurt like that. Hurt my soul because my soul didn't stop them either. I was spitting vomit out my nose, and I was choking. And hatred poured into me, burning in me and over me, and I hated them, and I hated me.

Yet I was the only one I punished.

They say forgive and forget. I can't do that, not that nice church way. But I have let their power go. Every sick cruel second is with me, but I get by, and I say, "Yes, I remember. But that is no longer my burden to carry."

I kind of felt that way when I learned to be a social worker, when I learned to give. To-give and for-give. Yeah. That was me.

When that Terrence man stayed with us, that time with Anna Caine and Joshua, he helped me to find the words. That is important. You can feel and feel, but it is important to have the words after all.

I can love Anna Caine now, and feel pity for her, but for a long time, I hated her, and it showed. But I want people to know that she did noble things in the end.

It wasn't her fault Joshua got stuck down south, but I would not argue with his daughter Miriam about that. Miriam is a good cousin to me but stubborn.

Anna Caine got Joshua back for us in the end. She had a house and a garden and maybe two dogs; she had settled down, and she had good neighbours. She gave that up to come back here, and that can't have been an easy decision with the virus and all. This new virus will take the world one day, but for now, we are trying the old things we did at first, and we are pushing it down and pushing it down, but one day, when we are too tired to push or just tired of pushing, it is going to burn right through us all.

But for now, there is time. I am going to gather the last stories of Anna Caine, and lots of people will think there is going to be sadness and death, that maybe they got the virus or froze or fell through the ice or got eaten by polar bears, but I want you to know it is a happy story.

My counsellor said people like happy endings, and you are going to get one.

Maybe more than one because lots of people have a story about them.

I have picked the best ones.

ACCORDING TO TERRENCE

Lord, it is good that we are here. I gaze about me in wonder for there are all those trees on the harbour. Trees, a great pulsing line of trees, and there are guns firing too, and suddenly, I am terrified because those are people, not trees, perhaps a hundred people in scattered family groups, and surely they have come to drive us back for we bring the plague.

But the guns are firing in unison to the sky. It is a salute, a tribute, a welcome. Joshua has found his way out of Egypt and a long journey he has had of it.

A woman is running in front of them, long hair streaming free, arms stretched above her head, and this must be Miriam, dancing out the victory at the Red Sea, or running to meet her father, as the case might be.

Joshua gathers his firstborn in his arms and sways there on the ice, and this other one, a little shorter and plumper, approaches; this must be the daughter Dinah, and now the arms encircle her and two bundled little girls, the newest grandchildren.

And there is Aaron, and a younger man with him, his brother Simeon, both grinning but not entering the ecstatic embracing and laughing and crying that mark this grand reception on the ice.

There are nods and smiles for Anna Caine, who seems rooted to the ice, and waves and greetings for me as well. Yes, here I am, he who made this journey possible, and for a moment, I allow a little pride. Yet, I am just the instrument, the final step in the formula, the pawn, perhaps, of my Creator.

How can the sun be so dazzling on the ice and the wind so cold?

I am tired to the bone, and I would rest, Lord. Being your instrument has stretched me, and I puff, just a little, almost waddling in these travel clothes.

M

How can I describe what it is like? It is like a long brilliance of sun and wind, a passing among family groups who shift and part like performers in an elaborate dance, weaving close to their own, swinging wide of all others, yet there is no conscious distancing. They know this dance well.

I have a corner in the older children's room, and Anna has the other. It is like being in the cabin again, but now Joshua claims his own room, the room of his marriage, ten years alone but his and Leah's still. His daughter Dinah and her younger children share a room, and her older ones are sleeping over at their Aunt Miriam's. I feel we have taken their room, but nobody else seems to mind. The cots are narrow, child-size, but they are luxurious compared to the bunks we endured for two weeks.

Aaron and his partner have built a small place on the edge of his father's lot, and his brother Simeon stays with them. I do not think Anna was quite aware of the partner, either. This woman, Johanna, is a quiet and unobtrusive person; I think she might be like Aaron's stepmother, Leah. All our wives seem to be Leah to Anna Caine's Rachel.

Miriam is an intense young woman, mid to late thirties, close in age to Aaron. She must be a good principal, I think. She is decisive, and she seems to genuinely like children. They follow Ms. Miriam, chatting, and she is always smiling then.

Miriam does not smile for Anna Caine. She looks past her, addressing others, eyes sweeping past her. I would say Miriam is uncomfortable with her father's one-time lover, and she is not truly comfortable with me. When Miriam glances my way, her eyes quickly move on, and I feel like a jilted lover or a failed husband, and I suppose I am.

I am supposed to leave on the next plane, but that is not straightforward. There is the medical checkup, and there is the plane schedule. The next plane comes through tomorrow, but all pending medicals will be conducted by the doctor who is arriving on that plane, so I will take the plane the following day. This is a formality, for I have been screened and quarantined, but this is the way of things, so I have two days in Endor. Sharing a room with Anna Caine. Well.

I am so tired, Lord. I want to stay here, far from the anger and stress of the city. I want to send for Sarah, and we will wait out the virus here, welcome among Joshua's people, and we will shoot partridges and chop wood and become young together. I will honour Sarah as she deserves to be honoured, even though I cannot love her as I loved Anna Caine.

I feel awkward as friend and ally to Anna Caine, but it is, in truth, not so bad.

Anna asks me not to puff when I walk, and I try to tell her it is the weight of these clothes. And it is the woodsmoke.

I am well, but I am weary, and sometimes, when I try to breathe deeply, the air seems to stop in my throat.

Joshua recognizes this. The day of the plane that is bringing the doctor, Joshua and I walk to the church and then the churchyard. There are neat crosses slicing through the hardened drifts. We stop by his grandparents' grave, and he tells how his father missed his northern home too much, and dulled his heartache with brew, and how his grandparents claimed Joshua and raised him. His grandfather had faced the so-called Spanish flu, and although it dragged him to the edge of death, he was one of very few who survived. This grandfather taught Joshua to be strong, and his grandmother taught him to be fair. A good set of examples, and he has tried in his life to honour them.

He moves on to Leah's grave, gently brushes traces of snow from the lettering of her name. "She was Leah," he says. "I was strong with her. My life began with her, and it will end with her. Here is where I will lie when everything is over.

"Anna Caine." He pronounces the name like a solemn blessing. "She was a friend to us. And then, there was a change there, a twist. I do not think it was meant to be, but there it was. And I am sorry I brought you pain."

"You brought me to Sarah," I murmur. "She was how it was meant to be. Your Leah, my Sarah. Our Anna. But she was always her own Anna, if we are honest."

Joshua nods. "Yes. Her own Anna. Yes. That is true, I think. But our Anna too?"

"Our Anna," I affirm, "who walked with each of us when it was time. And now, here she is again. Only we are all together."

"No." Joshua touches the lettering on the cross again. "You must look after Anna now. You must not let her follow me. This is not her journey, and she must see.

"She cannot throw away all her choices; that makes all her life a mistake, all my life a mistake.

"I think we all have good lives; we must not throw them away, like they are nothing. We should honour that spring, when all those things happened, and then honour all we have done since. I have had a good life as a husband and father, even though I sometimes thought of Anna instead, and I think you have had a good life with your Sarah, even if sometimes there is Anna in your mind.

"And Anna has been a good teacher in many places, even if she does not accept it. She wants to have love, but she sets it up with walls.

"I think this is hardest for her."

Love with walls. Joshua sees the human condition in all its painful beauty. Humans are the ones who construct love with walls around it. I am humbled.

The air is cold, and I wheeze, just a little.

"Your heart?" he says. "It does not like our cold, I think."

"It finds its work harder these days," I explain. "This did not start here."

He turns from me and stares across the harbour at the low mountains that rise along the horizon.

"I have another favour to ask," he says.

M

My medical has gone well. That is, there is no virus, no contagion, pulsing within my body, to be breathed into the medical plane and dispersed through the population. The logistics of this testing baffle me, for were we not tested, and monitored, and quarantined in the wilderness? Do they fear there is a latent speck, hovering? Lurking?

This long pandemic has run from terror to caution to apathy to passionate claims reminiscent of the more volatile medieval movements, and now we are back to terror. This time, we have knowledge and experience in our hands, but we are terrified, because even though we do understand what this strain or wave or new virus is, with all our knowledge and expertise and experience, we are powerless before it.

It is consuming us.

Perhaps it is God's own plague, and perhaps I should not have been flippant about it.

Yes, my medical has gone well; the weariness of my heart is well-documented, so that does not affect anything.

It just affects me when, for example, I am pushing a big wooden sled in the slush. I am not good at these things, for I do not get the oxygen my body demands.

M

I watched my plane leave this morning. Anna does not like sharing the children's room with me, but Anna is going to bunk in with Aaron and his partner Johanna for the duration. It will be good for mother and son to have time, and for her to bond with Johanna, a tall, thin woman with a shy smile and a loose ponytail down her back. She seems young, somehow, gentle without the gloom that settles over the family. Simeon welcomes Anna, reminding her of the Christmas she read to him. Dinah is more relaxed with this arrangement, and I confess I sleep better without Anna listening to me breathe, without her casting secretive looks toward Joshua's door.

Yet I suspect that Anna would rather I were the one transferred to the other house, and she become the matron of Joshua's house. After all, they wintered together in Anna's isolated little house, and we would do well to remember that Joshua's daughters Dinah and Miriam were not there.

Miriam is an enigma. On the surface, she is calm and warm, but there is a cold core of tension within her. She is fond of Aaron, and she is devoted to the father they share, but there is a quiet resentment of Aaron's mother. Perhaps Miriam senses that her mother, like the biblical Leah, was ever in the shadow of another woman. How did Joshua's Leah feel, O Lord? What was her life all those years, the dutiful wife who was not quite Anna Caine? She walked all those years as one bearing witness to the perpetual hurt of a gentle and faithful woman, just like Jacob's Leah in the biblical story—I wonder, was Jacob kind to his Leah?

Joshua is a man of honour. He chose his Leah, to live with her all their married years, to lie at her side in sleep in the churchyard. And on this journey together, if he touches Anna or looks at her, it is as friend thanking friend for being there when the future is sweeping in and threatening his resolve. And she is simply present, a companion who drinks in every moment on this first and last great journey together.

So why am I still here?

I remain because Joshua asked a favour. It is a small thing, but a necessary thing, and I will accomplish it.

And I stay because I am weary of the clash and seething cauldron of my life. As we crossed the harbour, I felt a pull. This is where I am meant to be. This is where I will live, and walk the shore, and talk with interesting people, like that cousin, Mattie. She makes me think of Tonya, although I never met her, a phoenix woman rising from the ashes of her horror and lifting her wings to the sky. Mattie's wings beat for the children in her care, and I want to walk beside her and learn from her presence.

I called Sarah this morning and asked her to start arrangements for her to come here. We can be content here, and she will not be Leah; she will be my first and forever Sarah. We will walk along the shore and grow older far from the fury and chaos enveloping the world. We will retire and volunteer in the library and the church, and our door will always be open and welcoming.

Sarah says that sounds very pleasant, but should she shut down the house and what should she do with "that car?" Who will escort her, and what will we do if I change my mind as I start to miss my classes and my pastoral care work?

She recommends that I wait a month, "while the Kalluk situation is settling," and then we will make a good decision.

I think she means get Endor out of my system, and I will be glad to get home to the Northwest Arm and walk along the water with her, my northern fancies finally fulfilled.

M

Easter is upon us, with all its attendant traditions. Joshua appears rested, stronger than he looked in Halifax, and I suspect he is rallying for the end, which is not the same as a remission. Anna seems quite sure that the cancer is leaving his body, but as he refuses further testing, we really do not know.

We have another week here together in Endor, and already Aaron is gathering supplies and gear for the journey North. He is a quiet man who keeps his own counsel, a young man with an older man's subtle wisdom. He does not argue or debate, although perhaps he does this within himself or with Johanna. His brother Simeon will accompany them, to help Aaron with the journey home.

Simeon explains that their father will want to go until he collapses, and it will take two of them to get him home.

Aaron clarifies that their father will still be very much alive and probably well, but he is going to be extremely tired.

They are all needed, Aaron says. Each will need the other.

I am tired of puzzles. Sarah always speaks plainly.

ACCORDING TO MIRIAM

I am the first daughter of Joshua and Leah Kalluk, and I want to tell you the story of my father's last journey. Before I begin, I need to say that I have never liked the way Anna Caine behaved as a mother, and I have never liked the way she behaved as a teacher. I have seen her type in my career, so interested in our culture and strutting around on the surface but grabbing what they want when they want.

My mother was carrying me in her belly while my father was sleeping with Anna Caine. That is the truth of it. But it was Anna Caine's idea, something she wanted, and he just fell in with her. But my father saw the truth of things, in the end. He saw that my mother loved with all her being, more than anyone else I have ever known. He saw that, in the end.

I was not pleased when my father asked Anna Caine to be his medical escort. "Then what am I to do?" he said. "I can't be there alone; you know that sometimes the cancer is filling my head, confusing me, and then there is the chemo, and all the medical talk, and she is good at those things. She is a friend; she is linked to us, through Aaron. She will help. And I want her there."

And when he saw that this put tears in my eyes—me, the principal, with tears in my eyes—his voice got very gentle. "That was long ago," he told me. "We should have all stayed friends, never a couple, but now we can be friends. I want friends. I do not look for another wife. Anna—she was like a moment. I liked her, I loved her, but not the love that comes from long life together. That was your mother, Miriam; there is no other like her, in this or any world.

"I will go to Leah when my time comes. But Anna was our friend long ago, and she can help."

When I asked why she was going North with him, he shook his head. "That is not her journey to make," he said. "Her journey is here, and then she must go home."

"She will climb into the *Kamutik*, like she climbed into your bed," I snapped. I wanted to hurt him, for all the times he looked at my mother and I knew he was remembering. "She will crawl into your coffin," I told him. Oh, I regret. I regret that last sentence, because my father was a man of honour, and I had made his courage cheap and dirty.

My father stared out across the harbour. "Aaron will take me as far as my body will let us," he said. "It is not long, now. It is coming for me. I must go now, but I do not think we will reach Hebron."

I cried long and hard and loud, and he held me because we knew that this was our last good talk together, and when he came back from his quest, he would be lost to me.

M

Now, that last Easter time was the greatest I have known, a great feast in my parents' home, with Dinah's toddlers scampering wild like kids that age do, to let their nerves out, with my Beth and Dinah's older girls plugged into their devices, my boy too old to scamper and not plugged in just yet but wanting to wrestle his uncles, and Simeon told him that Anna Caine was a good storyteller, but I decided to ignore that. Anna herself looked all tense and stared at everyone; I wondered if she was like that in a classroom because that must have been stressful for her students. Terrence, though—he was a man like no other I have seen. He and my son became good friends right away, and even my twelve-teen Beth took off her headphones and told him about her hopes for journalism school. Journalism! I was surprised, and I wondered why she kept this from me and my husband.

How did that Terrence ever wind up engaged to Anna Caine and how did he manage to escape?

I disciplined myself be kind to Anna Caine. She got my father home.

My father announced at the table, that Easter, that he was leaving on Tuesday. Oh, he would miss the games of Easter, but the time for North must come a little early.

Everyone said how well my father looked. His eyes met mine across the great feast table, and he smiled at me, and I said the good Northern air was making him strong again. My words fell over one another, chopped and toneless, but everyone smiled and nodded at them, like a great truth had been shared.

M

The Tuesday came. We all came down to the ice to wish them a safe journey. Joshua would lead them out on his snowmobile with a packed *Kamutik* in tow. Aaron would ride with Simeon at first, on his machine to one side, extra gas and gear strapped to the *Kamutik* behind them.

As we gathered there, Terrence came forward. He and my father shook hands, and then my father stepped back, head bowed. Terrence raised one palm high, and he whispered words for my father only. I do not know what he said, but I knew that this was a blessing—not a cheap church blessing but a blessing from the depths of creation.

Now we have a custom—not always, but sometimes. We like to grab onto the box, hanging on as the machine pulls away, laughing as only we can laugh, and then we peel away one by one to tumble onto the ice and run as far with our travellers as we can.

So, my father knelt straight and proud on the seat of his machine. He pulled his goggles down, but he thrust his hood far back, and he was smiling and so happy. Ah! The journey was beginning, and he was eager and excited. "*Hebronimiut!*" he exclaimed, and we all cheered and rushed to clamber up on the runners to hold the box, and he tipped back his head, and he laughed. And I swear I heard the great laugh, the laugh of my childhood and growing up, ringing across the harbour and echoing in the mountains, and I do not know if he really made the laugh that time, but it was *his laugh* that was ringing, and my heart leaped up, and it soared.

And even when Anna Caine jumped straight into the *Kamutik* box and Terrence behind her, laughing and puffing like a fat puppy, I still soared because nothing could take this moment. It was ours.

My father pulled his hood to his face and seized the throttle. First, though, he looked straight into the box, and I thought, at first, he was nodding to Anna Caine. No. He was nodding to Terrence crowded behind her.

We began to move.

"Me!" yelled Mattie, peeling away and laughing. "Goodbye! Good luck!"

Other cousins were tumbling free, scrambling and wallowing behind.

"Now me!" yelled my sister. "I love you, my father."

We were going faster, and now it was me.

"Remember!" I hollered, loud as I could, but my tears were muffling me.

The machine accelerated, and I saw Terrence rise to his knees.

"Our turn!" he roared. "Into His hands, my friend."

And he wrapped his arms around Anna Caine and flung them both sideways into the snow.

The *Kamutik* wobbled wildly but righted, and my father drove on.

Anna Caine raced down the ice, screaming, while Terrence knelt in the snow. His head bowed and his shoulders shook; I thought that he was crying, but it must have been the pain.

My father grew smaller, became a speck, and was gone.

ACCORDING TO AARON

I was sorry when my mother got left behind that day on the ice, but it was also like a great weight had been lifted. I had been with my father on these trips before, and it was like he went into a trance out there. Some modern-day *angak-kuk,* up there in the mountains, staring past the horizon. My mother pictured herself ministering to him, but sadly, she would just have been in the way.

I was sorry for my mother and not just a little. In all my memories of her, she was always a little sad. Always like she was listening, waiting. Now, this time, when she came to Endor with him, I think she was trying to make up for whatever it was they went through all those years ago.

It has been awkward, being their son. They were friends, maybe, but friends on different shores, maybe in different countries. Coming up the coast, it was not like escorting my aged parents on an outing; it was like making one trip and then going back for the other one and making a second trip. When I imagine them sharing a house and raising me together, I am grateful for the life I have had.

But I heard my mother screaming on the ice behind us, and that was the same scream that was rising in me, for that man, driving there, was passing from us all.

Mattie wanted me to tell her how it was out there, and all I could say was that it was hard. It was like we were blundering along, fumbling our way, but my father was looking straight ahead and seeing something grand.

And then there was the hollow shell of the journey home. It weighed heavy on me, heavy on Simeon; they say you must let it out and let it all go, but there are some things best honoured by silence.

I honoured my father. I honoured his journey. I honoured his life and his death.

My sister Miriam hugged me hard and said I did well. She'd always known me best, since we'd met on Simeon's birthday.

ACCORDING TO SARAH

Easter has drifted past, and we are deep in the liturgical season. I find solace in the rhythm of the liturgy, although when the faithful gather to fix the building yet again, I think of Terrence. *Meet in a stable, meet in a parking lot or a field, cast yourself into the arms of God and remember the desert years, when there was a tent, not a temple, for the Most High.*

It is hard to see daffodils, wobbling and pungent, grass greening, and side-walks clear, and know that, in Endor, snow still heaps along the roads, and people still travel over heavy ice on snowmobiles.

By now, I should be packing for retirement to Endor, to live out the fantasy of safety and shelter that Terrence, my husband, dreamed when he arrived there. Or raking the yard and bracing myself for his solitary rambles on windy nights, a restless and windblown, frustrated hero.

Instead, I find myself sifting through his papers in his little study upstairs: scraps tucked away in books, crammed on shelves, stuffed in drawers—the intricacies of a dear and haphazard filing system. I have long yearned to organize his work, to categorize and catalogue, but now that I can, I think I prefer to sift. There is charm in a grocery list tucked between the pages of a sermon, in a worn brown envelope on a shelf near the desk, alone. An envelope frequently touched and referenced, I would say. I draw out the pages it contains, and of course, it is about Anna Caine. No, it is a letter to Anna Caine, but not about her. The writer sounds so angry with life, so pained. I see she is a student, explaining her English project. And here it is: *A WINNIPEG NATIVITY, A Christmas Play for Grade 12 English by Marta Raymond.*

Oh my. It is not a very pleasant story, with drug dealers and nurse addicts wasted on Christmas Eve, with runaways and hurt people, but . . . oh! I see Mary and Joseph scrounging on the streets of Bethlehem, and this was how it was for them—not fine blue robes and halo glowing, perched side-saddle on a well-groomed and patient donkey. *They were like this. They were raw and desperate, and Terrence, my Terrence, understood.*

I am glad Anna Caine sent him that play. I run a search on the author, Marta Raymond, and discover an intense and intelligent face staring back from a graduation photo. She became a teacher in her hometown; she took an award-winning high school drama group right to Winnipeg. She was an honour to her community and her People; her obituary messages are rich in gratitude and love. She died of virus complications two years ago, deeply loved and missed by all who knew her.

I wonder if Anna knew. I suspect that Terrence did. He would.

I like sitting here, in my husband's study; I feel close to him here. And I will walk along the Northwest Arm sometimes, pull off my scarf, and let my hair tangle in the wind.

I sit here, and I weep. I weep for the day I drove away from the airport. Again and again, I slam the brakes and park sideways in the lane; I teeter to the departure lounge, wobbling in my dress boots, and kiss him with wanton abandon. *"I will join you,"* I breathe into his ear. *"We will have a new life, there in the presence of mountains."*

First, I will get rid of that car. I do not want her coming here. I will send it to the airport, and she can manage the bill.

I understand that Terrence fell or jumped from a moving sled, and Joshua's daughter said, when she called, that it happened when he was restraining Anna Caine from following the party going North, or something like that.

His heart started stretching some time ago, but he was still strong. Straining in that bitter, cold climate and wrestling on the ice with that woman—what was he thinking?

I am angry with Joshua, who should have just gone home last fall when he had the chance. And with Anna Caine, for involving Terrence. And with my husband, who this time took his servant role too far.

I am most angry with myself, because again and again, I dash from the car, and I tell him, and it does not happen.

Terrence Sutherland, beloved husband and disciple. A shadow coming home.

He should have guarded his heart.

And mine.

ACCORDING TO ANNA
(NORTHERN MAGNIFICAT)

My soul magnifies the North.

My spirit rejoices in you, my friend, for you have made all things new for me.

I see you in a shimmer of light, straight and strong, there on the ice. You grip the throttle with power, and the snow wind is on your face.

Your laughter rises from near the shore, and it rings across the harbour and vibrates off the mountains.

And I am glad, glad, my friend, that I bear witness to this moment, and I love you with all the love that is in my being.

All the years fall away, and there you are, eyes open to the light, your body lithe and taut, your muscles rolling beneath the skin, and here on my knees, I am granted a vision of what you will always be.

You are Joshua, and you are Thunder on the Land.

My heart cannot contain this whole; it can only beat in rhythm with the earth.

I thought I was your companion, your helper, your escort-organizer. And, yes, I was, and I did well, but you have passed into legend, and you are greatness on the Land.

I stand and feel the heartbeat of creation surging in unison with mine, and your heartbeat is there, and this is dazzling.

The little love of that first spring is but a prelude to the love that pours through me in this moment when you merge with creation.

I watch until you are gone, and when the light no longer washes through me, when the rhythm no longer pulses in and around me, still I stand, and the horizon itself is a blessing on me.

Now I know why you forced me to stay behind.

It was so that I would enter the moment, the moment we were born for.

Yes, you will return, and your body will lie in the churchyard.

But your spirit is free upon the Land, and I will find you there. I will reach and find you from anywhere in the universe.

I find Terrence huddled on the ice, and I cradle him until the nurses come.

My spirit is free upon the Land.

I do not love. I am love.

ACCORDING TO JOSHUA

I have walked in the ways of my ancestors, and I have honoured their lives.

The journey is cold, but I do not feel it. When my mind grows weary, and the mountains blur on the horizon, Aaron is there, his hand strong on the throttle. Simeon is here, his eyes watching . . . for I have taught my sons our ways, and they are strong in many worlds.

I do not come to Hebron.

I do not need to.

I am there, always, my spirit poured out upon the Land.

I stare, and there is a shadow but no face; this must be my son, but my eyes no longer look on this world. They roam the Land. I hear the laugh of Anna Caine, the laugh of youth, the laugh that brought the Land to Life. I belong not to Anna Caine but to the laugh that frees the Land. I walk in that laughter, and a dazzling light rises on the horizon, and I know that it is us, understanding at last.

I belong to my Leah, and I yearn for the day when we will rest, side by side.

But there is a dazzling piece of light, bursting over the Land, and that is where I am with Anna Caine.

There is no place for love.

I do not need to love.

I am love.

ACCORDING TO MATTIE

And now, the ending of the story and the blessing belongs to me, Mattie
Amarok, cousin of Joshua Kalluk, keeper of the stories of Anna Caine.

Aaron and Simeon brought their father home a few days after they set out.
They said he was the happiest they had ever seen him, but then he didn't know
anymore, and they brought him home to prepare.

I saw my cousin Joshua, when he came home, and his face was all peaceful.
He gave his daughters and his grandkids hugs, and he knew them.

He and Anna Caine just looked a long time at each other, and they were both
smiling something all secret, and I know I was thinking, *Here we go again*.

But you know, I do not think anyone saw that except me.

Miriam, when she talks about it, says he just walked past Anna Caine.

But that look, it was something special, something secret. Something that
wasn't like those old times, and not like friends but something new.

And Terrence, he wasn't doing so good, but he was still with us. First heart
attacks either kill you or scare you bad, they say, but he was just so weak. He and
Joshua shook hands, and Joshua knew him too.

Now these are the strange things. Anna Caine, for all her fighting to be with
my cousin, went back home. Yep. She had this kind of silly and holy look, and
she came through town and said goodbye to everyone on the road she met; she
came right up to me, and she put her arms around me, and she said she'd come
up sometimes, but I think that was just goodbye talk. Then she tucked Terrence
into the plane and took him home. Back down into the virus lands, where it's
going to get better or worse and come for us or pass us by. We will know when
it is time.

I guess, technically, Terrence took Anna home, since he was the travel escort.

Boy, I would love to see the family reunion for that one. I hope his wife is patient because he is going to be an invalid now.

Joshua said it would be safer for Terrence at home.

And maybe for Anna Caine, but it did seem strange, her giving in, like.

Maybe it was one of these "remember me like I was" moments.

Anna Caine went back to her house and probably those dogs, and someday, if the virus isn't so bad anymore, Aaron and Johanna will go see her.

That is a good thing. Then Anna Caine will have grandchildren, and they can look after her.

So, we all settled down again and waited. We have always been good at waiting.

Even when Joshua's eyes were failing that long spring, he was always facing North, looking out his window across the harbour.

His mind never failed, but he was shutting down inside. They kept saying he should go to the hospital soon, but he never said anything those times. Cancer people usually die in hospital; they have tubes and machines, but that was not my cousin Joshua's way.

I was the one sitting with him the last day. Dinah was at the store, and everyone else was at work or school. Dinah's little kids were playing around their grandfather's chair. My cousin just smiled at me. *"I am going to Leah soon,"* he said. And then he said, *"Anna is the North. I am there, always."*

That didn't sound disrespectful, the way he said it, but I sure don't think I will tell Miriam that part.

He closed his eyes and got very still.

I sat with him until Dinah came home, and I let her call Miriam and send for her brothers.

Yes. Anna Caine did do selfish things, but she did noble things too.

And she and Joshua weren't in love, at least after they figured things out.

No, they didn't have to be in love.

They are love.

Taima!

APPENDIX:
JOSHUA'S FAMILY TREE

**Lisetta and Ida were sisters; they were born in Hebron
but lived much of their lives in Endor.**

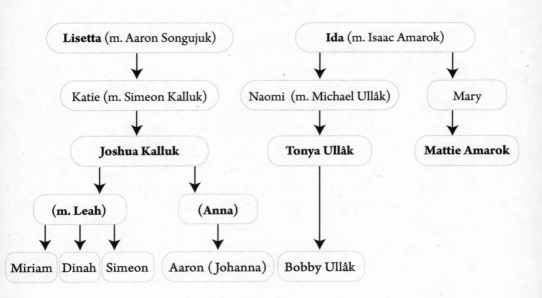

*Miriam (Kalluk-Peterson) Children: Beth and Marcus
Dinah: four children, not named in text

ACKNOWLEDGEMENTS

I want to thank the FriesenPress team for their incredible support, creativity, and patience. Thanks especially to my publishing specialist for their encouragement and guidance, to the editor for their skill and insight, to the designer for creating a cover of beauty, and to my promotions specialist for their past and future support.

Thank you to the people of home for supporting my writing journey and my many wanderings. Thanks to the many cousins and friends elsewhere who have been there for me.

Thanks to the writers and reviewers who have encouraged, shared, and supported me on this journey. Thank you to author A-M Mawhiney, for marketing collaboration and support.

I thank my son, Noah, and his partner, Boni, for their special presence in my life. And his father, for the joy he finds, no matter what the day brings.

To my Lady of Wasaya, my departed writing companion: I will remember always, my friend.

I am grateful to the communities where I worked during my teaching career for their open welcome, understanding, and acceptance. I give special thanks for the late Elder Rachel Chakasim: survivor, woman of grace and strength, and friend.

To people of Indigenous ancestry: I acknowledge that I cannot speak for Indigenous people. I can only write from my own world, with mere glimpses of the pain and betrayal that you bear fully, every moment. Please know that I write with love, from the heart, and with gratitude for the grace that I have received in your presence.

~~Anne (Michelle)

ABOUT THE AUTHOR

With degrees in theological studies and education (additional qualifications in special education), author Anne M. Smith-Nochasak spent over thirty years teaching in Indigenous communities, where she learned to challenge the limitations that are placed on students and delight in each child's potential as those communities do.

Although Anne has always enjoyed writing, now that she is retired, she considers it to be her favourite hobby next to reading. Still, as often as she can, she enjoys gardening, kayaking, hiking in the woods, and any work that brings her outdoors. She currently lives in a wooded area in western Nova Scotia with her golden dogs, Shay and Flo.

In 2021, Anne M. Smith-Nochasak was recognized as one of The Miramichi Reader's "Best Books of 2021" for her first book: *A Canoer of Shorelines* (FriesenPress 2021).

For more information about the author, or to connect:
Instagram @SmithNochasak
www.acanoerofshorelines.com

Printed in Canada